WHAT YOU DID

EVA RAE THOMAS MYSTERY - BOOK 2

WILLOW ROSE

Cover design by Juan Villar Padron,
https://www.juanjpadron.com

Special thanks to my editor Janell Parque
http://janellparque.blogspot.com/

**To be the first to hear about new releases and
bargains from Willow Rose, sign up below to be on
the VIP List.** (I promise not to share your email with anyone
else, and I won't clutter your inbox.)

- GO HERE TO SIGN UP TO BE ON THE VIP LIST :
http://readerlinks.com/l/415254

Tired of too many emails? Text the word: "willowrose" to 31996 to sign up to Willow's VIP text List to get a
text alert with news about New Releases, Giveaways, Bargains
and Free books from Willow.

Prologue

I t wasn't easy to run for your life in a prom dress. Carina lifted the hem of what had once been a beautiful oceanic blue mermaid evening gown; the very same one that had, a few hours earlier, been adored by hundreds of her fellow students' eyes as she was called up on the stage to be crowned prom queen. One of her beautiful Manolo Blahniks, of the first pair she had ever owned, had lost a heel on the asphalt before she made the turn onto the golf course. As she had pushed herself through the grass and the other heel had sunk into the moist and swampy Florida ground, she had ripped both shoes off, panting agitatedly as she heard the steps of her follower approaching in the darkness. She had lost her crown near the entrance to the country club as she ran there, shaking the doors, hoping that maybe someone was in there and could help her. But all the doors had been locked, and that was why she ended up running toward the golf course, her pursuer breathing down her neck.

Carina was a track runner, and as she ran across the golf course, she soon sensed that she had lost him. As she reached a small lake followed by a row of trees, she allowed herself to slow down for just a second. She stopped and listened, thinking she could hide between the bushes, at least till she caught her breath. Her lungs felt like they were on fire, and she was wheezing to breathe.

Stupid allergies!

She feared he might hear her heavy breathing and panting since it sounded so loud in her own ears. Unable to see any movement across the open area behind her, she took a few deep breaths, trying to calm herself down. As she managed to breathe easier, Carina fought not to panic. Her heart pounded against her ribs.

What happened to the others? Where are they?

There had been three girls walking home together when they left the school and the prom. They all lived in the neighborhood right behind the school and had decided to make the five-minute walk home together. There were, after all, three of them, and the area was very safe. Nothing ever happened in Cocoa Beach. As long as they stayed together, they would be safe.

Why hadn't they stayed together?

He had come as if out of nowhere. None of them saw him. They were chatting and talking about the night. Ava and Tara were both telling Carina how beautiful she had looked when doing the mandatory slow dance with Kevin, the prom king. Carina had listened and enjoyed the sound of jealousy in their voices when they talked about her, but the fact was, it had been the most awkward moment of Carina's seventeen-year-long life. Kevin was the boyfriend of her best friend Molly, and all the time she had been dancing with him, she had been looking at her friend, wondering if she looked like she enjoyed it too much. Molly had left during the dance and Carina hadn't seen her since. She had texted her as soon as the dance was over, trying to explain that she only danced with him because she had to…because it was expected of them. But Molly hadn't answered, and Carina had grown worried about her and wondered if she was mad at her. She had seen it in her eyes right before she left. The anger and resentment. She knew that look a little too well since they had been best friends since they met in Kindergarten.

I am so sorry, Molly. I didn't mean to hurt you. You have to believe me; I didn't enjoy it at all.

The girls had screamed when the masked man grabbed Ava and held a knife to her throat. Carina had panicked. Both she and Tara had screamed, while Ava whimpered behind the knife. Then Carina had kicked him. She had no idea where her strength and courage had come from, but she had lifted her Manolo Blahnik and placed a kick right where it hurt the most, and the guy had bent forward in pain.

That was when they began to run. He had reached out and grabbed for Tara, but she had managed to get loose from his grip, screaming helplessly. It was one of the last things Carina saw before she lost track of the others. At what point they got split up, she didn't even know. She just knew they had run, and, in the beginning, she had thought the others were right behind her, but as she ran onto the golf course, she realized she couldn't see them or hear them anywhere.

Now, as she stared into the darkness, she wondered if she had, after all, managed to escape her pursuer.

Had he given up?

Sweat ran down her back, and her blonde hair felt soaked. Her knees were still shaking while she tried to figure out what to do next. She couldn't stay there. If he was still out there, he'd find her.

A movement in the bushes made her gasp. A shadow ran across the grass in the moonlight, holding up her dress in the same manner Carina had earlier.

Tara!

Carina stepped out from her hiding place and wondered if she should yell her name, but as she opened her mouth to speak, a shadow stepped out from behind a tree and grabbed Tara. He swung her, screaming, in the air, then slammed his fist into her face. Carina watched while gasping for air as Tara fell to the ground and she couldn't even hear her scream anymore.

Carina felt her bones tremble, and she knew she should run; every part of her screamed for her legs to move, to get her away from there, yet they didn't. It was like they were paralyzed.

Was Tara still alive?

She watched as the man bent over the motionless Tara for a few seconds before he lifted his head and she felt his eyes on her. She couldn't tell if he was actually looking at her or not, but she felt those evil eyes like knives on her skin.

Swiftly, he rose to his feet and bolted toward her. She immediately knew she couldn't outrun him. Yet, she tried. She turned around and set off, but just as in her many nightmares, it was like she barely moved forward at all. Hands reached for her ponytail, and she was pulled forcefully back and into his arms. When she felt his hand on her neck and smelled his warm breath on her skin, she closed her eyes and prayed that she would feel no pain.

Chapter 1

T WO WEEKS LATER

"GREAT NEWS. I FOUND HER."

My eyes grew wide. They stared at the woman in front of me, behind the cluttered desk. Her name was Rhonda, and she was a private eye that I had hired to track down my long-lost sister.

Sydney was kidnapped from a Wal-Mart when I was only five years old and she was seven. I had recently learned that she might still be alive since it was our mutual biological father who had taken her, and it was believed they had left the country back then. It had taken me a few weeks to gather the courage to start the investigation and hire someone to do it for me. Rhonda had been at it for six months, searching for both my dad and my sister. So far, I had barely heard from her in all those months, and I assumed that was because she couldn't find anything. Her words and excited bright eyes staring at me from behind the deeply furrowed face surprised me.

"Really?"

Rhonda nodded. She grabbed a file from the pile next to

her and placed it in front of me. She pushed it closer, and I felt my heart begin to pound. I wasn't sure how to react to any of this.

"Take a look for yourself."

I could hardly breathe. I stared at the file, my fingers unable to stop shaking. I bit my lip, then looked up at Rhonda.

"And you're sure it's her?"

Rhonda nodded. "It wasn't an easy case, this one. But with a little help from a colleague in Europe, I traced your father to London."

"And Sydney?"

Rhonda cleared her throat. "He changed her name. She became Mallory Stevens over there. His name is now James Stevens."

"Mallory? So, that's her name now?" I asked, wrinkling my nose. I loved the name Sydney. It was going to take some getting used to, but then again, a lot of this was. It was about to turn everything in my life upside down once again.

Rhonda shook her head. "She changed her name again… when she moved to Florida."

I almost choked. "Florida? You mean to tell me…that… that…she's *here*?"

She nodded and fiddled with her pen. "It's all in the files."

"And she changed her name…again? So, what is she called now?" I asked, almost unable to take in all this information at once. My life had already been turned upside down quite a lot the past year since my ex and the father of my three children, Chad, had decided to leave me for a younger and blonder version called Kimmie. After the break-up, I had moved myself and the children back to my hometown of Cocoa Beach to reconnect with my parents, only to learn that the man I believed was my father wasn't, and that the man I had loved like a father was a vicious killer who had murdered several children. Now, he was dead, and my mom was still living with the children and me, refusing to go back to the house where they had lived together. I couldn't blame her. I wanted to burn that house down and see all the lies go up in flames along with it.

"So, what's her name now?" I asked.

Rhonda leaned forward, grabbed the front of the file, and opened it. Then she pointed at something on the middle of the first page, tapping at it with her long well-manicured purple fingernail.

I stared at the name in front of me, then up at Rhonda, my eyes scrutinizing her.

Was she pulling my leg?

"But...how...that's..."

Rhonda nodded. "I know. I had to check a few extra times myself to make sure, but there's no doubt. It's her. This woman is your sister."

Chapter 2

THEN:

"Artie. Talk to me. What are we dealing with?"

Gary Pierce approached the local sheriff, who was standing by his car. Surrounding him, his deputies looked nervously at Gary. They were standing by the dirt road leading to an old farmhouse in Riverdale, Maryland.

"Tony Velleda, forty-eight, is being held hostage. Kidnappers forced their way into his home yesterday when he was there alone with his eight-year-old son. The kid was then bound on his hands and legs and left in the home when the kidnappers took his father. The boy managed to free himself and alert the neighbors, who called for authorities. The kidnappers took him across state lines, and as far as we have been informed, are keeping him at the farm up there. We know there are four armed men and the hostage. We know that at least one of the kidnappers has gang connections and another is still on parole for assault with a lethal weapon. These guys don't mess around."

"Neither do we."

Gary felt his gun in the holster. He felt the thickness of his vest like he often did before going into action. It was a strange thing to do, he always believed, but he couldn't help himself.

It was like he needed to make sure it was thick enough to actually stop a penetrating bullet...like he didn't completely believe it would.

"We're going in," he said and nodded at the sheriff. "Have your men ready."

Minutes later, they were walking up the dirt road, Gary leading them. As he held his M-4 assault rifle out in front of him, preparing himself for what awaited him inside that small house, he thought about his wife Iris and their newborn son, Oliver. He was no more than three weeks old and the most adorable thing in the world. Just this morning, when Gary had left the house to go to work, the boy had smiled for the first time, and Gary had cursed himself for having to go to work on an important day like today.

"Please, let this go down well," he prayed under his breath. "Please, let me see that smile again."

Gary snuck around the house, then found an unlit window that he broke with his rifle. He removed the glass, then crawled inside, pointing the gun through the darkness. His partner, Agent Wilson, came up right behind him, sliding in after him. They found a door where light came out, then walked closer and peeked in through the crack.

Gary spotted three men, armed to the teeth, and another man sitting in the middle of the room, blindfolded and bound to a chair.

Gary signaled Wilson, then grabbed the door and they burst inside, both yelling:

"FBI! GET DOWN!"

The three men in front of them threw down their weapons, then cast themselves on the floor, heads down, arms lifted.

Gary turned around to search for the last guy, when he appeared in the doorway behind them leading to the bedroom, holding a rifle between his hands.

"Throw down your weapons, Officers. NOW."

Gary swallowed, almost panicking, then did as he was

told. Wilson followed, but as the weapons landed on the floor, his partner pulled out a handgun, turned it at the kidnapper, and shot. One clean shot that went straight through his head. The kidnapper sunk to the floor with a thud, rag-doll limp.

Chapter 3

"So, there you have it, Greg. It still remains a huge mystery to the citizens of Cocoa Beach. What happened to the prom queen, Carina Martin, and her two friends, Tara Owens and Ava Morales, on prom night after they left the high school? Maybe this new evidence they found today will help the detectives get closer to an answer."

I turned off the TV and threw the remote on the couch. It was on as I came home from my visit to Rhonda's, file still under my arm, and no one was watching. Before I turned it off, I paused to hear if they had any news in the case of the disappearance of the three teenage girls who went missing after prom night two weeks ago. It was all everyone talked about lately, and I had to say that the reporter on News13 was right; it remained a strange mystery. They had been gone for two entire weeks now, and still, there was no trace of the girls. The theories went from them being kidnapped to them having planned this themselves to escape the pressure of senior year and exams. The last part was way too far out for my taste, but that left us with the first option, and I really didn't like that either. Matt had been on the case from the night they never came home, and their parents anxiously called CBPD to ask them to set up search teams.

Matt and I had been dating for a little more than six months now, and things were going really well. We were enjoying spending time together and hated being apart, something I had never experienced with Chad. The connection Matt and I shared was so much deeper, which was only natural since we had known each other since pre-school and his house had been my place to run to when things got tough for me at home as a teenager. But we had been nothing but friends back then, and now we had finally decided to be more than that. Twenty years apart was apparently what we needed in order to figure it out.

My book was coming along well too. Between unpacking and getting settled, I had managed to almost finish it, and I couldn't wait to be done. I was writing about my—not biological—dad, a serial killer who had managed to deceive the people he loved and hide what he was up to in plain sight, committing these atrocities right under my mother's nose. Writing his story had been a process for both my mother and me since I kept coming to her with my questions into his childhood and their lives together. I think it was therapeutic for my mom to talk about him and what had happened, but I sensed that it also drained her emotionally.

Originally, I was supposed to be writing about some of the worst serial killers in the country seen from the perspective of an FBI-profiler, but when my publishing house learned about my new storyline, a true crime story told by one of the implicated, they threw away the contract for the first book and we signed a new one. And they gave me a huge advance on top of what they had already paid me. That's how excited they were. This one was so commercial and had bestselling potential, they told me. I wasn't opposed to it becoming a bestseller. I could use the money to support myself and the kids. Chad hadn't been in the picture much since he left us, and the few times he remembered to pay alimony, it barely covered half of the rent for our house. Having three children and being a single mom was expensive.

"Knock, knock."

Matt peeked inside, holding a bottle of wine in his hand. I smiled when I saw him. I could hear the children rummaging around upstairs, and Alex yelled something at one of his sisters. It was Olivia who yelled back and then slammed her door. She was now fifteen and had no patience for her six-year-old brother, or her twelve-year-old sister, Christine. Or for me, for that matter.

Matt jumped at the sound of the door slamming. I was so used to it, I barely reacted. Instead, I smiled at Matt again and grabbed the wine from his hand.

"What's the occasion?"

He shrugged, then leaned over and kissed me. "It's Friday, and I have the weekend off."

I sent him a look. I knew the wine was for me and not him.

"I'll order some pizza. There's beer in the fridge," I said.

His face lit up. "I was hoping you'd say that."

Chapter 4

"Yum, meatloaf!"

We walked into the kitchen, and Matt laid his eyes on the dish on the counter.

"I love meatloaf," he said and approached it. "Did you make this?"

I put the bottle on the counter and shook my head with a wry smile. "Me? Cooking? If that's why you're dating me, I might as well come clean right now. I don't cook, I'm afraid. I thought you knew this by now."

"It looks delicious," he said. "Why don't we just eat that instead of pizza?"

I found the bottle opener and opened the wine. I poured myself a glass, then gave him a look, and he nodded.

"Ah, I see. Your mom made this, right?"

"Yup."

"And there is absolutely no meat in it?"

"Not an ounce. No meat, no dairy, no gluten. Only plant-based ingredients. She cooked for us all earlier because she was going to Winter Garden to play cards with her girlfriends."

Matt sighed with dissatisfaction. "It looks so good, though."

"Be my guest," I said. "But I have been eating vegan for

this entire week now, chewing my way through plant-based dishes so much I fear there might be palm trees growing out of my ears. I, for one, am ordering a pizza with loads of meat on it and enjoying the fact that my mom isn't here to disapprove or get hurt by the fact that I can't stand her cooking."

Matt shrugged, then grabbed a plate. "I'm gonna try some. It's good for you."

I sipped my wine and watched as he grabbed a piece, then found my phone and ordered a family-sized pizza, making sure there'd be enough for the kids and Matt in case he changed his mind. Once I was done, I put the phone down and looked at Matt, who seemed to be enjoying the vegan meatloaf.

"This is good," he said. "I don't know why you're complaining about your mom's cooking. I think it's really good."

I sat down on a stool and watched him take another piece and finish it while sipping my wine.

"So, where's Elijah tonight?" I asked.

Matt found a stool and sat down too. He stopped chewing, and his eyes grew weary. Matt had been a single dad ever since the mother of his child was murdered in the fall. He had never had a close relationship with the boy since he hadn't learned of the boy's existence until he was three years old, and the mother finally told him. She and Matt had a one-night-stand some nine years ago, and he thought he'd never see her again. Now, he was taking care of the eight-year-old boy on his own, and it had completely changed his life.

"He's with my mom," he said. "She took him to the movies, giving me the night off."

I leaned over and grabbed his fork, then took a bite of the vegan meatloaf too. I chewed, then made a face. Nope. Just as bad as the rest of her cooking. I sipped my wine, washing away the bad taste. There was a big part of me that wished I could enjoy my mother's cooking; there really was. I could shed a few pounds or fifteen, but I just didn't enjoy it. And if I was honest, all this healthy eating somehow made me snack more between meals, and I found myself gaining weight after my mom moved in, instead of losing it like I wanted to.

"How are things between the two of you?" I asked. "Is it getting any better?"

Matt looked down at the plate, then shook his head. "He hates my guts."

"He does not. You're his dad."

"I'm telling you; he hates me. He won't let me help him with anything, and he most certainly won't talk to me. He won't even let me tuck him in at night. He spends most of his day with my mom after school since I am at work and every day when I come home, I hope that things will be better, that he'll have warmed up to me, but he hasn't so far. I think he blames me for Lisa's death."

I reached over and put my hand on top of his. "He lost his mother, the only parent he really knew since you had him so rarely."

"And whose fault was that?" Matt asked. "It sure wasn't mine. I begged her to let me see him more, but she always came up with all these stupid excuses. It was like she enjoyed disappointing me…like she only told me about him to hurt me."

"But she did tell you, so she must have wanted you involved on some level," I said. "Maybe it was just hard for her."

Matt ate some more from his plate, then shook his head. "Yeah, well…"

"Don't give up on him. You're all he's got. Give him time. His life has changed a lot in the past six months, and he doesn't know where he stands. He probably misses his mom terribly, and you're the only one around he can take it out on. Give it some time. I'm sure he'll come around."

"It's just…it's nothing like I imagined it would be, you know? Being a father, full-time I mean. It's really…hard."

"Welcome to the club."

I chuckled and sipped my wine, sending a loving glance toward my own children upstairs. Mine weren't doing too badly lately. Alex seemed to have found his peace with his new surroundings. Being a part of the gifted program TAG at school meant they were giving him more challenging assignments, and that seemed to have calmed him down a lot. He still yelled often when he spoke, and it was still hard for him to sit still for more than a few minutes at a time, but he seemed happier. The girls seemed to be doing better, too, than when we first got here. They never spoke much about their father anymore, and I didn't really know if that was a good or a bad thing. In the beginning, they went up to Washington to visit him and Kimmie at least once a month, but the past two months, the girls hadn't wanted to go when I asked them. Especially my oldest, Olivia, seemed like she couldn't care less about her father, and that wasn't like her. I wondered if something had happened the last time they were up there. I felt sorry for Alex since he missed his father, but I couldn't really send him up there all alone on a plane. Maybe other six-year-olds would do fine, but not my Alex. It wouldn't end well for any of the passengers on that plane.

"I saw on the news that they found another shoe they believe is Carina Martin's?" I said, trying to change the subject. "This time all the way at the east end of the golf course in some bushes?"

Matt walked to the fridge and grabbed a beer. "Yeah, it was the second shoe. We found the heel on the asphalt and the remains of the first shoe on the night she disappeared."

"But that means she went even deeper into the golf course than you thought, right?"

He nodded, opened his beer, and sat down. "Yeah. It was found close to a bushy area where lots of golfers usually lose their balls. It's like a small forest part that is nearly impassable. I thought we had that place completely combed through, but it's just so…big, you know?"

I nodded. "So, do you think she might have been hiding in there?"

"I don't know. She could also have gone in there with

17

some guy. It was prom, you know? People do some pretty crazy things on prom night."

"But you found the crown by the entrance to the country club, right?" I asked.

He nodded and sipped his beer. "We've found broken shoes in multiple locations spread throughout the golf course. We found Tara Owen's purse with her phone in it and part of Ava Morales' dress that was ripped off was floating in one of the small ponds."

"It's almost like Hansel and Gretel following the bread-crumbs," I mumbled.

He looked up. "What was that?"

I shook my head. "Nothing. What about the two other phones? Have you been able to locate them?"

He shook his head.

"Social media accounts? Anything that might give you a lead? Anyone they chatted with?"

"We're still working on that part," he said. "The forensic lab is taking care of it. They're still working on their computers and getting their cell phone histories. Young people today have so many social media accounts, it takes forever, but so far they haven't found anything useful."

"Have any of the girls had issues with other students at the school? Have they received any threats? Trouble at home with parents or relatives? Any mental illnesses?"

"No, no, and no," he said. "The three girls had perfect attendance, and they were straight A or A-B honor roll. They were well-liked and popular, especially Carina Martin."

"What about boyfriends?" I asked, sipping from my glass.

"Ava Morales was dating a guy from the school, but he wasn't at the prom since he was in Orlando to say goodbye to his grandmother who died the night before. The two other girls didn't have boyfriends. Some of the other students say that Carina was with Kevin Bass that night and that she was stealing him from her best friend."

"And this Kevin Bass, have you talked to him?"

"I think we've talked to pretty much everyone who was at

the prom. Kevin was on the cleaning committee and left a lot later than the girls. He was cleaning up with a bunch of teachers until about an hour after the party."

"It sounds like they were running," I said, pensively. "The way the shoes were scattered all over the area. I mean, it's not easy to run across a golf course wearing high heels, so it would be natural to take them off to be better able to run."

He swallowed. The look in his eyes told me he knew I was right, but he didn't like to think about it.

"But if they were running, where were they going?" I said, thinking out loud. "There really isn't anywhere to go. The golf course is surrounded by water," I said.

"We've had diving teams in the river for days on end, searching through every area of the river and the canals leading to the residential areas. You know this, Eva Rae," he said. "They haven't found anything."

"I know; I know. I'm just trying to figure out why you'd want to run across a golf course in the middle of the night, wearing your very expensive shoes and dress unless you were being chased."

"Or drunk. Or high and foolish," he said. "According to their friends, the three of them had been drinking before they went to the prom. Carina Martin even smoked marijuana with her friend Molly Carson behind the performing arts building right before she was crowned prom queen."

"That sounds like prom all right. They had an argument; didn't they?" I asked. "Carina and Molly? Over Kevin? I remember you told me so…or did I read it somewhere? Maybe Melissa told me. Molly is her daughter, you know."

"Yes. That's right. They did. We've been looking into her."

"Molly?" I asked, startled. "Melissa's daughter, why?"

"Because of the fight. Maybe it turned bad later on. Maybe she could have chased Carina, and maybe she fell and hurt herself and Molly hid her body? Molly's father does have a concealed carrier's permit. She might have taken his gun and gone off, or it could have been an accident."

I shook my head. "I hope you're kidding me. Not Molly. Not Melissa's daughter."

Matt took in a deep breath, then ran a hand through his thick brown hair. He hadn't been surfing much lately because of a growing workload, and his hair wasn't as blond as it used to be.

"Did she have an alibi at least?" I asked.

"Yes, but not a very good one, I'm afraid. Molly Carson went home while the prom queen was still dancing with the prom king. Lots of people saw her leave. She called her mother, who picked her up and took her home, and she went to bed after that, Melissa said. And I have to say that after talking to her friends and teachers, it would be very much out of character for Molly to hurt anyone. They all describe her as someone who takes care of everyone else, always has a shoulder to cry on. When I questioned her, I got the feeling she wouldn't be able to hurt a fly."

I drank my wine. "That's not much of an alibi, though. It could be argued that she might have climbed out of the window."

Matt gave me a look. "I know. That's what worries me. Well, that's one of the many things that bothers me about this case. As much as I would like to rule out Molly as a suspect, it's not possible."

"You don't really think a seventeen-year-old girl killed three of her friends over some boy, do you?" I asked.

He sipped his beer, then shrugged. "I've seen stranger things happen, but of course, I don't. As long as we don't have any bodies yet, there is still hope. But then you're looking at a possible kidnapping. And where does that leave us? I just don't understand why there hasn't been any ransom request made."

"Unless it's a sex offender," I said. "You already checked all that live in the area, didn't you?"

Matt nodded while finishing his beer. He put the empty bottle down.

"Yes. And we also spoke to the parents, over and over

again. No fights, no reason for the three of them to want to run away."

I sighed. This was a true mystery, one that had me intrigued, yet scared to death. I had two girls of my own. I wanted to figure out what happened to those three girls as much as anyone, even though it annoyed Matt to talk shop when he was off.

He glanced at the file on the counter next to me.

"How did the meeting go with Rhonda?"

I swallowed and looked away.

"Oh, my," he said. "She found something; didn't she? That's why you have the file?"

I shrugged. "Maybe."

"Did she find Sydney?"

I lifted my eyes and looked into his. Then, I nodded.

"Really? That's wonderful, isn't it? Isn't it, Eva Rae? Why do you look like that?"

"Like what?" I asked.

"Like you're upset and not happy. You've been wanting to find your sister all your life, and now you finally have the chance. Why don't you look thrilled?"

I glanced at the closed file on my counter. I wondered what to tell him…if I could tell him the truth. I needed to process it myself first.

"No reason," I said. "I'm just tired; that's all."

"Yeah, right," he said. "Who do you think you're fooling? Not the guy who has known you since you were three years old. Something is up. Spit it out, Eva Rae."

I sighed, then reached over and grabbed the folder between my hands. I stared at it for a few seconds, then opened it and showed him the first page, pointing at the name in the middle of it. He looked at it, then up at me, his eyes growing wide.

"You're kidding me, right?"

I shook my head. "Nope. This is her name now. And she lives here in Florida, apparently."

Chapter 5

The room they were being kept in was small and stuffy. The air felt moist and tight. Carina's chest heaved up and down as she fought not to hyperventilate. Ava and Tara were still sleeping on their mattresses on the floor next to her. Carina felt dizzy as she had every time she woke up in the tight room with the massive concrete walls surrounding her.

She had lost her sense of time since there were no windows in their prison. But she remembered, still with great terror, when she had woken up after her prom night. She had been on a carpet, a beige carpet, she remembered. Her head had been pounding like crazy, and she felt disoriented. She had called for her mother, then spotted Ava, who had also woken up, lying next to her. Then, to her terror, she had realized she had something around her neck, a chain. Panicking, she had tried to pull it off and then started to scream.

A masked person had approached her, then slammed his fist into her face to make her shut up. It had worked. She had fallen backward and not regained her sight properly until she felt a pull on her chain so hard that she could do nothing but follow along, crawling on all fours. There had been a hallway of some sort and what else? Oh, yeah, a bookshelf. There had been a bookshelf that he unscrewed and removed. Then, the masked man had rolled the carpet away underneath, and a slab of concrete was revealed with a frame around it. The masked man attached a bar with a hook to the slab and began cranking it open. Carina watched, her eyes swimming, and trying to focus as a hole appeared beneath it. Then the masked person spoke.

"Get in."

Carina had tried to focus on the hole and tried to keep her panic at bay, but now she couldn't anymore. She screamed again with the result that he hit her again, then kicked her in the stomach.

"GET IN!"

Whimpering, Carina climbed down into the hole, and soon the man followed her into the darkness. They walked through a small tunnel that led to a tiny door leading to a room the size of a closet with three mattresses on the floor.

The man pulled her by the chain and attached it to a metal bar inside so tight that she couldn't reach the door if she tried. She could get up and walk to the corner, where he had left a bucket for them to pee in and another one with some sort of kibble for them to eat and a bowl of water for them to drink from like animals. The first couple of days, Carina had refused to eat and drink, but then realized that, if she wanted to survive, she had to do what the others did. She had to become the animal this kidnapper treated them like. Still wearing the remains of her ocean blue mermaid dress, she crawled on all fours till she reached the bowl of water and drank greedily before the others woke up, her chain clanking against the metal bar on the wall when she moved. The bowl was changed once a day, so whoever came to it first got the clean and cold water. One day, Ava had mixed up the two buckets and peed on their food instead of in the toilet bucket. For that, she received a beating by the masked man that left her unconscious for two hours.

Now, as Carina was watching the two of them sleep, eating as much as she could before they woke up, she started wondering how long they had been down in that hole. Her nails were growing long, and her teeth were so sticky she could carve stuff off them with her fingernail. Not to mention the bad smell coming from their unwashed bodies. But as much as she would like to know how long she had been there, another question was beginning to press on her, one even more urgent than the first.

How long did he intend to keep them down there, and what would happen to them when he grew bored with them?

Chapter 6

The pizza arrived, and I went to get it, then yelled at the kids to come down and eat. As I returned to Matt in the kitchen, he still wouldn't let it go.

"But this is huge, Eva Rae. This is massive; don't you think?"

"I don't know," I said dismissively while putting the pizza down. It smelled heavenly, and I grabbed a piece directly from the box. Matt looked into the file again and shook his head, then pointed at the picture of my sister.

"I can't believe it. Kelly Stone is your sister? As in Kelly Stone, the actress? She's like famous, like really famous as in Hollywood famous."

"I guess she always seemed kind of familiar," I said. "I watched her in that movie *The Highway* and the one about that time traveler guy."

Matt lifted his eyes and glared at me. "So, what's your problem? Why aren't you ecstatic?

"Because…" I said, and put the pizza down. "First of all, I'm still processing all this, okay? Secondly, I'm disappointed; that's all. Because I can never go visit her."

"Why not?"

"You don't just walk up to some famous Hollywood

actress and go *hey, by the way, I'm your sister. Do you remember that you were once kidnapped in a Wal-Mart?*"

"Sure, you can," Matt said. "It would be shocking to anyone; why is it harder just because she's famous?"

I shrugged, then heard the children's steps on the stairs and signaled for Matt to keep quiet.

"PIZZA!" Alex exclaimed loudly as always.

"With lots of meat on it," I smiled and handed him a piece.

Alex's eyes gleamed as he looked up at me. "I won't tell Grandma; don't worry," he said and stormed to the table and sat down in a chair.

"Really, Mom? You're teaching him how to lie now?" Christine said as I handed her a piece.

I smiled wryly. "Eat your food."

"Meat, Mom?" Olivia said as she approached me, earbuds still in. I could hear the music blasting loudly from them as she pulled one out. "Really? I was kind of getting used to being vegan."

I stared at my daughter. "You're kidding me, right? You used to hate your grandma's cooking."

"Who hates Grandma's cooking?" a voice asked from the doorway. I turned to see my mother standing there, car keys in her hand, her purse over her shoulder.

Shoot!

Her smile was frozen as her eyes landed on the pizza, then on Alex's greasy face, strings of cheese hanging from his chin.

"So…I take it you're having a pizza party, huh? I'm sorry if my food is so terrible that you feel like you have to celebrate when I'm out."

I felt like crawling into a hole. She was hurt.

"Mom, I…I…"

"Save it, Eva Rae," she said. "I've had a long day. I'm going to bed."

She turned around and was about to walk away when Matt yelled across the room.

"I tried your vegan meatloaf, Mrs. Thomas, and it was really good."

I shot him a look. Was he seriously kissing up to my mother?

He shrugged. "What? It's true."

My mom looked tiredly at us. "That's wonderful, Matt. I'm going to bed."

"Mom...I..."

But it was too late. She had left. I felt awful. My mom had been so nice to cook for us every night and, no, it wasn't all terrible; some of it was quite good, actually. But I guess I hadn't really shown my appreciation to her. Fact was, I loved having her at the house, at least most of the time when she didn't criticize me. And it was good for the kids. I was finally close to her again and catching up for all the years we had lost. The last thing I wanted was for her to be hurt. She'd been through so much already. As we all had. And I felt like I was hurting her feelings constantly.

Was I doing it deliberately? To punish her for ignoring me all of my childhood? Because there still was so much unsaid between us?

I felt ashamed.

I drank my wine when Matt came up to me, handing me Rhonda's yellow folder.

"Maybe this could cheer her up, huh?" he said. "A little mother-daughter project?"

I stared into his eyes, then leaned over and kissed him. "You're kidding me, right?"

"Not at all. I think this could be good for both of you."

"I just...I don't feel like it's the right time now. I don't know if I'm ready yet."

"There will never be a perfect time to do anything like this. Think about it," he said and kissed me back, the kids making disgusted sounds behind us.

"Get a room; will you?" Olivia said and pretended to be gagging.

"Yeah, and a car," Alex said, imitating his sister.

I ignored them and laughed. It had taken them a little time to get used to their mom dating again, but after that, they had all been so nice to welcome Matt into our lives, and I knew they liked him, especially Alex, who always asked him to play with his firetrucks with him, and who loved anything with sirens and blinking lights. He had come around on the day Matt took him for a drive in his police cruiser. After that, there was no turning back for the two of them. Sometimes, I felt that Matt wished that his own son, Elijah, was more like Alex and that he enjoyed hanging out with him a lot more than with his own son, which was incredibly sad. I wanted Matt to have that connection with his own son that I felt with my children even though I was gone for a lot of the time when they were growing up. Their trust in me was slowly returning, and now my only regret was all the moments I had missed with them. I was hoping to be able to make new memories with them that we could cherish for the rest of our lives

I glanced at the folder in my hand, realizing that my priorities had changed drastically. I was all about family now, and that also included my sister, famous or not.

Chapter 7

"Where are we going, Eva Rae? Can't you tell me?"

I looked briefly at my mom, then shook my head. We were sitting in my minivan, the sun baking in through the windows, the AC cranked on high and Bruno Mars playing on the radio. It was a gorgeous day out, one of many when living in Florida, and surfers were crossing the roads, riding skateboards while carrying their surfboards under their arms. Beachgoers and snowbirds were carrying their gear, eyes gleaming at the thought of spending an entire day in the white sand.

"I'm not going to tell you, Mom. It's supposed to be a surprise," I said. My voice was trembling slightly in anticipation and nervousness, but I hoped she wouldn't hear it.

My mom snorted and corrected her skirt. "You know I don't like surprises, Eva Rae."

I had been awake almost all night, thinking this through, and by the time the sun rose above the neighbor's house across the canal, I had made my decision. Today was Saturday, so I had the entire day to do this. Matt was right; the right time would never come if I thought about it too much. I would always come up with an excuse to postpone it, and then I'd never know. If I wanted to face this woman whom I believed was my sister, I had to do it. I had to throw myself into it without any safety net.

"Why can't you tell me where we're going," my mom said after a short break and a deep annoyed sigh. We had left Cocoa Beach and driven past the Patrick Air Force Base on our way to Melbourne Beach, where Kelly Stone lived. Matt had told me that it had been in all the papers when she had bought the house a couple of years ago and it was very close to where the rapper Vanilla Ice had bought his house a few years earlier and had it remodeled during his TV show, *The Vanilla Ice Project.*

"Because I don't want to ruin the surprise," I said. "And, because if I told you, then you would never have come with me."

My mom snorted again. "That's not very reassuring, Eva Rae. You're not selling this very well."

I exhaled, trying to choke the butterflies in my stomach. I feared that I was making a mistake and contemplated turning around for a few seconds but then decided against it. This could end in disaster, yes, but it could also not. It could also end well.

I glanced nervously at my mother, then felt my heart sink. A gazillion thoughts rushed through my mind in this instant. It had been thirty-six years. Would we recognize her? Would she recognize us? What was she like?

My mom looked at her watch. "How far are we going? Did you remember to bring water? It's hot out. I don't want to dehydrate. How about sunscreen? And bug spray, did you bring that? If we're going to be outdoors, then I'll need that. You know how I swell up."

"You won't need that where we're going, Mom. And yes, I brought a couple of bottles of water in my purse. You won't dehydrate. Besides, we're almost there."

"Where? There's nothing much out here?"

My GPS told me we had arrived, and I drove up in front of a gate.

"What is this place, Eva Rae? What are we doing here?"

my mom asked. "What have you planned? I have a feeling I'm not going to like it."

I sighed and looked at her, then grabbed her hand in mine. She winced nervously.

"What is this, Eva Rae? You're scaring me."

"Mom. Sweet, dear, Mom. You asked what my plan was? To be honest, I have no idea. I don't think I've really thought this through."

My mom shook her head, her eyes scrutinizing me. "What are you talking about? Why are you being like this? What are we doing here, Eva Rae? What's going on? Won't you—for the love of God—just tell me?"

I swallowed. I hadn't really decided when to tell her and thought I could wing it, but now that we were there, in front of her house, ready to ring the intercom, I wasn't sure I could. How would she react?

"Mom…I…"

"What is this place?" my mom asked, looking out the windshield. Behind the wall, the treetops, and the lion statues towered a mansion. "Whose house is this?"

"It's…It belongs to Kelly Stone; you know the actress?"

"I know who she is. But why are we here?"

"Well, the thing is…I called her assistant earlier this morning and told her we were gathering sponsors for a charity surf event for orphaned children and that all the money will go to prevent human trafficking of children. She's agreed to meet with us and talk about it."

My mom gave me a look. "Why? Why would you say such a thing? I don't understand anything you're saying right now. Have you completely lost your mind, Eva Rae Thomas?"

I shrugged. "Maybe, but it was the only way I thought I could get her to meet with us. She doesn't like reporters and hasn't done an interview in years. She likes to keep private, so it's not easy to get to her."

"But why? Why do you want to get to her in the first place?"

I grabbed the folder from the back seat and held it

between my hands for a few minutes. What would happen if I told my mother the truth?

"Kidnapped children are an area close to her heart," I said. "She's donated millions to help prevent human trafficking over the years and helped build shelters for homeless children, so they don't have to sleep in the streets, where they can easily be kidnapped."

"Kidnapped children, but…what…why, why are you… lying to her like that?"

I exhaled again, then decided to go with another lie. "Because I'm actually thinking about doing this event and I wanted you to maybe do it with me. Would you like to do that?"

I swallowed and looked at my mom expectantly, biting my lip. Was she buying this?

"Why…well…Why didn't you just ask me that in the first place? You know I love arranging charity events. Why did you have to kidnap me and keep it a secret?"

I smiled and returned the folder to the back seat. "I guess I was scared you'd say no."

"Why would I say no to helping children? It's not like I have better things to do with my life these days. A project like this could be good for me and for us. And for the children, of course."

"So, you're in?" I said and rolled the window down, ready to press the button on the intercom.

She nodded. "Yes, I'm in. As long as you promise not to sneak attack me like this again, ever."

I sent her a forced smile, then turned around and pressed the button, while a loud voice inside of my mind was screaming at me.

What are you doing???

Chapter 8

As I had expected, Kelly Stone's house was beyond gorgeous. It was truly worthy of a Hollywood starlet. We walked up the stairs to the wooden double doors, where her assistant welcomed us. The house was directly on the beach, and as we walked inside the hallway, we were hit by the striking views from everywhere we turned. The Atlantic Ocean was glistening in the sun and looked very inviting through the Spanish arched window panes.

"Miss Stone will be right down," her assistant said and showed us into a living room that was big enough to fit my entire house. It was beautifully decorated and obviously done by a professional in the light beach style. For a second, I felt a pinch of jealousy of the woman I believed could be my sister. I was never good at decorating, and my homes were always a mess with toys and laundry lingering in the corners. I would never be able to have a home like this.

"This is nice; don't you think?" my mom said and took a quick glance around. "Very stylish."

"Yeah, well, if you have money like that, it's easy to live beautifully," I said, sounding a little more annoyed than I was. I knew my mom didn't approve of the way I lived, and she was constantly trying to clean up after all of us since she moved in, yet it still looked messy. This type of decor and house was more what she had been used to. It also meant I had grown up in a house where you were hardly allowed to touch the furniture. I had always promised myself that my children wouldn't grow up in a home like that. But that also meant I had to live with the mess. I just wasn't a very neat person. I never thought of it as being important. I preferred spending time with my children. Especially back when I was still in the FBI and used to work so much; I was barely home. Whenever I walked inside that house, my focus was fully on the children. There was no time to clean up or think about decorations. But I never could get my mom to understand that. She believed I was neglecting my family by working and not keeping the house.

"This is quite exciting," my mom said with a slight shiver. "We're going to meet a real movie star."

She whispered the last word like it was a secret. I felt a knot grow in my stomach while wondering how on Earth this was ever going to end well. How was I going to react when I saw her? Would she know who we were just by looking at us?

"Hello there," a voice chirped from the other end of the room. A beautiful woman in a light fluttering dress almost floated across the marble tiles toward us. I gaped at her, eyes wide open, stunned by her beauty as our eyes met, and I felt a pinch in my stomach. I didn't know if she felt it too, but I sensed that she did feel something because her smile froze for just a second. Her eyes lingered on me, then on my mom, *our* mom, before she shook her head and put the starlet smile back on.

Back in character.

"Welcome, welcome, I am so sorry for keeping you waiting."

She shook both of our hands, and we introduced ourselves. As Mom said hers, I wondered if this woman knew anything about us, or if she knew our names, but she didn't seem to react when hearing them. It was only when our eyes met that I sensed she paused every now and then, like she was trying to remember something, yet couldn't.

"Do sit down," she said. "I'm from London, so I think it's a little too hot to sit outside at this hour of the day. Can we just take the couch over there by the panorama window?"

We both nodded and smiled. I glanced at my mother as we sat down on the soft sofas with the massive pillows and thought I saw something in her eyes, but then it was gone.

"All right. What can I do for you ladies today?" Kelly Stone said and clapped her perfectly manicured hands. "My assistant said you have some charity event that you needed a sponsor for?"

Chapter 9

I stared at the woman in front of me as she spoke, telling us all about how big she believed the issue of kidnapped children was all over the world, while her expensive jewelry dangled from her wrists.

"It has always been very close to my heart, and not only the sex trafficking industry, but also the children who are kidnapped by a parent or close relative and taken far away. Many of them never see their families again. Those children grow up so neglected and always looking for that missing part of them. It's truly a cause that needs focus as well."

"And it's terrible for the families left behind too," my mother said, her voice cracking slightly. "To never see their children again and not knowing if they are dead or alive."

Kelly Stone paused after Mom was done. She stared into her eyes, and I wondered for a second if she knew. But then she shook her head lightly and leaned back.

"Where are my manners? You have been here for several minutes, and I haven't even offered you anything to drink. Where I grew up, that is highly impolite, and I must apologize. What can I get you? Coffee? Water? A glass of lemonade?"

My mom stared at her, her eyes following her every movement carefully like she was studying her. My pulse grew quicker.

"I'd love some lemonade," I said. "And my mom would too. If it's not too much trouble."

Kelly Stone turned to look at me. "Not at all."

Our eyes met again, and my heart was racing in my chest. There was no longer any doubt in my mind. This was her. This was Sydney. She looked very different than she had when we were children, and I suspected she had some work done on that face, but looking into her eyes, I knew it was definitely her. The realization filled me with so many emotions; it was hard to hold it back. I had been missing her for so many years, believing she was dead and gone, and here she was, doing awesomely for herself, perfectly alive and more beautiful than ever. I wanted to blurt it out, just tell her the real reason we were here, but I didn't. I was too scared of losing her again, of her getting angry at us.

She called for her assistant and told her to bring us both some lemonade. Then she returned and sat down.

"This is nice," she said with a light exhale. "Mother and daughter doing an event like this together."

"Yeah, well, we're sort of trying to reconnect after many years apart," I said. "I just recently moved back here to the area."

"That's nice," she said, smiling. "Do you have children?"

I nodded while it felt like my throat was swelling up. It was hard to swallow or even breathe.

"Three," I said, my eyes growing wet. I was fighting my tears but losing. "Two girls and a boy."

"How lovely," Kelly Stone said. "I bet they're excited to be close to their grandmother. Sounds like you have a nice family."

"Yeah…well…we do our best, I guess."

"It's not always easy, is it? Families," she said.

"It sure isn't," I said. "But it's so worth it."

Kelly Stone clenched a fist in front of her mouth and closed her eyes briefly, then gathered herself when the lemonade arrived. My mother grabbed her glass and emptied the entire drink in one gulp. I stared at her, startled. She usually never drank anything with sugar in it.

"Boy. I guess I was thirsty," she said, looking surprised at the empty glass in her hand. "Gotta be careful not to dehydrate at my age."

Kelly Stone's eyes grew wet as she looked at our mom putting the glass back down, making sure it landed on a coaster she found.

"It sure is getting hot out," Kelly said. "We all need to drink a lot to stay hydrated. Especially me who isn't used to the Florida heat just yet."

I sipped my lemonade as well, unsure of what to do or say next. I wanted us to stay as long as possible because I wanted to talk to my sister; I wanted to know everything about her now that I had finally found her, and I wanted her to know everything about me. But at the same time, I felt like I had to throw up. I was getting too emotional, and I wasn't sure I could keep it at bay for very long.

"I…I think we…Could I use the bathroom?" I asked.

Kelly Stone smiled and nodded. "Of course. It's right down the hall and to your left."

I got up and rushed down the hallway, then found the door leading to the bathroom. I shut the door behind me, then slid down to the floor, my back leaned against it, finally letting the tears escape.

Chapter 10

As I returned, my mom had gotten a refill on her lemonade and was taking it slightly easier this time, taking smaller sips. I wondered if the two of them had even spoken a word while I was gone; they were so quiet when I got there. I knew from Google that Kelly Stone didn't have any children, but still, I searched the place for pictures of anyone she might hold dear yet found none.

"Do you live here all alone?" I asked as I sat down.

Kelly shook her head. "My fiancée lives here too."

So, she did have someone in her life. That made me relax a little. I didn't like the thought of her being all alone.

"I'm getting used to him being here. I've always lived on my own. I was alone a lot when growing up," she said, tearing up, yet hiding it very well behind a bright smile. "Didn't have a big family or any…siblings. It was just me and my dad." She sniffled, then looked first at our mom, then me. "I don't know why I'm telling you all this. You must think I'm silly. I'm usually a very private person, and you have no interest in hearing all this about my…"

"Yes, we do," I said, then regretted it. I looked down as I spoke. "I mean. We don't mind at all. It's nice to know there is a human behind the actress, if you know what I mean?"

Kelly nodded. "I got carried away. I apologize. You're probably in a rush to get out of here and get back to the children. It is, after all, Saturday. Now, let's get into the details of this event, shall we? How much do you need to make this happen?"

I don't know where I got it all from, but I just threw out numbers. I had put together some imaginary plan before we left and showed it to her, not knowing if it looked remotely like anything plausible for a charity event. I didn't even know if Kelly Stone was simply just humoring me, but she went along, and before we knew of it, she had promised to fund the entire thing, as long as we kept her identity a secret. She didn't want it all over the media. That wasn't why she was doing it.

We said our goodbyes and soon after my mom and I were back in the car, and I turned on the engine. My mom was completely quiet as we drove out of the driveway and the gate closed behind us. I could hear my own heartbeat in my ears and wondered what the heck I had done. What had I expected to get out of this today? I knew I wanted to see her for myself before I decided anything. I wanted to make sure it really was her. I guess I thought that, when I saw her, I would know, and I was right. I knew it was her, but I hadn't thought this through enough. What would I do next? Did I have to put on this charity event? Did I come clean and tell her? How would she react if I did?

I rushed onto A1A and sped up toward Cocoa Beach, my mom sitting silently beside me.

Twenty minutes later, as I parked in my own driveway and killed the engine, she finally looked at me. Just as I was about to get out, she placed a hand on my arm. Tears were in her eyes as she looked at me.

"Thank you," she said. "For involving me in this."

"Mom…I…"

She nodded. "I know, sweetie. I know. You don't have to say anything. I think we should all sleep on it and then decide how best to handle this."

She exited the car and left me sitting back, baffled. What exactly did she mean? Did she know and just didn't want to tell me? Or was she actually talking about the event?

There was no way of knowing with my mom.

Chapter 11

THEN:

On the night he returned after the shooting at the farmhouse, Gary Pierce held his baby a little tighter than usual. His wife Iris stood behind him as he held the small bundle in his arms, a tear escaping his eye.

Iris put a hand on his shoulder. She had a concerned look in her eyes. "Did something happen today?"

Gary swallowed and kissed her forehead. He didn't want to tell her about it and have her worry.

"Just work, baby. Just work."

He sighed and pulled his wife into the hug, then held his two beloved ones as tightly as possible while the fear and anxiety slowly faded away. Today had been a close one. Staring down the barrel of that assault rifle had almost made him lose it. He had been certain he would never see his son and wife again. It was amazing how many thoughts could rush through someone's mind when staring death in the face. Most of his had been about Oliver and how he would miss out on all the important stuff in his life. He would never get to see him start to walk; he wouldn't be there when he had his first day of school or when he graduated. He wouldn't get to see what a handsome and smart young man Oliver would become and how he would constantly amaze him with his wits and how caring he was toward others. All those things, Gary dreaded he might miss. It was a constant fear that lingered inside of him every day when he went to work, not knowing what the day might bring.

And it had to be in Iris's mind too when sending him off every morning with a kiss and a coffee in his hand. It had to be tough on her as well.

They had told Gary and Wilson that they were heroes, that they had saved a man from his kidnappers and saved his life, so he could get back to his son. The man had been kidnapped to pressure him for money that they believed he owed them. It was gang-related and wouldn't have ended well for the man or the boy if Gary and Wilson hadn't been there, they were told. There had been a lot of shoulder claps and high fives and kind words, but all Gary could think about was how close it had been. It was the first time in the line of duty that he had been so scared of dying, and it frightened him. He never used to be afraid of anything, especially not on the job. As an FBI agent, you couldn't allow yourself to be afraid. Danger came with the job, and you knew that going in. It had never bothered him before. He barely thought about it. So, what had changed?

Gary stared at his wife and son, his heart pounding.

He had so much to lose now.

Iris stood on her tippy toes and kissed him, then stroked his cheek gently, while Oliver was fussing in Gary's arms, probably getting hungry when smelling his mother's presence. The child seemed so fragile in Gary's arms; it seemed almost impossible that he would ever make it in this cruel world. Yet that was exactly why Gary did what he did. He truly believed he contributed to making the world a safer place for Oliver to grow up in by putting the bad guys away.

If they don't get me first.

"I should take him," Iris said when Oliver's fussing grew to a squeaking that they both knew soon would be crying. After three weeks, they were slowly beginning to know the boy's signals and figure out what he wanted. They usually tried feeding him first, then checked if he needed a clean diaper, and if that didn't work, then he was probably just tired and needed to be put down for a nap. Still supporting his head, Gary handed the boy to his mother, who sat down and started nursing the boy. Oliver grunted, satisfied, as he ate, and his mother stroked him gently across his sparse hair while singing. Gary stared at the two of them, a huge knot growing in his throat, and realized this was the happiest moment of his life. There was nothing he wanted in life right now other than to be right there.

How did he get to be so lucky?

Chapter 12

"What do you think he wants from us?"

Ava spoke with a small hoarse voice that bounced off the walls of the small room. Carina lifted her head to look at her. They had all been thinking about it, but she was the first to say it out loud. When they first got there, they had screamed for hours on end and knocked on the sides of the room, hoping someone might hear them and come to their rescue. But soon they grew tired and could hardly keep their hopes up. It felt like they had been down there forever, and they began to wonder if it would ever end. Were they just going to die down here in this hole?

"You think he wants to rape us?" she continued.

The word made Tara sob loudly and hide her face, curling up on her mattress.

Again, Ava was only saying what they had all been thinking, yet hearing it made Carina very uneasy. She didn't want to think about it, yet she did, constantly. She kept thinking it was only a matter of time.

"I watched this show recently on Netflix about these girls who were abducted and kept at this man's house for eleven years."

Carina closed her eyes to try and calm herself down. The thought was terrifying.

"He raped them, and they even gave birth to his babies. Eleven years," Ava said, then paused. "I'll be twenty-eight by then. All my youth will be gone, wasted."

"Please, stop," Tara said. "Just, stop."

Ava looked at her, then bit her lip. "There are also those men who kidnap girls and then kill them when they get pregnant."

"Please, just stop, will you?" Carina said. "Just stop talking about things like that."

Ava stared at her, the chain around her neck clanking as she lifted her head. That was when Carina realized tears were streaming down Ava's cheeks. The small lightbulb underneath the ceiling gave them just enough light to see their food and where to pee, but it wasn't very bright.

"We need to encourage one another," Carina said and placed a shaking hand on her arm. "So far, he hasn't wanted to touch any of us, so maybe that's not why we're here."

Tara sat up, the chain banging against the bar on the wall where it was attached.

"Of course, that's why we're here. Why else would you kidnap three young girls our age? He wants to rape us till we scream and then he'll kill us. Don't you understand?"

Carina did, and she also knew that the two others were probably right. But more than that, she knew that thinking about all the terrible things that might happen didn't help them one iota. It only made them weak and paralyzed with fear, and that was exactly what this guy wanted them to be. She had seen it in his eyes when he pushed her down the hole. He wanted them to fear him, to know that he was in charge. He had that power trip in his eyes that she had seen once when her dad was harassed by a cop who had pulled them over. Ava's dad was black and used to them treating him that way, and even them thinking Ava couldn't be his since she had fair skin and didn't look anything like him. But she was. Ava just looked more like her mother.

"Aren't you scared at all?" Ava asked her.

"Yes, of course, I am," Carina replied. "I'm just saying

that right now we need to keep calm. Panicking will get us nowhere, okay? I want to make it out of here alive, and I think that if we stick together, then maybe we can outsmart this guy somehow."

Tara stared at her, her mouth open. Her entire body was shaking, even though it was very hot in the small room, and the air was sparse. Carina suffered terribly from claustrophobia, and it took all her strength not to panic completely.

"But how?" Tara asked.

"I don't know yet," Carina said. "But I want you both to keep alert. He comes down here once a day, the way I figure it since he took our phones and watches. But I think it's about once a day. We keep our eyes and ears open when he does, okay? It's all we can do right now. And then—most importantly—we don't panic."

Chapter 13

The sun hit my face through my curtains on Sunday morning. I turned over in bed and put my arm around Matt. He had ended up going to the station after all and had worked late. He had come over right before I was about to turn in. I had stayed up an hour longer, talking with him in the living room, telling him about my meeting with my sister, before we started to kiss intensely and soon—after a couple of glasses of wine—were all over each other. We had ended up upstairs in my bed and then fallen asleep.

It slowly occurred to me what had happened, and that Matt was still here when I opened my eyes.

"Shoot," I said.

Matt woke up with a broad smile on his lips. "Good morning to you, too."

He leaned over to kiss me, but I pulled away.

"You're still here," I said.

He sat up and ruffled his hair. He didn't look less cute in the morning; I had to admit. I stared at his abs. Chad had never had abs like that. Not that he was fat or anything; he wasn't, but he wasn't buff or even well trained like this. I suddenly became very aware of my own chubby thighs and a bulging tire of a stomach that still bore very visible marks of having given birth to three children.

"That I can't argue against," he said, grinning.

"No, no, you don't understand. The kids," I said. "They can't know you're here...that you spent the night."

Matt exhaled and rubbed his head. "I'm sorry, but we fell asleep after..."

"Not so loud, they might be listening," I said. "They can't know."

His eyes landed on me. "You really think they don't know? We've been dating for six months, Eva Rae. I'm always around. I've just never been here all night."

I looked at him, then covered myself up with the sheet. He put his arm around my shoulder and pulled me into a deep kiss. "I like waking up with you," he said in a whisper. "I want to do it more."

"What about Elijah?" I asked.

"What about him? He stayed with my mom last night."

"But are you ready to tell him about us yet?" I asked.

He wrinkled his forehead. "What do you mean? He knows we're dating. He likes you. I think he likes you better than me, to be honest. But I think that he likes anyone better than me these days."

"But do you want him to know you spent the night here?" I asked. "I'm not sure I'm ready to tell my kids that we...that the two of us are..."

He chuckled. "Having sex. Just say it, Eva Rae. It won't hurt you."

"Shh," I said. "My mom is in the house too. She might hear us."

"So, now your mom can't know either? How long do you plan on keeping this a secret?"

I swallowed. "I haven't really thought about that. It's just that my family is...well, old fashioned."

"So, they don't have sex?" he asked. "Your mom must have had sex at some point since she did give birth to both you and your sister."

"Shh," I said.

Matt laughed. "You can't even say the word out loud, can you? Sex. Come on, say it. Sex, sex…"

I leaned over and placed my hand on his lips to make him stop. "I swear," I said, laughing. "If you don't stop, I'm gonna tape your mouth shut."

His eyes were grinning at me, and he broke loose, holding both my wrists, fighting me off, pushing me down on the pillow. Then he stared into my eyes, and I felt myself blushing while staring at his lips, craving them, my body overwhelmed by such deep desire for him. Holding me still, he leaned over and kissed me deeply. My body grew soft, and I gave in to him once again.

Chapter 14

We told the kids – and my mom – that Matt had come over to take me out for a run. That was why he was here early in the morning on a Sunday. He did have his gym bag with his training clothes in the back of his police cruiser where he always kept it, so he could go to the gym after work. He brought it in, and we both got ready. Me mostly because I wanted to make this little white lie look plausible, even though I could tell my mother saw right through it. Still, she was polite enough not to say anything, only give me a look to make me feel shameful. I'm not sure Olivia bought it either, but Alex did and maybe Christine.

I didn't care, I thought to myself as I got dressed for our run. I needed this little lie to remain for a while. Maybe it wasn't as much for them as it was for me that I lied. I wasn't sure I was ready to move on fully yet, at least not admit that I was. I wasn't sure why, though. Chad was clearly having sex with Kimmie and had been for a year before we were even separated. I was just still trying to figure myself out, and somehow hiding the fact that Matt and I were…intimate… made it easier. It also made it less serious somehow, and I think I needed that.

"You ready?" Matt asked, doing jumping jacks in his

sneakers on the kitchen floor. He looked like he could run a marathon without even getting out of breath.

I smiled awkwardly, remembering the last time I had gone out for a run right after I had just moved back. I had been sore for a week afterward, and my knees had been stiff. I used to love to run, but the extra weight made it a lot harder than when I was younger. I used to be the fastest on my team when just starting at FBI's Behavioral Analysis Unit. But that was before the last two children, and before life got so busy that I had no time to keep in shape. I had always thought it would be easy for me to get it back since I had always been in good shape when I was younger.

"I guess," I said with a shrug.

I glanced at my mom, who was making her gluten-free pancakes for Alex. She had barely spoken to me after we went to see Sydney—or Kelly—the day before, and her eyes kept avoiding mine. I wondered what was going on inside of her.

But then again, I had wondered about that my entire life.

Matt and I left the house and ran down my street. By the time we had passed four houses, I was already panting heavily. The air was so moist it made it hard for me to breathe. I had forgotten how the Florida air was so tough to run in, especially when you weren't used to it.

Matt, who was a few feet ahead of me, slowed down so I could catch up and we turned down Minutemen Causeway. I followed him, barely able to keep up with him.

"Come on, Eva Rae. You wanted this to seem legit, right?" he said with a grin, running backward in front of me so he could see me. The look on his face reminded me of when we were younger and would run races to compete at the school's track. Back then, I had always been faster than him. Well, at least before we hit high school. After that, he got stronger and usually beat me, but only barely.

"You need to sweat to make it look like you were actually running."

I stuck my tongue out at him, then pulled myself together and sped up. I ran past him, and he whistled, impressed.

"I see you've still got it."

"Catch me if you can," I said, speeding up, pushing myself so much my knees began to hurt.

Matt laughed behind me, then started to run faster, and soon we were racing down the sidewalk, past the high school, and continued toward the golf course at the end of the causeway. I managed to keep ahead of him almost all the way, right until we reached the beginning of the grass when he sped past me, and I had to stop. Panting, I threw myself in the grass, wheezing for breath, feeling lightheaded, and my heart pounding in my chest.

Matt came up to me, also panting. He sat down next to me. "Not bad, Eva Rae. For a girl."

I chuckled, remembering he always used to say that to me when we were younger, and I hated that. When growing up, I had always gotten so angry when he said that, and he had known it and used it to provoke me.

"You try giving birth to three children, and then we'll talk, all right?" I said.

That made him laugh. "Touché."

He lay down next to me, and we stared at the clear blue sky for a few minutes while catching our breath, or at least I did. Matt was quickly ready for more, whereas I was done. My body was hurting all over and my cheeks so red they must have looked like they were about to explode.

"You want a rematch?" he asked after a few minutes.

"Not in a million years," I said. "I want water, and then I want coffee and food."

He laughed again, then stood to his feet. He reached out his hand toward me when I spotted a group of kids sitting behind a bush not far from us. Four children, not much older than Alex, were playing with something that made my heart freeze the moment I realized what it was.

"Oh, dear God."

Matt's eyebrows shot up. "What is it?"

I didn't have time to explain. I rushed toward the children. The one holding the item hid it behind his back as soon as he saw me approaching. His lips started quivering when I spoke.

"Hey, you. Yes, you kid. What was that you were holding in your hand just now? Yes, I'm talking about the thing you're trying to hide behind your back. Show it to me, please."

The boy's big brown eyes stared up at me. The three other kids looked at him, then up at me.

I reached out my hand. "Hand it over, please. You shouldn't be playing with that. It's dangerous."

The boy swallowed, then finally reached his hand toward me and placed the syringe in my hand. Matt came up behind me and looked down at it.

"What the heck?"

"We were playing doctor," the girl standing next to him said.

"This is no toy, kids. This can be very dangerous to play with. Where did you find this?" I asked.

The boy stared at me, then finally pointed.

"At the golf course?"

"We usually look for golf balls," he said. "In those bushes over there at the end of the course."

"Probably some addict who shot up out here," Matt said.

I bit my lip and stared at the syringe in my hand. It was almost empty, and there was dried blood on the tip of it.

"When did you find it?" I asked.

"Two weeks ago," he said and held out a small wooden box. "I kept it in this box. I keep all my treasures in this."

"He also found a phone," the girl next to him said.

The boy gave her an annoyed look.

"Show them, Evan. He's the police." She said the last part nodding toward Matt.

Evan sucked in air between his teeth, then opened his treasure box and pulled out a phone. With shaking hands, he handed it to Matt, who took it and looked at it, turning it in the light. As his glare fell on the back of it, his eyes went dark. He looked at me, then leaned over and whispered:

"I think it's Carina Martin's. Her mom described a case looking very much like this with the flowers across it."

I stared at him, then looked down at the syringe.

"I think we need to get both of these items to the station and have them sent to the lab. You'll probably need a team out here to go through those bushes over there and have this boy show you exactly where he found them. I have a feeling these are more breadcrumbs to your case."

Chapter 15

I left Matt to do his work and ran home as soon as I had turned the syringe over to the crime scene techs when they arrived.

My kids were done eating breakfast and had returned to their rooms as I entered, except Alex, who was sitting in the living room playing with his firetruck. He barely noticed that I returned and was deep into what he was playing.

"Where on Earth have you been?" my mom said as I walked into the kitchen. "You've been gone for an hour and a half. And don't tell me you went running for all this time."

I looked at Alex to make sure he wouldn't hear, then approached my mom. "Matt and I stumbled across what we believe might be evidence in his case."

My mom's eyes grew wide. "In the disappearance of those girls from the high school?"

I nodded and grabbed a gluten-free pancake that had been left on the counter. It tasted awful, but I ate it anyway, pouring loads of syrup on it. I watched my mom as her eyes grew weary.

"Awful story that one," she said. "Those poor parents."

"Now, we still don't know if they were taken or if they have just run away," I said, pouring more syrup on top of my pancake. "They did find a message for Ava on Instagram from a photographer who wanted to make her a model, but the parents told her she wasn't allowed to meet with him. The message was a couple of months old. The police are working the theory that all three of them might have just gone somewhere. Matt told me this last night, but it's not something you can tell anyone since it's a very loose theory."

"Eva Rae," my mom said.

I looked at her. "What?"

She nodded toward my plate. I had gone a little overboard on the syrup. "Are you really going to eat that?"

"Of course, I'm going to eat that," I said, pretending like I couldn't see what she meant.

"That is pure sugar, Eva Rae. It's not…good for you. Honestly, you eat like you're a child these days."

I sighed, then cut my pancake. "At least I went running this morning. I burned off some of all those calories already."

She gave me a look, and I sent her one back to make her get off my back. I had enough guilt nagging me as it was over my weight; I didn't need her looks or words to knock me out.

"Suit yourself," she said, then left the kitchen. I took another bite of my pancake, then pushed the plate away, realizing it really didn't taste that good with all that syrup on it. I threw the rest out, then planned to go upstairs to take a shower when something stopped me. As I was about to walk up the first step, I accidentally looked out the window through a crack in the pulled curtains facing my backyard, and that was when I saw it.

I am not lying when saying, my heart literally stopped.

Chapter 16

Boomer looked at the woman through his binoculars. He was keeping his distance; he was no fool wanting to be caught, but he just had to be there when she found it. He just had to see her face when she spotted his work of art.

He watched her run into the yard, screaming loudly. Eva Rae Thomas approached the girl, then pulled the chains, trying to get her loose, but had no luck. Neighbors in the yards across from her canal soon heard the screams and came out to look. Some were pointing toward her, others clasping their mouths in shock. Meanwhile, the screams continued, and it was like a sweet song in Boomer's ears. The chill went straight into his bones and stayed there.

"Someone, call 911!!" The woman screamed. "NOW!"

Several of the neighbors did. Some were yelling; others just stood there, paralyzed in fear.

Boomer took one last glance in the binoculars at her strained face as she fought to get the girl loose, pulling helplessly at the chains, before he realized it was time for him to leave. His presence would end up being noticed if he stayed longer, even if he kept his distance.

Boomer turned the small boat around and chugged away, taking it slowly, holding his fishing pole up to make sure no one would find him to be out of place. As he reached the end of the canal, he took a left, then continued down into the intracoastal waters, where the mangroves would be his cover. In the distance, he heard the sound of blasting sirens. Boomer grinned and took in a deep satisfied breath as a flock of pelicans swooshed by above his head.

Chapter 17

I was screaming and pulling the chains. My mom came running out to me, and as I yelled at her to call 911 and keep the kids inside, she ran back in to find a phone.

My hands were moving frantically back and forth on the poor girl's hands as I tried to liberate them from the swing set, which she had been chained to, and was hanging from. Blood was smeared on her face and seemed to be coming from her eyes, I realized as I tried to look at her. I reached up and felt her neck for a pulse and found one. The girl wasn't conscious, but she was alive.

Oh, dear God, what's wrong with her eyes?

I stared at the girl, who looked like a bug caught in a spider's web, the way she was displayed with her arms and legs stretched out. The chains were attached to each corner of the swing set, stretching the girl's body out. Her head hung slumped down on her chest.

"I called 911; they're coming," my mom yelled behind me. "What else can I do?"

"Get the bolt cutter in the garage. I need to get her down," I yelled.

My mom took off. She came back a few seconds later, holding up her long skirt as she rushed across the lawn, the bolt cutter in her hand, her usually impeccable hair standing out in all directions.

"Here. I hope it's the right one."

"It is," I said and took it. I rushed to the girl's leg, then used all my strength to cut through the chain till it snapped and her leg dangled freely. I hurried to the second leg, then put the bolt cutters on the chain, my hands shaking in shock and terror, then closed it around the chain and cut through. The second leg got loose, and my mom ran to the girl and held both of her legs, trying to lift the girl, so her arms wouldn't be strained so terribly. I sent her a grateful look, then crawled up on the swing and stood on it, while placing the bolt cutters on the chain holding the right arm and cut it loose. My mom shrieked as the body became heavier. She managed to hold her still, while I climbed onto the next swing and reached the second corner, then cut through the chain, sending my mom a look before I finished it to make sure she was ready to grab her. I could hear the neighbors gasp on the other side of the canal as the girl came loose and my mom balanced her, stumbling from the weight. I jumped down and managed to grab the girl in my arms before my mom fell with her. Shaking, I held her tight, pressing back my tears, when I heard Matt's voice coming from behind me.

"I came as soon as I heard your address mentioned over the radio. What's going on? Here...let me help you."

He grabbed the girl's legs, and we managed to put her down on the grass. Matt was sweating and panting as he looked down at her.

"Oh, dear God," he said and clasped his mouth.

I did the same as the hair was removed from her face and I realized who this was. My stomach churned, and I felt like throwing up.

"Oh, dear God, oh, dear Lord, no, no, no."

He looked up, tears springing to his eyes. "What did they do to her; what did they do to Molly?"

I swallowed anxiously as I spotted the paramedics running into the yard, carrying a stretcher, and I backed up to let them have their space to work. I stared at the girl while they assessed her condition, then got her hooked up on oxygen and soon rushed her away. I couldn't stop wondering what the heck was going on. Molly had been the only girl in that group of friends who had made it home, the one we had assumed had been safe.

Chapter 18

I went back inside to check on the children. Christine was sitting by the counter in the kitchen, Olivia holding her arm around her, while Alex was drawing on the floor, getting crayon smeared all over the tiles.

"Are you all right?" I asked and approached them.

Christine didn't look up. My eyes met Olivia's.

"She saw it," she said. "Through the window upstairs. After you screamed, she looked out; we both did. Alex didn't see anything. We kept him from the windows and closed all the blinds."

I swallowed hard. "I...I am so sorry you had to see that. Come here."

I grabbed both of them and pulled them into a hug. I held them for a few minutes, kissing the top of their heads. Christine was sobbing, her small body shaking.

"I know her," Olivia finally said as she broke out of the hug. She sniffled and wiped her eyes dry. "She's from my school, right? A senior."

I nodded and touched her hair gently. My beautiful daughter, who almost seemed too good for this world.

"Yes. Molly Carson. She's my good friend Melissa's daughter." I choked up as I said her name and stopped talking.

"Is she...is she dead?" Olivia asked, eyes worried. She looked so much like her father in this second, and I was briefly reminded of how deeply I had loved Chad once.

I shook my head, thinking about Melissa and how hard this was going to hit her.

"She was still alive when we took her down. She's on her way to the hospital now. I'm sure they'll take good care of her."

"So, she'll live," Christine said.

I bit my lip not to cry. "I...we don't know yet."

I held my girls tight while Matt entered through the sliding doors. Outside, our yard was crawling with uniforms, and soon the crime scene techs would arrive and would be combing through the yard and probably also the canal looking for evidence.

I let go of the girls and told them to go to the living room, where they wouldn't be able to look out at the window and see what was going on out there. They did, arm in arm, and took Alex with them. Matt pulled me into a hug and held me while I tried hard not to cry.

"How?" I asked him almost in a whisper. "How did someone manage to chain a girl in our backyard without us noticing anything?"

He shrugged. "If he did it at night. It was dark; we were sleeping."

"We were in the house all morning. And we didn't see it?"

"The curtains were closed, so were the blinds upstairs."

"But...If we had found her earlier, then maybe she'd have a better chance. What if she doesn't make it, Matt? This is Melissa's daughter. This is my best friend's daughter. Why? Why her? And why my backyard?"

Matt shook his head slowly, looking pensive.

"You think it's related to the disappeared girls, don't you?" I asked.

He shrugged again. "How can I *not* think that? They were a group of four friends. They were supposed to have walked home together, all four of them together, but one went home earlier."

I sucked in a deep breath between my teeth while thinking like crazy about all of this. One thought kept coming back to me:

Why my yard? Of all the houses this guy could have chosen, he chose my backyard, why?

Matt looked into my eyes. "I have to go," he said. "I have to go tell Melissa and take her to the hospital."

I nodded, feeling a knot in my stomach and throat. "I know. I'm coming with you."

He sighed gratefully. "I had hoped you'd say that."

Chapter 19

Matt parked the car on the street in front of Melissa's house and killed the engine. We shared a look, and both took in a deep breath.

At least the girl isn't dead. We're not here to tell her that her daughter is dead.

It wasn't much of a comfort. I had known Melissa since we were in preschool. Matt and I both had. Her husband had recently been diagnosed with MS, and they were fighting bravely to keep their heads above water. Melissa had recently taken a job at Surfnista, a local café to help out with the medical bills that were piling up. With the rate Steve was going, he wouldn't be able to work more than a few years, if even that, and then where would that leave them? Just last week, she was sitting in my kitchen telling me this. And I had told her everything would be okay; they would figure it out, and we would all help as much as we could. I knew Dawn and I would, at least, and Matt, of course. Dawn had no children and was back to dating Phillip, the captain at the fire station who lived on my street. She had also been a part of our friend group since we were children and we looked out for one another when it was needed.

But now, I was coming to her house to tell her this? It was

going to break Melissa's heart. It felt like kicking her when she was already down.

I got out of the car, and Matt followed me up to the door. I felt his hand touch mine briefly before I rang the doorbell. Melissa came to the door, still in her PJs, hair tousled, slippers on her feet, and a coffee in her hand.

"Eva Rae? Matt? What are you doing here at this hour on a Sunday? Did I forget something? Were we supposed to meet up? Wait, why do you look so serious, Eva Rae...you're... what's going on here, guys?"

I took a deep breath and pressed back my tears. "It's Molly. You need to come with us to the hospital."

She almost dropped the cup in her hand, but Matt caught it from her. "Molly? What do you mean? She's...she went to a friend's house last night; did...did something happen to her?"

Melissa's voice grew shrill as she spoke, and her face went pale.

"Tell me what happened, Eva Rae; is she... is she okay?"

"We don't know," Matt said. "It's too early to say. She was unconscious when she was found and taken to the hospital in an ambulance. We're here to take you there."

Melissa looked at me like she was waiting for me to tell her it was a joke, that we had been pulling her leg in a cruel prank.

"It's true, sweetie. You have to come with us. Now."

"But...Steve...Steve had an attack last night. He can't get out of bed; he's heavily sedated."

"We can drop the kids off at my place," I said. "They're too young to understand what's going on. My mom and Olivia can look after them. I'll help you get them ready, and then we'll leave."

Melissa nodded, her nostrils flaring. She was keeping it together, but only barely. She made room for me to enter and I rushed inside where three young children, two boys and one girl were scattered across the living room, jumping on the couch, screaming, and two of them fighting over a sword.

Chapter 20

"I almost envy Steve, that he gets to sleep through all of this."

Melissa spoke with a scoff. We were sitting in the waiting room where they had told us to stay until they had news on Molly's condition. I was holding her hand while Matt had gone to find coffee. Dawn had arrived too and was sitting on the other side of Melissa. So far, we hadn't spoken to any doctor and had no idea how Molly was doing. I had told Melissa about how I had found Molly in my backyard and she had listened, shaking her head in disbelief.

The wait and uncertainty made me sick to my stomach. I felt so terrible for Melissa and wanted so badly to do something to help her out, to remove this pain.

"It's mostly all the scenarios that you constantly go through in your mind, you know?" she continued. "What if she doesn't make it out of there. What if she dies? How will I get past this? How will I ever live without my firstborn? How am I supposed to do that, Eva Rae?"

Melissa turned her face to look at me. The despair in her eyes made me want to scream. As a mom, I knew exactly how she felt.

Please, let her live, God. I'll do anything, anything!

I parted my lips and wanted to say something to soothe

her pain, but the words I could think of didn't seem sufficient at all. I wanted to tell her it was going to be all right, that I was sure the doctors were doing everything they could, but it was all just clichés and meaninglessness.

Matt returned with our coffees, and we took them. I sent him a grateful glance and saw the sadness in his eyes as well.

"Why don't they tell me anything?" Melissa asked when she had taken her first sip. "We've been here two hours, and we have heard nothing. How come they haven't told us anything, Eva Rae?"

"I don't know."

I took her hand in mine and squeezed it. Melissa exhaled and shook her head while a tear rolled down her cheek.

"I'm sure they're doing everything they can," Dawn said and sipped her cup.

"Can't they just tell me if she's alive or not? Everything else we can deal with as it comes along, but I need to know if she's alive."

"I'm sure they'll be…"

I paused when I saw a doctor come through the door, dressed in green scrubs. My heart ached when seeing the serious look on his face. He rubbed his stubble and looked at Melissa, who rose to her feet, still holding my hand tightly.

"Mrs. Carson?"

Melissa nodded, her skin turning paler by the second. "Yes, that's me. How is she, Doctor?"

"She…I'm afraid that her eyes are gone."

"Gone?" I said. "What do you mean gone?"

"I'm afraid they have been removed."

Removed? How?

Melissa's body began to shake. "She's…she's blind?"

The doctor nodded.

"But she's alive?" Melissa added.

"Yes."

Melissa breathed, her chest heaving up and down rapidly. "But she can't see?"

He shook his head. "No. And I'm afraid we believe she has also been raped."

Chapter 21

After the last sentence, it was obvious that Melissa didn't hear any more of what was being said. Her knees went soft, and I felt her collapsing, so I reached over and grabbed her in my arms. Dawn and I helped her get to a chair and sit down, while Matt finished talking to the doctor. The doctor told him they were taking blood samples to check for diseases and infections that could be transmitted through sexual contact and, of course, for pregnancy.

Melissa was shaking all over, and we just sat there while she gathered herself. As the tears finally started to roll, I pulled her close to me and into a hug. We sat there for quite a while, Melissa's body trembling between my arms until Matt returned and sat down next to her.

"There will be a sexual assault nurse examiner, a SANE, who will make sure to do a forensic exam," he said and looked at Melissa, eyes wet, biting his lips, his nostrils flaring. Matt fought his tears, then spoke through gritted teeth.

"I will get this guy, Melissa, you hear me? He's not getting away with this."

Matt got up and crumpled his empty coffee cup, then threw it in the trash with a loud groan. He then kicked a chair in anger and held a fist up to his mouth. I couldn't blame him. He was just displaying how I felt.

Frustrated, helpless, angry.

Melissa sniffled and wiped her eyes. "Well, at least she's alive, right? I mean, I ought to be happy about that, shouldn't I? Why aren't I?"

"It's a lot to take in right now," I said.

She swallowed and tried to hold it back, but more tears sprang from her eyes, and she broke down again. I reached over and held her in my arms while she sobbed.

"My baby was raped?"

"I am so sorry," I said.

"My baby was attacked, raped, and now she's blind," she said. "My baby will never be able to look me in the eyes again. I will never see hers again, ever. She had the most gorgeous eyes. They were beautiful and would sparkle when she smiled. She won't see her siblings as they grow up, and she'll never see the stars at night anymore. She always loved watching the stars. Why…why would anyone take that from her? What has she ever done to them? Why would they take her sight from her? I don't understand, Eva Rae. Who could be so cruel to do this? Who? And why? Her life is ruined. It's completely destroyed."

"Lots of kids live good lives even when blind," I said, but the words felt so empty. I was so frustrated in this second. I could feel her despair; it was unbearable not to be able to fix this for her. She was my friend, going through the pain of her life. And I just sat there, doing nothing but coming up with empty phrases and clichés that meant nothing.

Then I said what I really wanted to say all along. I lifted her face and looked into her eyes, while I spoke the words that I could put meaning behind. Words that I knew weren't empty and indifferent.

"I will catch this guy, Melissa, do you hear me? I will do everything in my power to get this one. Matt and I will do it together. He will not get away with what he did to Molly. I promise you this here and now. Do you understand what I'm saying?"

Melissa sobbed, then smiled and nodded behind a curtain of tears. "Thank you, Eva Rae, thank you so much."

Chapter 22

"It's so hot in here; I can't stand it!"

Ava squirmed on her mattress, and her chain clanked against the bar behind her.

"I feel so disgusting and clammy, and the air we breathe is so heavy; it feels like I'm suffocating."

Carina looked at the wall next to her. She had scratched a mark in the foam for every time she believed a day had started, right after their captor had been to change their bucket and give them fresh water and food. Fifteen scratches on the wall told her they had been down there for a long time, too long. The stench of their bodies brought tears to their eyes, and Ava was right, the air was almost unbreathable. The chain around Carina's neck was hurting her and had gnawed into her skin, leaving sores that were painful to the touch. She felt like crying every day she opened her eyes inside of this hell, and sometimes she gave into it and let the tears roll down her cheeks while wondering if they would ever make it out of there. But she didn't do it while her friends were looking. She had long ago decided that she was going to be the strong one. In a place like this, they needed one, and she knew she was able to be that. The two others panicked several times a day and screamed and cried, and sometimes even yelled at her for not panicking, but Carina kept her composure.

One of them had to.

"I can't stand it here!" Tara said, lying on her side on her mattress. "I can't take the smell; I can't take the air, and I can't stand the sight of these brown walls."

"I know," Carina said to both of them, trying to cheer them up. "But today, we'll try the thing we talked about, okay?"

Tara sat up. She was so pale in the dim light from above them. She was the skinniest one of the three, and she had been losing weight since they got there. They all had, but it seemed to be going faster with her. Carina was worried about Tara and how much longer she would last. That was why she had decided that today was going to be the big day.

"Really?" she asked.

Carina nodded. "We've talked about this long enough now. It's time we do something before we go insane."

"But I thought you said the plan wasn't perfect yet," Ava said.

"It isn't, but I have a feeling it never will be," Carina said. "We lose a portion of our strength every day, and I fear that if we wait too long, we might not be able to pull it off."

"I agree," Tara said.

Carina could see her collarbone above her ripped prom dress. It was sticking out more and more each day that passed. Her cheeks had fallen in, and her eyes were big as they landed on Ava.

"Did you hear that, Ava? It's time."

Ava nodded. She was way more robust when they were captured than both Carina and Tara, and she seemed to be holding up a lot better than either of them. Still, her eyes were matte with exhaustion, and she was winded from the lack of oxygen.

"It probably won't be long till he gets here, so I want you to go through the plan with me once again, and then keep yourselves ready."

Both girls nodded excitedly. Carina went over the details again before they all leaned their backs against the wall and stared at the door in front of them, waiting for it to open and that nasty man to show his masked face again.

Chapter 23

T HEN:
It was a nice day. The sun was shining from a bright blue sky, and it was finally warming up a bit as spring showed its picturesque face. Winters were long and dark, Iris Pierce believed, and this one had been extraordinarily long, even though it had been the best in her life. Having a baby had been the greatest achievement. Most parents probably thought so, but they had waited a long time for this baby. They had tried for five whole years before they had finally succeeded in conceiving. It had almost destroyed both her and Gary, not to mention their marriage. Not being able to get pregnant had been by far the biggest shame in Iris's life. Who was she if she wasn't able to give Gary what he so desired? Not a woman, not a wife. Not in her eyes.

Iris wrapped Oliver in a blanket and walked outside to put him inside his carriage. The sun shone brightly in his face, and she made sure to turn the carriage around, so he wasn't in the direct sun, then pull down the mosquito net. She looked at her son in the carriage and felt her heart melt as their eyes met. He looked so much like his dad already, and that often made her laugh. He was like this miniature version of Gary, a wrinkled and prune-like version of him. But he was also so incredibly gorgeous that her heart could hardly contain it. And neither could Gary. She saw it in his eyes when he came home from work and picked up the boy. She saw the deep pride in them. But she also saw something else lately that had startled her a little. She had seen fear, a deep worrisome fear growing inside of him, and she wondered if it had to do with his job and what he saw there. She sensed his job was getting to him somehow. She wondered if he feared something might happen to him, so he wouldn't be able to see Oliver grow up. To be honest, Iris often feared that too. Especially lately. More than once, she had caught herself waiting anxiously by the door as the clock struck six and she expected him home, unable to shake the worry until he was finally inside, hugging her and Oliver.

"Now, there. It's time for you to go to sleep," she said, smiling from ear to ear at her boy. She couldn't help herself. Everything about him made her so warm and peaceful inside. Her love for him was nothing like she had ever felt for anyone before, not even Gary, whom she loved dearly. This was different; this was deeper and so intoxicating, almost like a drug. She needed to be close to him; she craved his presence in her life and to feel his skin against hers. There was nothing in the world that made her feel like this, nothing.

Iris was going to take him for a walk downtown and maybe buy an ice cream for herself at the park, now that the weather was so nice. She liked to take a walk with the carriage at least once a day, and Oliver slept so well inside of it while she got some much-needed exercise and fresh air. Being cooped up inside with the baby was wonderful, but she was also slightly scared of losing touch with the world around her. She needed to get out.

Iris grabbed the carriage and was about to begin her walk when she realized she didn't have her diaper bag with her. She left the carriage for a second and rushed inside to look for it. She walked into the kitchen and found it on the counter, where she had packed it with clean diapers for the ride, just in case. It was funny, she thought to herself with a chuckle, how her small and elegant purse had been exchanged for this big ugly bag filled with essentials for the baby and not her anymore. It was just like her own life. It had been mostly filled with taking care of her own needs, and now she barely even cared if she got something to eat or showered, as long as the baby was happy.

Iris threw a glance at the mirror in the hallway and chuckled again at her appearance. As long as she didn't meet anyone she knew, she was fine, she thought to herself, then hurried outside, grabbed the carriage by the handle, and placed the bag underneath it.

"All right, Oliver," she said. "Let's go for that walk; shall we?"

She hadn't expected the baby to answer because why would he when he was only three weeks old? Yet there was still something that caught her off guard, and she lifted the mosquito net to look inside the carriage, to check on her son, or maybe just catch another glimpse of him like she so often did when he was sleeping.

But the carriage was empty.

Chapter 24

We set up a "war room" at CBPD by Matt's desk the very next day. As we had been reading through case files and going through a ton of details in the case, Chief Annie approached us.

"I heard you were in the building, Eva Rae," she said and walked closer. She pulled me into a hug. Chief Annie was a heavyset woman with a hug that felt like it would crush you. She also had the kindest deep-set brown eyes that lingered on me, and a smile to make me feel welcome.

"Good to hear that you finally decided to come onboard. I told Matt to ask you as soon as those girls disappeared. I wanted you."

I flushed, feeling flattered. "Thanks."

"Good to see you, Eva Rae," Annie said and squeezed my hand. "You look great."

That made me smile. I had a yard filled with crime-scene techs that had worked all night with lights out there and dogs, not to mention the divers in the canal that were keeping me awake. I had fought with the kids all morning to get them out of the house on time, and still, Alex and Christine had missed the bus. Then, after dropping them off in my PJs, I had been stuck in traffic driving down Minutemen Causeway, and as I came back to my house to get dressed, I had discovered water all over the bathroom floor and realized my toilet had a leak. I had called the plumber and told my mom to make sure she was there when he got there. She had been in the middle of reading the paper and drinking her coffee, then politely told me she was going to visit her friends today and play golf in Winter Park, so I probably shouldn't count on that. This meant I had to wait till the plumber got there to let him in before I could leave with his humungous bill in hand, and it wasn't until I arrived at the police station that I realized—because Matt politely told me so—that I had a huge coffee stain on my shirt, right on my chest where everyone would see it. I also had only brushed my hair in the car and hadn't even put on make-up, simply because I forgot to, so to tell me I looked great had to be a very polite compliment.

"Thank you," I said. "You too, Annie. But you always look great."

"We should do lunch one of these days. Maybe I could get you to come on board as a permanent solution," she said, then looked at her phone in her hand. "Whoops. Gotta be somewhere, like five minutes ago, I'm afraid. We're having our monthly *Coffee with the Mayor* event tonight at city hall next door, and we need to find out who will be guarding it."

She looked deeply into my eyes.

"Find my girls; will you?"

"I'll do my best."

Annie left, and I turned to look at Matt and the whiteboard by the end of the wall. We had hung up photos of all four girls. Carina Martin, Ava Morales, Tara Owens, and Molly Carson. The sight of their high school photos staring back at me made my heart drop. I sat down and rolled my chair toward them. Underneath their picture, Matt had written **PROM**. I stared at the word.

"They all went to the prom that night," I mumbled. "Could he have been at the dance? I know we talked about this before and that you interviewed all the teachers and chaperones present, but why were they all at the same dance right before three of them disappeared? Could it be that they were all four supposed to disappear that night?"

"And then he came for Molly later?" Matt asked.

"Maybe she knew something or saw something that he wanted to stop her from telling."

"But why not kill her then? Why not bury her somewhere or throw her in the river where the gators would eat her?" he asked.

"You make a good point. The part about her being placed the way she was, in my backyard, makes it feel so personal. Like he wanted me to find her there. Like there was a reason for choosing my yard and not someone else's."

"Because you knew Molly?" he asked.

I bit my lip and stared at Molly's photo. Her gorgeous brown eyes stared back at me, and I felt a pinch in my stomach when realizing I was never going to see them again, and neither was her mom.

"Yes, maybe, but maybe it was something else. There's something that seems kind of disturbing to me," I said and got up from the chair, then studied the picture of Molly that Matt had taken at the hospital, where she was lying with bandages across her eyes. We hadn't been able to interview her yet but kept the photo to remind us why we needed to stop this guy before he hurt any of the other girls if he hadn't already done so.

"What do you mean?" Matt asked.

"It didn't really occur to me earlier, but now I can't stop thinking about it. It's the eyes," I said.

"What about them?"

"I…It's just. There was a case once that I worked on. It was early in my career. We tracked down this guy who poked out the eyes of his victims before he raped them, so he would be the last person they remembered seeing, and so they wouldn't be able to recognize him in a line-up. He left them in the street, blinded and assaulted, helpless, unable to find their way back home. Often, they would run into the street and get hit by cars."

"So, could it be him again?" Matt asked.

"It could if I hadn't shot him in '09 as we raided his house."

"Okay," Matt said, "so he's dead, but maybe it could be someone copying him?"

I nodded. "That is definitely a possibility. But why would he target me in that way?"

"Because you got rid of his hero, the one he idolized, and he wants you to know that he is taking over."

I turned to look at Matt. "Look who's the profiler now."

"I took psychology in college," he said, smiling. It felt good to see him do that since we had both been so gloomy since we found Molly. There hadn't been anything to smile about so far.

"You might be onto something," I said. "This guy wants my attention; that's for sure. And he's got it."

Chapter 25

J ane Martin looked at the clock on her stove. It was three-thirty in the afternoon. The realization made her bend over in agony and pain. This was the time she would usually go pick up Carina at the high school. She would drive up into the pick-up line and wait for her to come to the car, blushing in embarrassment since all the other kids her age would get into their own cars and drive off. But Carina hadn't been able to pass her license test yet since she had flunked twice, and so she was pretty much the only kid her age who was still being picked up by her mother, much to her embarrassment. It had also been a nuisance to Jane since she had started working as a campaign manager for a local politician and she had enough on her plate these days.

But not anymore.

Not since Carina went off to the prom and never returned home. Jane hadn't left her house since that night when her daughter disappeared, and she wasn't going to.

"You have to start living soon," her husband, Scott, had told her so many times these past few days as he went off to work himself, pecking her unlovingly on the cheek. "We can't stop living just because our daughter ran away. We still have a son, and he needs us."

Scott was determined that Carina had run off with her

friends, that they had taken off on some trip to Las Vegas or maybe just Miami to go clubbing, and that they would be back soon. And the stuff they found at the golf course? Well, they had been drunk and goofed around out there before they decided just to take off. They were young and carefree, was his opinion.

It had been seventeen days now. Who went clubbing for seventeen days? What teenager had that kind of money?

"I think something happened to her," Jane had said over and over again. "I can feel it in my heart. She's in pain. She's hurting. A mother knows these things."

But Scott hadn't wanted to hear it. "I did the same thing when I was her age," he said.

"You went on spring break in Miami," she replied.

"But I lied to my parents and said I was staying with my best friend and his parents."

She shook her head. "How is that the same?"

Jane exhaled and looked out the window at the canal behind her house. A boat chugged past. An elderly couple was sitting behind the wheel, smiling, with their fishing poles stuck on the roof. They were probably coming back from fishing on a nice, beautiful day, maybe having caught themselves a couple of trout for dinner.

Jane and Scott used to go fishing, and it was their plan for retirement once that came along. Just the two of them, out on a boat going off-shore fishing off the coast with not a care in the world. That was the dream, and it was obtainable. Except now she feared it would never be. She would never be carefree again if Carina didn't come back. She wasn't sure she'd survive that. The past seventeen days had been so tough it felt like she would die.

Jane exhaled and made herself a cup of coffee. She stared at a box of Oreos that her son had forgotten to put back in the cabinet. Usually, she'd take a couple, maybe eat the entire pack, but not today. She had lost a lot of weight since Carina had disappeared, and normally that would have been an accomplishment for her, something she'd be thrilled about, but now, it didn't matter. She had no appetite, and she didn't care anything about food anymore. It was so useless anyway. Their neighbors from across the street had been so nice and brought them food to eat, so they didn't have to worry about cooking, and she had tried to have some of the chicken pot pie last night, but it hadn't even tasted good. It was like it was growing in her mouth, and she had kept chewing and chewing at it, unable to swallow it. She had ended up spitting it out in the trash, then going for a glass of Chardonnay instead. The wine kept her calm and helped her sleep. Drinking wasn't a solution; she knew that, and it could become a slippery slope. But right now, it was the only thing she could get down, and she needed it. That and her coffee to get her through the dreadful day.

Her doorbell. Her first thought was that it was Carina, that she had finally come back. Jane almost dropped her cup on the tiles. Then she realized Carina would never ring the doorbell. Or would she? What if she was embarrassed? What if she had come back and was afraid they were angry with her, so she didn't dare to walk right in?

It could be.

Jane put her cup down on the counter, feeling her pulse quicken, and rushed for the front door, images of Carina's beautiful face flashing through her mind. There was nothing she wanted more right now than for her husband to have been right about their daughter.

Jane grabbed the door handle and swung the door open when her hope froze instantly. Outside stood not Carina, but a FedEx guy.

He smiled.

"Mrs. Martin?"

She nodded, disappointed. What had Scott bought now that they didn't need? Another useless tool for his garage that he would never use? Something electronic that would end up gathering dust on his desk? Or was it Frank, their youngest? Had he been on Amazon and bought something silly?

"That's me."

"I have a package for you. I just need you to sign right there."

She grabbed the pen and scribbled an ugly signature on the display, then took the package.

"Have a nice day," he said and tipped his hat.

"Thank you," she said, even though she knew she wouldn't. This day would be just like the sixteen previous, filled with despair and pain, longing for her daughter to come home.

Little did Jane know as she put down the box and opened it, that this day was about to be a lot worse than all the previous ones.

Chapter 26

"When are you coming home, Mom?"

I looked at the whiteboard by the wall behind Matt to see the girls looking back at me, almost accusingly. We hadn't gotten anywhere all day.

Some help I was.

Guilt ate at me for not being at home with my children like I had promised them I would. Christine had come home from school and found my note written on our activity board in the kitchen, where I wrote I was going to help Matt out on a case today.

"I don't know, sweetie," I told her. "But Grandma is there with you today."

"You know I don't like being alone with her," she said. "She's creepy and weird. She keeps telling me to make better choices when I grab a snack, and then she looks at my ripped jeans and makes jokes asking me if *I paid full price for them 'cause then I would need my money back*. Stuff like that. It's annoying."

"She's just from another generation," I said, remembering my old ripped jeans back in the nineties that my mom would look at with a grunt.

"You mean she's old," Christine said.

"Yes, she's old. And maybe she's a little weird, but give her a chance, please? She's the only family we have right now, and we should cherish her. Who knows how long she'll be around? We'll regret it later on in life if we don't make the best of what we have with her."

"Did you read that off Facebook or something? Besides, we do have other family. We have Dad, and his mother is our grandmother too. And she's not so weird."

That shut me up. I had always loved Chad's mother and had to admit that I missed her terribly now that I wasn't with her son anymore. I had more than once wanted to pick up the phone and call her and ask her for advice these past six months when my life was in ruins, but then stopped myself, realizing that she wasn't my mother-in-law anymore, that we weren't family anymore. The thought almost made me tear up.

"Yeah, well, they're all in Washington," I said, trying to sound diplomatic and not blame Chad any more than necessary. I had long ago decided I wasn't going to be that kind of an ex. I wasn't going to say bad stuff about him to the children. He was their father, and they adored him, and I wanted them to keep liking him. But it was a fine line that was easily crossed, I had learned. Especially since I was still so angry at him for leaving me like that, without even a warning, and for cheating on me, of course. "They're not around right now. So, try and make the most of Grandma, okay? Play a board game with her or maybe cards? And try to include Alex. He doesn't have many friends yet, and I worry about him being lonely."

"You worry about him being lonely? What about me?" Christine said, almost whining. "I hate all the girls in my school. There's no one I like here. I miss all my old friends, and I miss Dad."

Ouch.

"I know you do, sweetie. I know you must miss him a lot," I said as Chris Cooper approached Matt's desk. Chris Cooper was another detective at CBPD and also an old friend from school. He looked serious first at me, then Matt. I held up a finger to let him know I'd be right there.

"Do you want to go up there soon?" I asked. "I can call him and ask?"

She went quiet.

"Christine? Why don't you want to go up there lately? Did something happen?" I asked. "You haven't been up there in almost three months. Don't you want to see your father?"

"I want to see him, Mom. I miss him; it's just…" she said.

"Listen, I'll call him today and ask, okay?" I said, trying to end the call. "I'll call and ask him when you can go see him again."

"Okay," she said, almost in a whisper. I could tell she was sad and needed to chat more, but I didn't have the time right now. It broke my heart. I wanted to know what was going on.

"We'll talk more when I come home, Christine, okay?"

"Okay," she said again and hung up.

I did too, then lifted my eyes and met those of Cooper. He handed us a note. "You need to go to Jane Martin's house. Her husband called. It was urgent."

Chapter 27

The Martins lived in a beautiful newly-built riverfront house at the end of our island by the golf course. The husband was a partner in a big local law firm, and I recognized his face from one of the billboards on 520 leading to Orlando, even though he wasn't smiling the way I was used to. Today, his face was heavyset, and his eyes were burning in anger as he greeted us in the doorway.

"I don't know who is behind this, but if it is some kind of joke, then I'm gonna..."

"What's going on, Scott?" Matt said.

"You better see for yourself," he said. "Come on in."

"This is my partner, Eva Rae Thomas," Matt said. "She's FBI and working the case with me."

Scott gave me a look, then moved aside so we could come into the big hall. Inside, the house opened up to the most spectacular views of the intracoastal Banana River and the Thousand Islands in the background. Boats were anchored in the distance, probably fishing or going swimming, maybe diving from the rooftops. I remembered my own youth when we always went out to Ski Island and partied with the others from our high school, bringing our coolers with beer and shots. The only life on the islands were snakes and tortoises, and most importantly, there were no police to check for underage drinkers.

We walked to the kitchen where a blonde woman sat on a stool by the counter, crying. In front of her sat a brown package.

"Jane?" Matt said and approached her. She lifted her eyes and spotted him. "What's going on? Did something happen?"

Jane sniffled and wiped her nose on a Kleenex, then nodded. "I…There was a man at the door, a FedEx guy; he brought me this package. At first, I just thought it was something Scott ordered off of Amazon, or maybe our son did, but my name was on it, so I…opened it."

Matt nodded. "And what was in it?"

Jane sobbed, then pulled herself together. She reached inside the box and pulled out something. It looked like fabric of some sort. It was red and silky. She held it up so we could see. The golden letters said:

PROM QUEEN 2019

My heart dropped, and I looked at Matt, then back at the mother.

"It's the sash," Matt said.

"The one Carina got right before she…disappeared," Jane said, then broke down again. I walked to her and put my arm around her since the husband didn't seem to want to. He just stood there like he was paralyzed and stared at the sash on the granite countertop.

"I've seen the pictures," Jane continued. "On Instagram. I've been going through them over and over again from that night. All her friends posted pictures from that night. She wore this on the stage when she was crowned, and I never got to see her in it. I would have been so proud. She really wanted to be prom queen since I was prom queen back in the day too. She knew I was going to be so happy for her."

"If this is someone's idea of a joke, then I am going to kill them," Scott said, fuming.

"I don't think it is a joke, Mr. Martin," I said, still holding his crying wife. "I think this is very serious. Was there any card with the package?" I asked Jane. She shook her head, and Matt peeked inside the box.

"Nothing in here."

"And there have been no text messages or emails demanding a ransom or anything like that?" I asked her, then looked up at her husband.

They both shook their heads.

"Nothing," Jane said and clenched her fists. "What do these people want from us? Why have they taken our poor baby? Why?"

With no ransom request or any demands at all, I had no answer for that. It didn't fit the MO of a sex offender either. I couldn't stop thinking about Molly and how on Earth these cases were connected because I was certain they had to be. Four teenagers from the same group of friends couldn't be a coincidence. But what was this person's goal?

What did he want?

Looking at the sash on the counter and the tearing up mother, I had a feeling we would find out soon, and it wasn't going to be pleasant.

Chapter 28

Boomer whistled while he drove down Minutemen Causeway, the town's small main street. He saw the many police cruisers as they passed him on their way and knew exactly where they were going. Meanwhile, he stopped at a red light at the end of the road, where it met A1A, and he spotted city hall and the police station on the corner.

While he waited, he took a sip of his soda and emptied it, throwing the empty can out the window while thinking about Eva Rae Thomas. He grabbed his phone and looked at the app, tracking her exact whereabouts. Yes, she was there. She was at the address where he had just delivered the sash. Boomer pulled his lips slowly upwards into a smile. It was all going the way he wanted. They were all playing along like the good little dolls they were. But things were moving slowly, he thought. Too slow. It was about time that he speeded up the events.

Shake things up a little.

That was exactly what he was about to do, he thought to himself as the light turned green and he turned right into the intersection, then hit the brakes and stopped the truck, placing it sideways, so it blocked the entire street. The car behind him honked loudly. Another came around the corner behind it and honked aggressively, but Boomer didn't listen.

He got out of the truck, making sure the cap covered his face for the surveillance cameras, then walked onto the sidewalk. Swiftly, he turned a corner and fell into a crowd of tourists waiting to cross the street. He took off the cap, then followed them, hiding in the crowd as they moved across the street toward the beach, hearing the aggressively honking cars behind him as the traffic was getting completely blocked.

Chapter 29

"I just got off with FedEx," I said and looked at Matt. He had called for the Sheriff Office's Crime Scene Unit, and they took the package to the lab to see if they could extract any evidence from it. They were right now working the kitchen and securing the package and the sash.

"They're trying to track the driver down, but according to their headquarters, there were no deliveries on this street yet today. Not even in the entire area. This address is last on their route and wasn't scheduled until a few hours from now. But get this. They did, however, have a truck stolen a couple of days ago from their office in Viera on the mainland. Could that have any connection?"

Matt looked at me and exhaled. "I should say so. I just talked to Cooper. You won't believe this. They found a FedEx truck parked in the middle of A1A in an intersection, right in front of the police station. Someone left it there. It's blocking traffic. The driver was gone."

"Don't let them touch anything," I said, my eyes growing wide. Things were moving a little too fast for my liking. I felt like I was losing control of the case...like someone was pulling the strings.

"You think it's our kidnapper, don't you?" Matt asked.

"You think he came here, delivered the package, and then left the truck for us to find; am I right?"

I nodded. "I think he was here. I think he wanted to look at her face when she got the package. He wanted to look her in the eyes."

"Wow," Matt said. "That's sick."

I swallowed. "I don't think there is anything well about this guy. Why do you think he left the truck in front of the police station? Because he's telling us he is in control. There won't be any fingerprints on it, but he wants us to look for them. He's toying with us. I don't have a good feeling about this guy."

"I'll call them back and make sure the truck is taken through forensics," he said. "When I spoke to Cooper, he was still waiting for the tow truck."

"Okay," I said pensively, then looked at Carina's parents, who were sitting on the couch in their living room, barely looking at one another. I approached them, then sat next to Jane. She was staring at her fingers, fiddling with the tissue between them.

"Did you have a good look at the man from FedEx when he was here?" I asked. "Did you see his face?"

She nodded. "Sure."

"How would you describe him?"

She sighed. "I don't see why…"

"Just humor me," I said. "We need to find him."

"You think it was him; don't you? You think it was the guy who kidnapped our daughter?" Jane spoke with a quivering voice. Her eyes grew wet, and soon the tears rolled down her cheeks. "You mean to tell me he was…here? He was here at our…our doorstep? The man who took Carina? Our Carina, our daughter?"

"We don't know if…"

"He was here?" Scott Martin began while rising to his feet "He was here?" he turned to look at his wife. "And you…you did…you did nothing? You just signed and took the package?"

"Please, Mr. Martin," I tried. "There was no way your wife could have known…"

"No, he's right. I could have stopped him," Jane continued. "I could have called the police, and maybe he would lead us to her; am I right? But I didn't. I just signed the darn thing, took my package, and shut the door. I looked him straight in the eyes and then went on with my day. I looked into the eyes of my child's kidnapper and…did nothing!"

"You need to calm down, Mrs. Martin," I said. "We don't know if it was the same man or not. It could also be someone he paid to give you the package. No matter what, we need to find him. The package you received wasn't sent via a normal FedEx office. There's no return address and the guy who brought it wasn't a FedEx deliverer. What he was, we don't know, but the truck was most likely stolen, and the guy was someone pretending to be from FedEx. Whether it's the man we're looking for or just an accomplice, we don't know, but we have to find him. He's our only lead right now. So, please, tell me, what did he look like?"

Jane Martin stared at me, blinking her tears away. Her nostrils were flaring. She glanced briefly at her husband, who was sitting with his head bent to his knees, holding his head like he was afraid it would explode.

"I guess he was…tall, like Matt, about six feet two or so," Jane said, her voice trembling as she spoke. "He was pretty buff, you know? Maybe from carrying all those packages all day. His hair was blond."

"Did you look at his eyes?"

As I said the words, a loud blast sounded from outside, and the windows shook slightly. I looked at Matt as the shaking stopped.

"Was there a rocket launch scheduled today?" I asked, remembering those days as a kid when we went outside to watch them be sent off from Kennedy Space Center. Rocket launches were part of our daily life when growing up on the Space Coast.

The couple didn't seem alarmed either, and Jane continued.

"They were steel grey. And he had very straight teeth. And a beard. Not a big one like a homeless person, or the hipsters, but a small well-trimmed goatee."

"Anything else? Any tattoos?"

She shook her head. "No. At least none that I could see. He was in uniform. He seemed friendly. Like he knew me."

"Did you know him? Had you seen him before?"

She shook her head. "I don't think so. Even though there was something familiar about him."

Matt approached me. "I need to talk to you."

As I looked up at him, I realized something was wrong. He was pale, and his eyes were black. I excused myself quickly, then got up and walked with him.

"What's going on?"

"The truck," he said, his voice shivering.

"What about it?"

He swallowed. His hands were shaking, and I grabbed one of them. "What's going on, Matt? Did something happen? Matt? Talk to me. What's going on?"

Chapter 30

"You've got to get that finger further down."

Carina sat on the mattress next to Ava as she plunged her pointer finger deeper into her throat.

"Hurry up. He'll be here soon. You've got to make it look real," she urged her. "Try with two fingers if it doesn't work."

Ava tried again, this time using two fingers, pressing them into her throat, whimpering as she gagged.

"There you go. It's working."

"You can do it, Ava," Tara said.

Ava gagged, and soon after, yellow bile came out of her, mixed with mostly water. They had let her drink most of what was in the bucket to fill her stomach up enough so she would have something to throw up. They didn't get much food down here, and the little she usually had wouldn't yield much. They needed her to throw up more than once.

As Ava gagged again and threw up on the mattress, the stench quickly filled the small room and made the two others feel sick to their stomachs as well.

As steps approached behind the door, they all exchanged a look.

"Here he comes," Carina whispered. "Just do as we planned. It will work. It has to."

Ava whimpered and nodded, then as they heard the bolt

on the door open, she closed her eyes and pressed the two fingers down her throat again, and as the masked man entered, she bent forward and threw up once more.

"What the heck…?" he yelled as it landed on the floor in front of him. He sniffed and then held his nose. "What's that stench?"

"Ava is sick," Tara said.

"She's been throwing up all night," Carina added.

"And she's been shaking all over. She's sick," Tara continued. "I think she's really sick."

"She might infect us as well," Carina said. "Then we'll all get sick."

"We might die," Tara said.

"She needs to see a doctor," Carina said.

Ava gagged again and threw up, throwing herself forward, so a bunch of it landed right at his feet.

The masked man stared down at Ava, a gun clenched in his hand. He bent down and knelt in front of her, holding his hand up against the surgery mask like he wanted to make sure it was still there to protect him in case she was infectious.

"Are you really sick, little girl?"

Ava gagged, but nothing came up this time. Then she nodded with a sniffle, snot running from her nose.

"She needs to see a doctor," Carina repeated. "Please, sir. She might die down here if she doesn't get help."

"And then we'll die too."

Tara looked at Carina like was she asking *Too far?* But Carina didn't think it was too much.

"All right," the man said. "I'll take you upstairs."

He leaned over and grabbed Ava's chain on the bar, then unlocked it with his key. Ava sobbed and cried as he led her out the door, like she was a small dog he was taking out for a walk. As the door slammed shut behind them, both of the remaining girls sat back, sweat springing from their foreheads, silently asking themselves:

Did it work?

Chapter 31

THEN:

"Iris? Iris?"

Gary parked the car outside their house and rushed up the driveway, stumbling over his own feet as he hurried toward his wife. She was sitting on the porch, her head bent. He had been at the office when she called, and luckily not out on assignment. It had taken him fifteen minutes to get home, a drive that usually took thirty.

Gary knelt next to her, and Iris finally looked up, her eyes red-rimmed. All she had said on the phone was that Oliver wasn't in his carriage. She had been screaming it hysterically, and Gary had told her he'd come right away.

"I got here as fast as I could," he said. "What's going on?"

"Oliver is gone," she said.

"I don't understand; what do you mean...gone?" he said, heart pounding in his chest. How did a baby just disappear? Had his wife lost it? Had she put him somewhere and couldn't remember? Was it some sort of postpartum depression? Gary had heard about women who suddenly couldn't figure out even the simplest tasks after giving birth, who got so depressed they couldn't take proper care of their child. He had even heard from a colleague that sometimes they tried to kill their own children since he had once been called out to a case like that. Worst thing in the world, he had said. A mother killing her own child. It doesn't get any worse than that.

Iris shook her head. Gary felt like shaking her, trying to get her to explain this to him, to tell him where their son was.

"I came out here...and then he wasn't...he wasn't in his carriage anymore. I just went in there to get my bag. I was gone for one minute, tops, and then he was...gone."

Gary rose to his feet. He walked to the carriage and looked inside. Oliver wasn't in there. Gary looked on the tiles and the grass surrounding it, in case the child had fallen out.

"How could he suddenly be gone?" Gary asked. "I mean...he can't...he can't even hold his own head up, let alone crawl out of the carriage on his own. He's too small."

Iris looked at him, despair in her eyes. "I...I don't know. He was just...gone."

"And you're sure you put him in the carriage? I mean, maybe you didn't. You haven't been sleeping much lately, sweetie, maybe you left him inside and just thought you put him in the carriage."

She swallowed. "No, I put him in there, and then I went inside. Besides, I've looked everywhere inside too. Oh, God, Gary, please tell me I'm just losing my mind, that he is still here somewhere. I'm panicking; please, do something."

"I'll search the house," he said and stormed into the hall-way, heart racing. He ran upstairs first and looked through all the rooms and closets, thinking that if she was as confused and worn out as he suspected, then maybe she had left the child somewhere in there. And if the baby was asleep, they wouldn't be able to hear him.

A baby doesn't just disappear like that.

Unless she hurt him. Unless she did something bad and just blocked it out.

The thought was so terrifying that he couldn't finish it. Gary shook it off and continued into the nursery, looking at the changing table and in the bathroom, desperately lifting any blanket or towel he could find to make sure the child wasn't underneath it. He also checked the bathtub and even the garbage bin, just in case. But there was no sign of his baby boy anywhere.

Gary ran a hand through his hair, desperately trying to think straight, but the panic that was spreading like wildfire inside of him made it impossible. It was getting harder to keep the anxiety at bay, and soon there was nothing but chaos inside of him.

He ran downstairs and found Iris standing bent over the carriage, looking inside of it, like she thought the child might still be there; she just couldn't see him.

"Iris?" he said.

Iris didn't answer. She stood like she was frozen and stared into the carriage and, as he came closer, she pulled out something that made his blood freeze.

A hand-written note.

Chapter 32

The flames and charcoal-gray smoke licked at the sky as we approached the intersection in front of city hall and the police station. The firefighters, who lived and worked in the building next to city hall, had pulled out their engine and were spraying water on it, Dawn's boyfriend Phillip leading them in the action. Meanwhile, paramedics put someone into an ambulance and rushed off, the siren blaring in the air as we exited Matt's cruiser.

We ran toward Chief Annie, who was standing with two of Matt's colleagues, a safe distance from the fire. Spectators had gathered on the corner, and a couple of uniforms were keeping them back. It looked mostly like tourists in their bikinis and trunks with beach chairs slung over their shoulders.

"What happened?" Matt asked, panting and agitated.

Annie looked at both of us. I could tell she was emotional. "It just exploded. The FedEx truck blew up. Cooper had... Cooper was just..."

She paused to gather herself. My heart knocked against my ribcage. This was bad. This was really bad.

"Cooper?" Matt said, his voice growing shrill. "Something happened to Cooper?"

Annie nodded. It was hard for her to speak, and her lips shook as she tried anyway.

"We were waiting for the tow truck, and the FedEx truck was blocking the entire street. This is our most high-traffic area in the entire town, so it was becoming a problem. I asked him if he could check and see if there might still be keys in it, so we could move it. He went to take a look inside the truck, and that's…that's when it went up in flames. He was flung out and landed on the asphalt, flames engulfing him."

Annie's eyes teared up as she said the words. She clenched her fist and placed it in front of her lips, pressing down hard to keep herself from breaking down. Chief Annie was tough and not one to get emotional usually, but this had her at the end of her rope.

I had known Cooper since we were kids too, not well, since he wasn't a close friend of mine, but still. I felt Annie's despair from where she was standing. She had to be blaming herself for telling him to go in there; she had to feel an enormous weight of guilt.

"Was he…?"

She nodded heavily. "He was still alive when they took him away. But severely burned on big parts of his body. It's hard to say if he'll survive being burned like that."

"Dear Lord," Matt said. He worked closely with Cooper, and I could tell he was tearing up. I went to hug him. I held him tight while we stared at the burning delivery truck in the middle of the street, all of us wondering what kind of sick bastard would do this. Who in their right mind would booby-trap the truck and blow it up right when he knew someone would be inside of it? One thing was certain. This was getting very personal, and now he'd have the entire police force breathing down his neck, not to mention the entire town, who always stood behind our men in uniform.

Chapter 33

A bomb squad arrived from the county's sheriff's office, and the area was combed through in the search for more explosives, using dogs. The schools were put on lock-down, and all of downtown was blocked off. A forensics team arrived to gather bomb debris for analysis. About an hour later, the area was declared clear, and we could go back inside the station.

We had just walked in through the glass doors when Lisa, who managed the front desk, stopped us.

"Detective Miller?"

Matt stopped in his tracks and looked at her. Lisa seemed perplexed. A lot more than usual.

"I know it's terrible timing right now, but…"

"What is it, Lisa?" he asked.

"Well, the Turners are here with their daughter. They said you asked them to come in?"

Matt rubbed his stubble. "I completely forgot."

The Turners were the family that Melissa thought her daughter Molly was having a sleepover with on the night she was blinded and raped. Lisa nodded in their direction, and I turned to look. Three people were sitting in the row of chairs leaned against the wall. One of them was a younger girl wearing a crop top and jean-shorts so short it looked like she wasn't wearing any pants at all when sitting down.

"Mr. and Mrs. Turner?" Matt said and approached them.

They stood to their feet, faces strained.

"What happened out there?" Mrs. Turner asked. "We had just gotten here and sat down when we heard the explosion, and we were told to evacuate the building and go out the back. They just let us back inside. Was anyone injured?"

Matt nodded heavily. "A colleague got hurt. He's been taken in for emergency treatment."

"How awful," Mrs. Turner said and looked briefly at her husband like it was his fault, then returned to face Matt again. "I am so sorry."

Matt nodded. "As are we all, Mrs. Turner. If you'll follow me, I think we'll take this in the interrogation room."

"The interrogation room?" Mr. Turner said. "But…"

He received a look from his wife and stopped. The Turners followed us through the police station, their daughter chewing bubble gum and blowing bubbles as we showed them inside of interrogation room one. Matt found a couple of extra chairs. He brought them in, and we all sat down. Matt exhaled, and I could tell he was struggling to keep it together. He opened Molly's file.

"If you don't mind me asking, why are we here?" Mr. Turner said nervously. He was a small man in brown cargo shorts and a light blue shirt from Salt Life. He had a nice tan. My guess was he was a boater or a fisherman, or maybe both.

"It's regarding Molly Carson," I said.

They looked surprised at one another, then at their daughter. "Molly? What has she done?"

"She didn't do anything," I said and swallowed to remove the knot growing in my throat when thinking about Melissa's poor daughter. "It was more what was done to her."

"Something happened to Molly?" Mrs. Turner said, her eyes growing wide. She looked at her daughter, who suddenly sat very still and wasn't chewing her gum anymore.

"What happened to her?" Mr. Turner said. "We haven't heard anything; have you, Leanne?"

His daughter shook her head. She was beginning to look flushed, and I sensed she was scared.

"We were hoping you could help us clear that up," Matt said.

"Us? But...how?" Mr. Turner said, looking at his wife, then at us. He folded his hands in his lap and leaned forward. I sensed a nervousness, but that wasn't uncommon in people who weren't used to dealing with the police.

"She was at your house for a sleepover the night before last," I said, scrutinizing them.

"A sleepover at our house?" Mrs. Turner said. "But... we've been out of town all weekend. We went to North Carolina just outside of Charlotte. We're looking at houses since we're moving up there this summer."

I wrote it down on my pad. "And you have witnesses that can confirm that?" I asked.

Mr. Turner nodded. "Of course, plenty of people saw us up there, including the real estate agent who took us around town all weekend. Witnesses, huh? Are we being accused of anything because, if so, I'd like to have my lawyer present."

"No one is accusing you of anything," I said, "We're in the middle of an investigation, and it doesn't hurt to have an alibi."

"But..." Mrs. Turner said, looking pensive. "Is...it bad, is...Molly dead?"

I shook my head and looked briefly at Leanne, who hadn't moved an inch and was barely blinking.

"She's not dead."

"Oh, thank God," Mrs. Turner said and clasped a hand to her chest.

"But something terrible was done to her, and we're trying to find the person who did it. So, what we can establish is that Molly lied when stating she was spending the night at your house, right?"

Mrs. Turner nodded, fighting to keep her composure. It was

obvious they knew Molly very well, and she had probably been friends with their daughter for many years. Mrs. Turner was visibly affected by the news. I was happy they had a solid alibi and that there was a reasonable explanation for them not being at their house when we sent a patrol out to pick them up right after we had found Molly and taken Melissa to the hospital. The fact that they weren't home had made them seem suspicious at first, but now it was perfectly normal. They seemed like a nice family, and I would hate for anything to destroy that picture. With everything I had been through over the past six months, I needed to know that there were still nice families out there who didn't lie to one another for thirty years or hurt children.

"We didn't know anything about this," she said. "Usually, the girls have sleepovers all the time, but this weekend we were gone, so…"

"And Molly probably knew that," I said. "Do you have any idea why she felt the need to lie to her parents about this?"

Mrs. Turner shook her head. "I don't really see why…"

She stopped then and looked at her daughter. We were all looking at Leanne, knowing she was the only one who could possibly know why Molly was lying, and who she was meeting when her parents thought she was having a sleepover at her friend's house.

Leanne shrugged. "I don't know. It's not like she's my best friend or anything; we just hang out sometimes."

"So, you're not part of her friend group with Carina, Ava, and Tara?" I asked.

Leanne shook her head. "No."

"Leanne doesn't go to the high school," her mother interrupted. "We do Florida Virtual school."

"So, she's homeschooled?" I asked.

"Yes. With all the temptations to vape, do drugs, and drink, we believed it was best for our daughter to keep her out of all that."

I stared at the woman, trying to imagine myself homeschooling my children. The thought was absurd. I loved my children dearly, but I also liked it when they were out of the house. We would only end up fighting non-stop, if not with me, then with each other. It just wasn't for me.

I turned to face the girl, sensing she knew more than she was letting on.

"Leanne, if you know anything about what Molly was up to, then you have to tell us. Was she meeting someone? Had she met someone online maybe?"

Leanne gasped lightly, and her eyes grew wide.

"Okay, she did," I said. "Who? Was it a man? Come on, Leanne. You might as well tell us. We will find out eventually when we go through her computer and social media accounts."

"Leanne, if you know anything, tell the police right now," her father said. He received another look from the mother, and I guessed she wasn't exactly used to being told what to do.

"I don't know, okay?" Leanne said and threw out her arms.

I gave her the look I usually gave my kids when I knew they were lying through their teeth and not getting away with it.

"Leanne?" I said.

"Okay, okay. She was supposed to meet this photographer. He had contacted her on Amino, I think it was, and he told her she was pretty and asked if she had considered becoming a model. He had seen her pictures and would like to take some professional ones. She could make a ton of money, he said. She asked me if she should do it. She said she'd ask her parents about it first, but I told her not to."

"Leanne!" her father said.

"Her parents would never understand," she continued. "They would never allow her to go. Not until they saw the pictures, then they'd see that it was real. If they saw her looking like some supermodel, then they'd realize that she could do this, and that this photographer wasn't some phony."

"So, you told her to lie to her parents," I said. "And to meet with him."

"Well, yes. I said I'd be gone all weekend, so she could tell them she was sleeping over at my house. They'd never know."

"And where was she planning on spending the night then?" I asked.

"She was supposed to meet this guy at dusk at a park so he could take the photos while the sun was about to set. It was the best lighting, he said. He was going to take her to Orlando, and they'd stay the night there, and she would meet some agents in the morning. They were going to stay in a hotel, he said. At the Hilton, that's where the meeting would take place. He knew all the big names in the business, he said, and it was important that she meet with them if they were going to sign her. Molly had always dreamt of becoming a model, ever since she was little. This was her big break."

"Except it wasn't," I said. "Instead, it destroyed her life."

"You sound like you think it's Leanne's fault," her mother said. "It's not like she could have known that this guy wasn't legit; she couldn't possibly know what would happen."

I stared at the woman, wondering about an article I had read recently about the parents of today. They weren't called helicopter parents anymore; no, today they were called snowplow parents. A snowplow parent will "plow" down any person or obstacle standing in their child's way. They were constantly paving the way for their children, removing every obstacle or disappointment that might appear, enabling them never to make responsible decisions or take responsibility for their actions.

I couldn't legally charge Leanne for encouraging her friend to lie to her parents, but boy, I wished I could at this moment.

Chapter 34

I managed to make it home in time for dinner. I rushed inside, threw my purse on the table, and turned to see all of them seated around my dining room table.

Alex saw me first.

"MOMMY!"

He was about to jump down from his seat when my mom stopped him.

"Your mom will come here. You eat now."

I smiled widely at the sight of my family, then rushed to Alex and kissed him. He reached up his small arms and grabbed me, wanting me to kiss him again.

"I missed you, Mommy," he said. "Where were you?"

"Yeah, Mom, where have you been?" Olivia asked.

I sat down in my seat, while my mom got me some food and handed me the plate. I stared at the green stuff, then wondered if there was such a thing as a kale-allergy and whether my mom would believe me if I said I suffered from it.

"I'm helping Matt on the case," I said. "They need me. And, frankly, after finding Molly out there...in our backyard, I feel obligated to help. Melissa is, after all, my best friend."

"There was an EXPLOSION downtown," Alex

exclaimed very loudly, yelling the word out. "Were you there, Mommy? Was there a FIRE? And firetrucks, huh?"

"Please, use your inside voice, Alex," my mom said.

I smiled at him. "Alex is correct. There was a truck that exploded right in front of city hall today. And, yes, I was there, and yes, there was fire and firetrucks and firefighters who put the fire out."

Olivia stared at me with big eyes. "I heard about it at school. We were on lockdown for hours. Then they told us all to go out on the football field while dogs searched the school. They say it was a bomb; is that true?"

"I heard someone was hurt," Christine said.

I took a deep breath, then nodded, sticking my fork into the green mass on my plate, dreaming about it being pizza or steak.

I might as well tell the kids the truth, I thought. *They'll only hear rumors from their friends, and that will be worse.*

"You're all correct. It looks like there might have been a bomb placed in that truck and someone did get hurt. An officer. One of our colleagues and Matt's friend."

Olivia gave me a look of concern. I knew that look a little too well. All my children had it right now, even Alex.

"I'm going to be fine," I said. "I was nowhere near the truck when it exploded. I don't want you to worry about me; do you hear me? I'm being very careful."

"Now, enough with the long faces," my mom said. "Eat your dinner before it gets cold."

We ate in silence, and it was nagging at me. The last thing I wanted was for my children to have to worry about their mother too. They had enough concerns in their lives as it was. This wasn't good for them. I hated the fact that they had seen Molly hanging in that swing set and knew so much about what was going on.

After dinner, I cleaned up while my mom went to the living room to relax. She turned on the TV and watched the news until Alex came and sat with her and she turned it onto *Peppa Pig* instead.

Christine and Olivia helped me clean up and, as I was loading the dishwasher, Christine came up to me.

"What did Dad say?"

"Dad? About what?"

I looked at her a little confused; then I remembered.

Oh, shoot. I was supposed to have called him! I promised her.

"You didn't call him; did you?" she said disappointedly. "I should have known."

Christine started to walk away. I stared after her, wondering what I could say or do, but nothing came to mind. Instead, I grabbed my phone and walked out on the back porch, then called him. It was dark out, and I could hear fish jumping in the canal. They did that a lot, especially as it got warmer. No one really knew why, but some people said they were catching bugs; others said they were running away from bigger fish like dolphins or sharks. I had never seen a shark in my canal, but there were plenty of dolphins.

"Chad, it's me."

"Eva Rae?" he said, surprised. "What's wrong? Is something up with the kids?"

"The kids, well…actually, yes, something is wrong. They miss you, Chad. They miss their dad, and you don't seem ever to have time for them anymore. They're asking when they're going to visit you again."

I knew I was putting it on a little thick since, technically, I was the one who was pressing for this to happen, but I sensed it was the only way to Chad's heart.

"Visit? Ah, well…It's just there's a lot right now. I've recently started a new job at a new insurance company, and I no longer work from home, so it's a little difficult to find the time, right now at least…I mean, as soon as things settle down a little, I'm sure…"

I sighed. "What the heck is going on, Chad? You used to be all about the children."

"I just…It's hard to find the time right now. I'm sure it'll get better when…"

"Don't give me that," I said. "This is not you, Chad. After

fifteen years of marriage, you don't think I know you? This is not you. This is her; isn't it? She's the one who doesn't want them there; am I right?"

He exhaled, and I knew then that I was right. Tears sprang to my eyes. My poor babies. They had to know by now; didn't they? They had to have realized by now that their dad had chosen his new girlfriend over them. That was why they didn't ask to go. It wasn't that they didn't miss their dad. They sensed he didn't want them there.

"It's just…well, three children are a little much. I can't blame her. We only live in a condo and don't have space for them. It gets very crowded when they're here, and it's a little too much for her."

I closed my eyes and bit my lip. I wanted to yell at him so badly but had to restrain myself.

"So, what are you saying, Chad? You can't see your children because they take up too much space; is that it?"

"No, no, of course not. Darn it, Eva Rae, you know how much I love them."

"Then why won't you see them? Why can't you make room to be with your own children, Chad? Explain this to me because I simply don't understand it. I don't even know who you are anymore."

"We're trying to figure it out, okay?" he said, annoyed. "I'll make it work somehow. I miss them too, okay? But it's… well, it's not that easy."

"I really want to believe you, Chad; I really do, but you're making it hard. You've got to find a way to spend time with your children. You're breaking their hearts. I see it in their eyes. You're not with them every day; you don't see the hurt in them like I do. You can't do this to them. I won't let you."

"You won't let me? What's that supposed to mean?" he said, suddenly sounding like I had offended him. "You're no better yourself, you know? Do I have to mention how little you were home when they were younger? Who took care of all the tantrums, all the homework, all the laundry, all the crying when tucking them in at night, huh? You're no saint in that area either. Don't you tell me how to be a good father when you've only been a mother for like ten minutes of their lives."

Ouch.

"I know I'm not..." I started but realized that the line had gone dead. Chad had hung up on me. Startled at this, I sat down on the porch swing, tears escaping my eyes. Inside, I could hear Alex scream something at one of his sisters, and soon someone was crying. I leaned back, closing my eyes for just a second before the door opened and Olivia peeked her head out.

"Mom? Alex pulled Christine's hair. I think you better come."

I swallowed the knot of tears stuck in my throat and nodded.

"I'll be right there, baby. Just give me a sec; will you?"

Chapter 35

S he was sitting on the porch swing underneath the porch light. Boomer couldn't stop staring at her. She looked tired and sad, yet so vulnerable and beautiful.

He liked to watch her and did it a lot. Earlier in the day, he had been in the crowd downtown watching too. He had seen the officer walk into the truck right when it blew up. People around him had screamed and run for cover when it happened. Boomer had watched when Eva Rae Thomas had arrived in the cruiser with her partner, the guy she was also dating, Matt Miller. Covered by the crowd on the corner in front of Heidi's Jazz Club, he had watched her closely until a police officer had told them to get out of there, that it was too dangerous for them to stand so close.

Boomer had moved away, still covered by the crowd. He had continued down A1A until he reached Juice N' Java, where he had bought himself a coffee and chatted briefly with the woman behind the counter whose name was Deborah about the horrifying blast they had heard.

"We all ran out there, but our boss told us to get back inside," she said, slightly excited but trying to hide it. "A car exploded, someone told me afterward. Something like that. Did you hear it too?"

"I sure did," Boomer said and paid with cash, making sure not to leave a trail.

"I guess everyone did," Deborah replied. "Good thing it was all the way down there and not right here that it happened. Must have been something wrong with that car or somethin', to go up in flames like that, causing an explosion. The cash register shook and everything. People were screaming in here. For a moment, I feared it was terrorists or something like you hear about in Europe and those places in the Middle East. Terrible world we live in. But Marty in the kitchen said it was just an accident. His brother is a cop, and he texted him and asked."

"Good thing it wasn't anything worse," Boomer said and received his coffee.

He tipped Deborah extra before returning to watch the scene from a distance. A news chopper was lingering in the air above the intersection, and reporter vans had arrived. Styled women in short skirts and high heels were elbowing their way up the career ladder and doing live reporting from the scene. The police had blocked off the entire intersection and big portions of A1A, while dogs sniffed the trash cans and drains. People around him were shocked and talking with fear in their voices, yet not afraid enough to not want to have a look for themselves.

When Eva Rae Thomas had walked back into the police station, it wasn't fun anymore, and he had decided to leave. He knew it wouldn't take long before the police would start questioning the spectators and looking for anyone who stood out, knowing that criminals often returned to the scene of the crime to watch their work.

Boomer had rushed up through the town and taken his pick-up truck, which he had parked behind the Chinese restaurant Yen Yen. He drove to Cape Canaveral, then walked down to the beach, where he sat in the white sand, looking at the pictures he had taken with his phone, pictures right during and after the bomb went off. He kept staring at the pictures, going through them again and again, his heart beating faster each time. Then he opened and looked at the ones he had taken of her, zooming in as much as he could on her face as she received the news from the chief of police. One of her colleagues had gotten hurt. One she cared about.

It hurts; doesn't it?

Boomer then opened the app he was using to trace her phone. He had been surprised that she had accepted him when he had asked for her friendship in the app, using a fake profile with the name of one of her old friends. He figured she had seen no harm in accepting this friendship, thinking it was someone she knew. It was almost too easy. And now he could follow her everywhere she went, constantly staying one step ahead.

Now, as she rose to her feet to walk back inside, as soon as the door slammed shut, Boomer started up the small boat and chugged away, cruising down the canal. He docked the boat further down in his usual spot by the ramp, then grabbed all his fishing stuff and put it in the pick-up truck and drove it home, listening to Taylor Swift on the radio. As he walked into the house after putting his stuff in the garage, he looked at himself briefly in the mirror in the hallway, then ran a hand through his hair and smelled his sweaty armpit before yelling:

"Honey! I'm home!"

Chapter 36

"We found the guy who wrote to Molly, the one who claimed to be a photographer."

Matt was at my door the next morning, looking like he hadn't slept at all.

"Come on in," I said. "I have coffee."

"Sounds heavenly," he said and walked inside with me. We entered the kitchen just as Alex turned his spoon with milk and cheerios at his sister and was about to sling it at her.

"ALEX!"

He stopped and turned to look at me, spoon still balancing in his hand.

"Don't you dare do that," I said. "Are you kidding me?"

"But she started it," he whined, letting the spoon fall into the milk. "She's *me-an*."

"Am not," Christine said.

Alex answered by sticking his tongue out.

"That's it," I said. "Both of you go upstairs and brush your teeth. Bus will be here any minute. GO!"

"You're so unfair, Mom," Alex said, then ran up the stairs, Christine right behind him, rolling her eyes at me.

I turned to look at Matt, then smiled.

"Coffee?"

He nodded, startled, then sat on a stool, wiping away a few lost cheerios from the counter.

"What was that all about?"

"That? I don't know. The usual, I guess," I said and poured him a cup. "Who knows what they fight about? I'm not sure they even do anymore."

I poured myself another cup. It was my third this morning. I hadn't slept much myself either and felt the exhaustion in every bone of my body.

"Does it frighten you?" I asked and nodded toward the stairs. "Seeing this?"

He shrugged. "I'm just not used to all this conflict, I guess. But that's probably what makes it so hard with Elijah, you know? Me trying constantly to avoid conflict."

"Ah, yes, conflict comes with the job, and a lot of it. You just can't let it get to you. They can hate you at one second, then turn around and love you dearly the next."

Matt sighed. "I'm afraid he hates me pretty much all of the time."

I put my hand on top of his, then leaned over and kissed him. "It'll get better. I promise," I said as our lips parted. "Now, what was that about you finding the guy who contacted Molly?"

Matt nodded. "Computer Forensics has her laptop, and they found him easily. He wrote messages to her on the social media app called Amino. They managed to pull the entire conversation."

"Never heard of it," I said. "I feel like every time I just learn about social media, another one pops up, and I'm lost again."

"I know," he said. "Our parents had it easy."

Our eyes met, and he immediately regretted his remark.

"Well, my parents had it easy," he said. "Anyway, this is like a social media platform for art lovers, so it seems very safe, but in reality, it's just like all the others. You post pictures of yourself and creeps find you. Molly was no different, she posted many artistic self-portraits as her art, and he saw the photos and thought she was beautiful enough to become a model. This guy has been writing to Molly for several months, and I guess that was why she chose to trust him. I can't blame her. When you read their conversation, he comes off as extremely nice. He's not even trying to push her into it. He cautiously warned her about bad seeds in the business and seems to know what he's talking about. Like he gave her all these references, numbers she could call if her parents wanted to check up on him, he said. Numbers that were fake, naturally. He even told her she could bring her parents if she wished or a friend. He didn't want her to think he was some creep that wanted to exploit her. She ended up being the one pushing for him to help her because she wanted this so badly. He kept telling her she should talk to her parents about it and said that he didn't want her to do the photos without her parents knowing about it."

"Yet, she did it anyway. He probably knew she would. He's clever, this one," I said and sipped my coffee. "Using reverse psychology. Making her think it was her idea and not his."

"Exactly," Matt said.

"So, when can we talk to this guy?" I asked.

Matt smiled. "How about right now?" He pulled a note out from his pocket with an address on it. "Forensics gave me his address. It's ten minutes away."

"Let's go," I said and was about to grab my purse when I heard the school bus sigh outside my door and peeked out just in time to see it take off. I turned to look at Matt.

"Right after I drive them to school."

I heard my kids' footsteps on the stairs. Olivia didn't have classes till later but was awake now too, and I could hear the shower being turned on. She would ride her bike to school, so I didn't need to worry about her, only the young ones.

"How about we all go in my police cruiser?" Matt asked.

Alex heard that and rushed down the stairs.

"YAAAY!"

"Really?" Christine asked less enthusiastically. "You want

me to sit in the back seat like some criminal? Everyone will stare at us. They'll all talk. I'm not doing it."

"I will; I will," Alex said, jumping up and down. He rushed to the front door while I sent Christine a reassuring smile.

"Nonsense, honey. It'll be fun. I'm just gonna run upstairs real quick and tell Olivia we're leaving, and then we'll go. Go ahead and get in the car. I don't want us to be late. Don't be so grumpy, Christine."

"I hate my life," Christine said, moaning, then followed Matt reluctantly.

I knocked on the door to the bathroom, then yelled at Olivia that I was leaving and received an *Okay* for an answer. I rushed down the stairs, past my mom, who opened her mouth to say something, then I pecked her on the cheek before she could and stormed out to the driveway where Matt already had the engine fired up and music blasting out the windows. Alex stuck his head out the window, looking like he was about to explode with excitement while his sister hid her face behind her hands.

Chapter 37

"I thought you'd let me see a doctor? I'm not feeling well."

Ava stared at the man wearing the surgical mask. He had entered the room where she had been kept for hours, alone. After taking her out of the room with the other girls, he had taken her into a bedroom and chained her to a pipe, then told her to lie on the bed, and then gagged her. It had been light out and then dark again before the light came once more, and the darkness came back while she had waited for him to take her to a doctor as she had asked. But he hadn't shown his masked face at all. Now, the room she was in had gone dark. She had prepared herself for another night alone in the bed when the door had opened, and light had hit her face again. The man had flipped the switch by the door, and a lamp had turned on, almost blinding Ava.

"Why are you keeping me in here?" she said, worried as he finally pulled the gag out. "I'm sick. Please, take me to see a doctor."

The masked man sat next to her on the bed, holding a knife in his hand. Ava saw it and felt her pulse quicken.

"You girls think I'm an idiot; don't you? Like I didn't know you were trying to fool me, pretending to be sick. Did you really think I would take you to see a doctor so you could tell him I was keeping you prisoner, huh? Do you think I'm that stupid?"

"N-no," she said, anxiety rising inside of her. He had known all along that it was a trick. The realization caused panic to spread inside of her. "I don't think you're stupid at all."

The masked man tilted his head. "Oh, look at you, trying to make sure I don't get mad, telling me what I want to hear. But the thing is, I am angry. I am a very angry man. You took me for a fool, and now you have to pay the price."

Ava whimpered and pulled back on the bed. She tried to pull loose from the chains but couldn't. She tried to scream, but after throwing up the little she had in her stomach and not having any food or anything to drink for almost twenty-four hours, she didn't have the strength to scream very loud, let alone fight back.

"Please, sir. I...I didn't mean to...I'm not..." Ava tried, but she was so exhausted she could barely think. Whatever kept her awake was fueled solely by her fear.

The masked man approached her, knife still in his hand.

"Now, the thing is, you weren't supposed to die till last, but now that you pulled this trick, I decided to take you first instead. How about that, huh?"

"N-no, please, mister, I am...I don't want to..."

"You don't want to what?" he asked, coming very close to her face. "You don't want to *die*; is that it?"

"Y-yes. Please. I don't want to die," she pleaded, crying now. "I just want to go home."

The man's face was close to hers now, and she could hear him breathing. Looking into his eyes, Ava suddenly recognized them and gasped loudly. Even though he was wearing a surgical mask, she could still tell that he was smiling.

Chapter 38

"So where are we on finding our bomber?" I asked as Matt drove out from the middle school's parking lot, where we had just dropped off Christine. She had blushed and put on her jacket, hiding her face in the hoodie as she got out. The entire crowd of kids that was rushing to school had stopped and stared at the kid arriving in a police cruiser. I had to admit; I felt a little bad for her. Middle schoolers were merciless.

"I'm guessing the lab isn't done with their analysis yet, but have we had any luck with the surveillance cameras from City Hall?"

Matt shook his head. "I had two of my men going through the footage all night. So far, all they've seen is the truck arriving, being parked in the middle of the intersection, and a guy running away from it."

"Any face? ID?"

Matt shook his head. "I'm afraid not. We could only see him from the back. It's almost like he knew where the cameras were. He was wearing a black baseball cap too. It's no use."

"Okay, we'll find him without it, even though it would be nice to put a face to him. Maybe Jane's description of the delivery guy to the artist later today will give us something. I feel pretty convinced he's the same guy who hurt Molly and who took Carina, Ava, and Tara. Say, wasn't there a photographer who contacted Ava as well about becoming a model? I remember you saying something about it at the beginning of your investigation."

Matt looked at me. "Yes, I checked him out. It's the same guy. Or rather, it's the same profile. It's called Space Coast Photography."

"So, he's hiding behind a company name to make it look legit. Easiest trick in the book, but also something young gullible girls might fall for."

"It was the same profile that contacted Ava on Instagram and told her he would like to take pictures of her, but her parents wouldn't let her go. They didn't believe it was real."

"So, he was a suspect earlier on. Did you ever talk to him?"

Matt shook his head. "He was gone when we went for him, and we never found him. A neighbor said they rarely saw the owner of the house, that they believed they had family up north and maybe was out of town."

"Had he seen the girls?"

"He said he often saw young girls come and go at the house, but he couldn't recall seeing our three girls specifically. Our hunch wasn't enough for a warrant, the chief said, since this was months ago, or we would have raided the house. We had a patrol stationed there for a few days, but there was no activity to report."

"I see," I said. "And what is this guy's name?"

"The house belongs to a Jordan Daniels."

Matt parked the cruiser in front of a small townhouse in South Cocoa Beach and killed the engine. I took off my seatbelt and felt my gun in the holster. This was the moment I hated the most about the job. You never knew what awaited you on the other side of that door. It could be anything from a nice old woman or neglected children to someone willing to end your life.

Chapter 39

T HEN:
　　"He says he wants money. Let's just give it to him."

Iris stared at Gary. He had called it in, and now the house was crawling with uniforms and the forensic team going through every corner of their home. As an FBI agent, Gary had been at dozens of crime scenes, but he had never ever imagined it would one day be his own home.

"It's not that simple, Iris," he said. He was trying not to hiss at her, but it was hard. He couldn't help himself. He tried not to be cross with her, he really did, but the fact was, he was blaming her for not keeping a proper eye on their son.

Why would she leave him out of her sight like that?

"We don't believe he has been inside the house," his supervisor, Agent Peterson, said coming up to him. Behind him stood Gary's partner, Agent Wilson, along with most of his other colleagues. Seeing all of them in his house wearing FBI jackets and gloves made Gary's heart drop.

"There are no footprints or fingerprints anywhere, no sign of anyone breaking and entering," Peterson continued. "Personally, I think he walked up from the street. He might have just passed by out there, then seen Iris as she put the baby in the carriage and thought there was his chance at making some easy money. My guess is that he is some drug addict or someone in deep gambling debt."

"So, you think that if we give him the money, then he might bring Oliver back?" Iris asked.

"I didn't say that," Peterson said with an exhale. "With someone like that, you never really know what their next move will be."

"But it's worth a try; isn't it?" Iris said. "In the note, it says he wants twenty thousand dollars. I have that in my savings from when my mother died. I can go to the bank right now and get the cash. It says in the note that he will bring back the boy *safe and happy* if we do as he says."

"It also says that he will kill the baby if we make *a wrong move*," Gary said. "God knows what a wrong move is in his book. Calling all my FBI colleagues probably isn't a *right* move to him."

Iris's expression changed. Her eyes were red-rimmed from crying, and her shoulders slumped. The hope in her eyes died out for a minute.

"So, what are you saying?" she asked. "Are you saying he might already have killed him?"

"Let's not jump to conclusions," Peterson said. "We have literally everyone looking for the boy right now. Besides, why would he kill him if he wants money? Then he has nothing to bargain with."

Iris nodded, head bowed. "Peterson is right. I say we give him the money and get our boy back. It's all I want."

She lifted her glance, and her eyes met Gary's. It was hard for him to even look at her right now, but as their eyes met, he felt himself grow softer. Maybe she couldn't have helped it. It didn't have to be anyone's fault. Bad things happened to good people sometimes. Accidents happened. At least that was what he always told relatives when he went to their houses to tell them about their loved ones having passed away.

We can't control everything in life. There was nothing you could have done to prevent this from happening. You must forgive yourself.

Iris's lips shaped half a smile as their eyes remained locked. "What do you say, Gary?"

He nodded, biting his lip nervously. "I say we do it. Let's give him the money and get Oliver back."

Peterson placed a hand on Gary's shoulder. "I'll set things in motion. We won't let him get away, Gary. You know we won't."

Chapter 40

"Yes?"

I stared at the small skinny woman in front of me standing in the doorway. She was wearing a long black skirt and a green tank top and had her dreadlocks wrapped in a very colorful scarf. In her hand, she was holding what looked like a very expensive and professional camera.

"We're looking for Jordan Daniels," Matt said and showed her his badge.

"That's me," she said indifferently. She was wearing heavy eyeliner and had a tattoo of an octopus licking up her shoulder.

"*You're* Jordan Daniels?" I asked.

She gave me a look. "It can be a girl's name too, you know."

I glanced briefly at Matt, then back at the woman. "Yes, of course, it can."

"So, what can I do for you?" she asked.

"We have a few questions for you if you don't mind?" I asked, sensing she would respond better to a female approaching her than Matt.

She looked at me, then nodded. "Sure. Come on in."

She let us inside her small dark house where all the blinds were pulled in each and every room. In the living room, she had set up a regular studio with lamps facing the backdrop to give the right light.

"I take it you work from home?" I said as we walked inside and she put her camera on the tripod. It was a cluttered place with many magazines spread out and photographs of young girls lying everywhere, yet it still came off as stylish with high-tech minimalistic furniture.

"I sure do," she said. "This is my studio. This is where I do most of my shoots if I'm not called out on a shoot somewhere."

Matt looked at the photographs on the long white desk leaned against the barren wall.

"You photograph a lot of young girls, I take it?"

"Those are the ones who are most in demand, yes," she said with a sly smile.

Matt showed her a picture of Carina Martin. "Ever seen her before?"

Jordan studied the picture, then shook her head. "Nope."

"So, she hasn't been here?"

"No. I would have remembered that. She's very pretty but not exactly a model."

"How about this one," Matt said and showed her a school picture of Molly Carson.

Seeing her picture again made my stomach churn. The previous night, before I went back home to dinner with my family, I had stopped by the hospital and sat down with Melissa over a cup of coffee. She was still in deep shock and had a heaviness to her face I had never seen before. She was barely keeping it all together with the kids at home and being at the hospital most of the day. Luckily, Steve had tried some new medicine and was up and running again now, so he could help her out, but he also needed to take care of his job, so he didn't lose it and with it their whole income. Molly was doing better and was out of the ICU, and she was awake, they said, but she hadn't said a word to anyone yet. We were still waiting for her to start talking so we could ask her about the pig who did this to her. The doctors didn't really know if she was unable to talk or if she just chose not to. Only time would tell, they said. They were hoping it was still just the shock that was blocking her, and as it wore off, she would begin to speak.

I prayed that they were right.

Jordan grabbed the photo and peeked at it. I studied her closely to look for any reaction. Jordan shook her head.

"Nope. Never seen her either."

"Are you sure?" I said. "Maybe take another look. Take your time."

She sat down, the photo still between her hands. She looked again and shook her head.

"Those eyes. I would definitely have remembered those."

Yeah, well that was all any of us could do now. Her mother would never see them again.

"I am sorry; I haven't seen her before. Why?"

"Are you the only one who handles your social media presence?" I asked. "Or do you have someone else doing it?"

Jordan smiled. "Look around you. Do I look like I could afford people working for me?"

"You could have an intern working for you maybe," I said.

"Well, I don't."

I grabbed a photo of a random young girl from her desk and held it up. "How do you find girls? Do you contact them?" I asked.

Jordan looked away as I asked the question, and I took note of her reaction.

"They come to me," she said. "They call me up, or they write to me because they want to become models. I tell them I can't promise them anything, but I can take some professional pictures of them that they can send to an agency. I sometimes help them find the right agencies to send them to as well. It's not illegal what I do."

"No one said it was," Matt said, still looking through the pictures of girls on the desk. He picked one up and looked at it closely, then put it down. I took out the photos of all four girls and put them in front of Jordan. "Could you look at all these girls and tell me if you recognize any of them?"

Jordan was getting annoyed with us now. I could tell by her agitated body language.

"What is this about?"

"Just do it for me; will you?" I asked.

She exhaled and looked at all of them, shaking her head. "I haven't seen any of them before. I am sorry."

"Try again."

"Seriously? It's not like it's gonna change. I told you I don't know any of these girls."

I smiled, trying to hide how much she was annoying me right now. "Just humor me. I want to be one hundred percent certain."

"Are you for real?"

I nodded. "I am very real, thank you. Now, take your time. Don't rush it. We have all day."

"Geez, you'd think you people had better things to do."

As she studied them, I turned to look at Matt, who showed me a picture he had found in the pile. I nodded to let him know I had seen it. Jordan lifted her head and looked directly at me.

"There. I have looked at them three times now, and I don't recognize any of the girls at all."

"And you're sure?" Matt said and approached us, still holding the photograph in his hand.

"I am sure."

Matt turned the photo and placed it on the table in front of Jordan, then slid it across it till it was right in front of her.

"Because this photo kind of looks a lot like this girl; doesn't it?" he said and pointed at Ava Morales's photograph.

"I think we need to have you come in for further questioning," I said.

"But…but I can't…I'm going out on a photo shoot this afternoon."

My eyes met Matt's, and I nodded.

"Let's take her in."

Hearing this, Jordan sprang to her feet and bolted for the door.

Shoot.

"We have a runner!"

I was quickly up and running after her, while Matt was slower to react. Jordan made it past him and opened the door. She leaped out into the driveway, then sprinted down across the lawn and into the street, Matt and I following her closely behind, hands on our weapons, ready to draw should it become necessary.

Agile Jordan sprang down the street toward the river, sprinting like she was some darn track runner. Who would have thought such a small girl had such force in her? I, on the other hand, panted agitatedly as I tried to follow her, cursing myself for not being in better shape like I had promised myself. I guess I hadn't exactly expected to be running after criminals anytime soon since I had actually quit my job.

Matt was doing a lot better and was soon ahead of me, almost within arm's reach of Jordan, ready to grab her. But just as he reached out his arm, she took a swift left turn and sprinted down Brevard Avenue instead. Matt lost speed and was soon left behind, while Jordan made it toward the river.

Oh, no, you don't.

Angrily, I sped up, pressing myself to the utmost, then as I was about to lose her, I threw myself at her, reached out my arm, and wrapped it around her neck, then pulled her backward using all my weight and stopping her in her tracks.

The next second, Matt pulled her to the ground. He was on top of her, turning her around, pressing his knee down on her back, and Mirandizing her.

Chapter 41

We let Jordan Daniels sweat for a while, then returned to our desks and sat down. The station was buzzing with activity as Chief Annie had called in help from the county's sheriff's office to find our bomber. I still believed it was the same guy we were searching for that had taken Molly and the three other girls, but Chief Annie wasn't fully convinced. It couldn't hurt to work several angles, she said.

I could hardly argue with that.

Matt brought both of us coffee while the adrenalin left our bodies. My legs were sore from running, and I think I pulled a muscle. I massaged my thighs as he handed me the plastic cup. I took a sip, then his phone rang.

Matt took the call while I read a text from Christine. She was upset because everyone was talking about her in school, and she had no one to sit with at lunch. I shivered, thinking about my own middle school years. They really were the worst.

I texted her back,

I AM SORRY, BABY. I AM SURE IT'LL BE BETTER SOON.

"That was the lab," Matt said when he hung up.

"Any news?"

"The syringe that the kids found. They've analyzed it and

believe it contained ketamine."

"A date rape drug?" I asked.

He nodded. "They also found traces of Carina Martin's blood on it. It matched the blood sample we had from Carina Martin's doctor that was taken a few days before she disappeared while she was in for a checkup."

"So, this was what he used to drug her, and probably the others too, when abducting them," I said, then glanced toward the interrogation room where Jordan Daniels was still waiting. "Or maybe she."

"The phone was also Carina's, as I suspected," Matt said.

"Okay, so now we can safely say that the three girls have been taken, am I right?" I asked and looked at the board behind Matt. "The theory of them having run away seems to be shrinking."

"I think it is safe to say," he said.

"Good. Did they have anything else?" I asked. "Any news on the bomb?"

He shook his head. "Not yet. But they got the results of the tests run on Molly Carson."

I sat up straight. "And?"

He shook his head. "Nothing. The rapist left no DNA. There was condom lubrication and no semen present. No DNA elsewhere on her either. Probably wore gloves when touching her."

"Of course, he did," I said and sipped my coffee. It suddenly tasted bitter. I glanced up at Molly's picture and felt guilty. I had promised Melissa I would catch this guy, but of course it wasn't going to be that easy. God forbid I had even one good lead to go on.

Matt sighed and finished his cup. He put it down heavily. "So, now what, Agent Thomas? What's our theory here? We have a woman in custody, but do we really think she raped and blinded Molly?"

"Maybe not. But I do think she might know who did," I said and finished my cup as well. I crushed it and threw it in the trash can in the corner.

Chapter 42

They heard footsteps. Carina was the first to hear them and open her eyes. Next to her slept Tara, who was now so skinny she was barely awake at all anymore.

"What was that?" Carina said and sat up.

Carina had lost track of time and barely knew if it was night or day anymore, but she did know that Ava had been gone a very long time. Carina worried about her and whether she had managed to get to a doctor's office. It was the plan that she should pretend to be sick and then alert the doctor once she got there. Since the day Carina had seen the masked man take her away, she had been waiting and waiting for someone to come. She had tried to stay awake for as long as she could, but the lack of food made her exhausted and, eventually, she had fallen asleep. Once she woke up, she had expected the police to come crashing down the door at any minute, but it hadn't happened.

Where are you now, Ava?

The wait was painful. Still, she kept her hopes up. The man hadn't been there since he came and took Ava. They had no more clean water and no more food. Carina felt her ribs and realized they were poking out now, and her stomach was in pain because of hunger. The worst part was the thirst.

Now, as she listened for more footsteps and didn't hear any, she thought that maybe it had just been another dream.

Carina crawled to the water bucket and poked her head into it. There was a little left on the bottom, and she lifted the bucket in the air, emptying it completely. Then she glanced at Tara, wondering if she should have left some for her in case she woke up. But maybe she wouldn't wake up at all, and then it would just be a waste. They would both die. At least Carina now knew she could get by for a little while longer, even though the dryness of her mouth and throat was painful.

Carina crawled to Tara and felt her neck. At first, she didn't feel her pulse, and she feared she had died, but by pressing harder into the paper-thin skin, she finally felt it.

She was still alive.

"Come on, Ava," she said. "Have you told them yet?"

Please, say they're on their way. Please, tell me they're coming. I don't know how much more of this I can take.

Carina sat down on her mattress and leaned her head against the back wall, a position she found herself sitting in constantly. She cried weakly and closed her eyes, dreaming about being on the beach with her friends, running around playing ball, eating chips, and swimming in the ocean. She had just drifted away when she heard more footsteps coming from above her head. Carina's eyes shot open.

"I heard it again," she said into the room. "Someone is up there. Someone is here!"

She tried to wake up Tara but had no luck. Now, she heard voices too, muffled voices, and more footsteps. Carina rose to her feet and started hammering on the walls. The foam was soft and made barely any sound, and soon she realized it was no use. Carina took a deep breath, then opened her mouth and started to scream.

"HEEEELP!!! HEEELP!"

There were steps outside of their door now, and she looked at it in anticipation, almost laughing.

"Tara. Tara! Wake up. They've found us. They're coming for us. Help is coming now."

But Tara didn't wake up. Carina stared at the door as the deadbolts were pushed aside.

"HEEELP!" she screamed. "We're in here!"

The door opened slowly, and a face appeared behind it. Carina almost cried with happiness until she realized it was the masked man. And he was alone.

He rushed toward her, then slammed his fist into her face. Carina felt the blow and sunk to her mattress, the room spinning around her.

"Don't you think I know what you've been up to? You think I would fall for your little trick, huh?"

Carina looked up at him, not sure she completely understood.

"A-Ava?" she asked.

As a grin spread behind the mask, she started to cry. "What have you done to her, you creep? What did you do to Ava?"

The man stared down at her but didn't answer. Instead, he walked to the door, found the light switch, and flipped it, turning off the small lamp beneath the ceiling, the source of all their light. Then he slammed the door shut, leaving Carina and Tara in complete darkness.

Chapter 43

"**D**id you call Dad?"

Christine had barely entered the house before she asked me. Her sweet eyes stared up at me in anticipation, and it broke my heart.

"You didn't, did you?" she said, disappointed. "I knew you wouldn't."

I exhaled and wiped my hands on a dishtowel. I had been cleaning up the kitchen since I got home. My mom hadn't been home all day since she was out with a friend shopping at the mall, so I decided to clean up from breakfast before the kids came home from school.

"As a matter of fact, I did," I said.

I had been thinking about this so intensely since I spoke to Chad, wondering what to tell the kids when they asked, and I had to admit that I hadn't come up with anything that wouldn't at some point end up hurting them.

"And? What did he say?"

Her eyes gleamed with excitement while I pondered what to do, what to say. I could hardly tell her the truth, that the woman her dad lived with now didn't want them there. She would only end up hurt and then hating Kimmie, and that wouldn't make their visits with their father any easier.

"You know what? Right now, he's a little overwhelmed

with his new job, and he has to work a lot, but he promised that as soon as it slows down a little, he'll have you come visit, okay?"

Christine stared at me, her smile frozen in place. I bit my lip, wondering what was going on inside of her. Did she buy it? It wasn't a complete lie. But it wasn't exactly the truth either.

"So…so…he didn't say when?" Christine asked. "Because summer break is coming up, and we could go up there for a longer time, maybe a week?"

"I…sweetie, I don't think…"

Alex came out into the kitchen and looked at both of us while standing behind his sister. I didn't want him to hear any of this and wanted to finish this conversation now.

"Hey, buddy," I said addressed to him. "Are you hungry? How about I make us some cinnamon rolls, huh?"

"Yay," Alex said, his eyes lighting up. He grabbed a stool and sat down at the counter with his firetruck in his hand. He looked at his sister, then at me. I forced a smile.

Christine's shoulders slumped, and I knew she didn't buy my excuse. We had been through this before, back in the fall when her dad had told her not to come, and she almost went anyway on her own but was stopped at the airport. It pained me that nothing seemed to have changed much. For a little while, I had believed things had changed since they actually went to visit him every month, and we seemed to have gotten into some sort of routine. It somehow felt even worse that he was now pulling out once again. The kids were going to feel like it was their fault. They were going to wonder if they did something wrong on their last visit.

"It's her, isn't it?" she asked. "She doesn't want us there."

"Who?" Alex asked.

"Kimmie," Christine said. "She doesn't like us. Remember the last time we were up there? Remember how she and Dad had that big fight in the kitchen when we were in the living room, and they thought we couldn't hear them, but we could?"

Alex nodded, bowing his head.

So, that's what happened. That's why the girls didn't ask to visit him anymore for several months. They didn't feel welcome. They knew they were the cause of their fight. They were in their way.

"I'm sorry, baby...I..."

Christine nodded. "I get it. Dad doesn't want us to come because she doesn't want us there."

"Daddy?" Alex asked. "He doesn't want us?"

"Of course, your dad wants you to visit. He's just trying to figure out a way to make it happen because they don't have so much room in the condo, okay? He promised me he'd make it happen somehow. Don't worry, okay?"

But none of the eyes looking back at me believed a word I had just said. Especially not Christine. She grabbed her phone and started tapping on it, disappearing into that world of her own that I couldn't reach her in, while Alex slid down from the stool, saying, "I'm not hungry."

"Me either," Christine said and turned around without even looking up from her screen.

I opened my mouth to try and say something but couldn't really find the right words. A knock on the door grabbed my attention, and as I walked to open it, both my children disappeared upstairs.

Chapter 44

The woman standing outside my door was dressed in a long gorgeous gown that reached the ground. To her side, standing a little behind her, was a younger man, dressed in a Hugo Boss polo shirt and what looked like very expensive Cartier sunglasses.

"Kelly Stone?" I said. "What are you doing here?"

"This is where you live, isn't it?" she asked.

"Yes, it is, but…"

I stared at the man near her shoulder. "This is Noah. He's my fiancée."

"Nice to meet you," I said, still flabbergasted. It wasn't every day that a Hollywood movie star knocked on your door.

"Can we come in?" she asked with her heavy British accent. I couldn't stop staring at her. I had been thinking so much about her since I had seen her at her house that day. Especially every time I saw her face in the check-out line at Publix, where she was often on the covers of many of the magazines.

"Yes, yes of course," I said and stepped aside. They walked past me, and I closed the door. I picked up some shoes and toys and threw them all inside a cabinet and closed the door.

"I'm sorry for the mess."

Kelly Stone stopped in front of Alex's teddy bear that was lying on the Spanish tiles. She picked it up.

"How old are they?" she said and looked toward the stairs.

I swallowed, still holding one of Alex's firetrucks under my arm. "Alex is six, Christine twelve, and Olivia fourteen, no sorry fifteen; she just turned fifteen. It's hard to keep track, you know?"

Kelly Stone looked at me. She had taken off her sunglasses and held them in her hand.

"Is it? I wouldn't know."

Remembering that my sister was two years older than me, and that meant she was now forty-three, I realized it was probably too late for her to have children. It wasn't impossible, but it had to be something that she wondered about as well. Had she chosen career over family? There was so much I wanted to ask her but didn't dare to.

"Are they here?" she asked, still looking toward the stairs. "The children?"

"The two youngest are," I said. "Olivia has a volleyball game this afternoon, so she won't be home until later."

Kelly Stone smiled, then looked down at the teddy bear.

Just tell her, you fool. Tell her you know who she is and that you're her sister.

"Can I get you anything? Coffee?" I asked.

She looked at me and smiled again. "We won't stay long. We have to get to the airport. I'm shooting a new movie in Canada."

"Canada, huh? Sounds cold," I said. "How long will you be gone? You know, in case we need to get ahold of you for… you know…the event."

Our eyes met, and I felt such a warmth spread in my stomach. God, how I wanted to tell her the truth right there, but for some reason, I didn't. I guess I was scared of how she might react.

"I'll fly back in a couple of days," she said.

"Okay, okay, that's good. I bet you have your own plane

and everything, huh? Not that it matters. You're busy and have to leave soon. What can I do for you? Is it about the event? Because my mom and I are working out the details as we speak, and we should have a program for you any day now."

"I know who you are."

I looked up, and our eyes met again. My stomach lurched.

"I...I'm sorry?"

"I know who you are and why you came to me."

I swallowed hard.

"I...I..."

"Why now? Why did you come to find me now?" she asked, still fiddling with the teddy bear between her hands. "After all these years, why now all of a sudden?"

My heart was racing in my chest, and I took in a deep breath to calm myself.

"I just recently learned about you, that you were still alive," I said, my voice quivering. "Up until then, I thought you were dead. My entire life, I thought you had been killed."

Kelly Stone looked at our mother's picture on the wall, then nodded toward it.

"What about her? Did she think I was dead too?"

I shrugged. "I don't know, to be honest. She never talked to me about it. We still don't talk much about any of it."

"You know, you were the reason I came here," she said. "To the Space Coast. I don't remember much about my childhood, but I did remember having a sister. My dad would never talk about any of you, so I had to figure it out on my own. But all I remembered was you on the beach, playing, and then watching rockets and shuttles being sent off into space. That's how I figured that you might be here, but I couldn't find you. I didn't know your name. My dad wouldn't help me, and we lost contact because of it. But now I do. Eva Rae Thomas."

"And you're Sydney Thomas," I said, tears welling up in my eyes. "That was your name back then."

Kelly Stone reached out her hand and stroked my cheek

gently, a tear running down her cheek. I fought hard to hold mine back. My lips were quivering.

"I might have been that once, but I'm not her anymore," she said as something changed in her eyes. A hardness settled in them. She put the teddy bear down in the recliner before she faced me once more. "And seeing you again causes me too much pain. I can't do this anymore. I need you never to contact me again."

What?

My eyes grew wide. Startled, I stood back and stared at my sister as she turned around and rushed out of the house, clicking along on her high heels on the tiles, her boyfriend giving me an apologetic smile, then hurrying after her. I stood in the doorway as they got back into the limousine and drove off, feeling like someone had just ripped a part of my heart out.

Chapter 45

Boomer watched the screen on his computer. In the right corner, he saw Eva Rae's young son, Alex, as he ran through the living room, screaming loudly, arms above his head, wearing only pajama pants. Seconds later, he saw Eva Rae come into the picture, then yell something at the boy, trying to grab him, but he jumped away from her, laughing. Eva Rae Thomas then placed her hands on her hips and, seconds later, the boy stopped, and she grabbed him, then tickled him till he screamed for her to stop. Then they disappeared out of the camera's sight. A few minutes later, they reappeared in the left bottom corner of his screen as they entered the boy's bedroom, and she was finally able to get him to lay down. He was still only wearing pants when she put the covers over him, and they prayed together before she turned out the light. Boomer had been in her house while she was at the police station to set up the small cameras under the ceiling. They were wireless, smaller than a pea, and looked like a screw in the wall. He got them off eBay for only twenty dollars per camera. Easiest thing in the world. He had placed enough of them in her house to be able to follow her every move. He could use his phone if he didn't have his computer nearby.

Easiest thing in the world.

Boomer grabbed a beer from the fridge and opened it. He stood still and listened to see if he could hear the girls, but there was no sound coming from under the house. Either he had soundproofed it well, or they were both dead. Right now, he didn't care either way. He was so angry at them for trying to trick him that he wanted them to die. He only wished he could have shown them what he did to their little friend. Then they would learn never to try anything like that again; they'd know he wasn't someone you took for a fool. Boomer was no ordinary kidnapper or sexual predator. No, what he wanted was different and so much more devious than what any of those fools could come up with. But so far, he didn't feel like he had really been able to show the world what he was capable of. It was about time he turned up the heat a little.

It was time for the next act.

Boomer brought another beer with him back to the computer, so he didn't have to get up again anytime soon. He was in for a long night of watching his favorite show.

He sipped his beer and leaned back in the couch as he watched Eva Rae Thomas walk into her bedroom and start to get undressed. Boomer smiled to himself and put a hand on his crotch as she took off her bra and he got a really good look at her naked. His obsession with her had grown unhealthy; he knew it a little too well. He also knew he had to tread carefully, but it was hard for him not to give in to it. He wanted to possess her; he wanted her to know he was in charge of her, of her life. And he wanted to hurt her. Not in a traditional way or even a physical way. No, he wanted her heart to bleed so terribly she wouldn't want to live anymore. Even if it meant taking it out on someone she loved.

Only then would he be fully satisfied. Only then would he have achieved his goal.

Chapter 46

I was tossing and turning in my bed. There was a full moon outside, and it shone brightly behind my thin curtains, lighting up my room, making it even harder for me to get some much-needed shut-eye. I couldn't stop thinking about my sister and the strange meeting with her earlier in the afternoon. I couldn't shake the feeling that there was something I could have said or done to make her change her mind, to make her want to see me again. But it didn't matter how many clever things I came up with to say; it was too late. She had left, and she had told me she never wanted to see me again.

I just didn't quite understand why.

Was it because I had lied to her? Had I destroyed everything and ruined all my chances of getting my sister back? Was it because I had pretended to be doing that event and I hadn't been honest and told her who I was? Or was it something deeper?

Was I ever going to find out?

I turned to the other side, to face the door instead of the window, then closed my eyes again to try and fall asleep. The bed felt suddenly strangely uncomfortable, and I twisted back and forth a few times to try and get into a better position. I closed my eyes again and tried to empty my mind of worries. Yet, as soon as I had pushed my sister out of my head, in popped my children. Their sweet faces were staring up at me, their eyes big and sad, asking about their father.

I was getting sick of this and of him ruining everything. Why couldn't he just take the kids every other weekend or at least once or twice a month? It wasn't that much, was it? They missed him so much. How did he suddenly become so heartless? Why couldn't I talk to him at all?

I turned back to the other side, pushing the kids and Chad out of my mind, trying to think about something that made me happy, something joyful. Matt came to my mind immediately, and I opened my eyes, then placed a hand on the empty side of my bed, suddenly missing him terribly. He was at his own place and had spent the evening with Elijah. I wondered how they were holding up and if they were finally able to bond. It was tough trying to get to know your son after eight years and then finding out he blames you for the death of his mother. No, Matt didn't have it easy either.

As I stared at the moonlight coming in through my window, I thought about the case and the three girls. We still had no idea where they were. And then I thought about poor Molly and Cooper at the hospital. Cooper had suffered third-degree burns on two-thirds of his body and had to have skin transplants, Matt had told me earlier. He also said that he probably would lose his right leg. I felt awful for him.

I took a deep breath, then wrinkled my nose. All day, there had been this smell in the house, and I couldn't figure out where it was coming from. My mom had noticed it too, and the kids. I suspected it was the opossum in the attic that had bothered us for months. I had tried everything to chase it away, even had a professional guy out here to set up a trap, but somehow it was too cunning and avoided getting caught. Since then, I had given up, but it had gone silent a few weeks ago, and I figured that maybe it had died. I'd have to find out how to get up and into the attic to see if that was what it was.

Again, I turned around, then looked at my phone to see what time it was.

Three a.m. I only had a few hours before I needed to get up and get the kids to school.

Come sleep, come on.

Finally, I dozed off, and then my phone rang.

Chapter 47

The number on my display was unknown, so I picked it up, thinking it could be important.

"Hello?"

Silence. I was about to hang up when I heard someone breathing on the other end.

"Hello? Is someone there?"

"Agent Eva Rae Thomas?"

The voice was deep. It didn't sound like anyone I knew. It sounded distorted like it was using one of those voice changing apps.

"Who is this? Identify yourself, please."

"I'm the one you've been looking for."

I shot up in the bed, eyes wide open. "What do you mean, *you're the one I've been looking for?*"

Silence followed before he answered.

It is a male voice, isn't it? It's hard to tell.

"You know what I mean."

I swallowed, my pulse quickening. If this was the guy who had kidnapped the girls, I had to play my cards right. I couldn't mess this up.

"Where are they?" I asked. "All I want is to bring them home to their families. They're scared, and I think you are too."

"I am not scared."

"Why are you doing this?"

"You'll see. You'll understand. Soon."

"What will it take to get the girls home safely. Money?" I asked.

"There isn't enough money in the world."

"Okay. But what do you need? There must be something you want. Otherwise, the girls would already be dead."

"Who says they aren't dead?" the voice said.

My heart sank. "Are they? Are they…dead?"

"As I said, you'll find out. Soon. Now, sleep tight; tomorrow, we'll know if you're a real princess."

The line went dead. I stared at my phone, my heart pounding in my chest. Had this just happened? Had he really called, or had I dreamt it?

No, he was real enough, and I was very much awake.

We need to trace this call.

I grabbed my phone again and turned the lights on to call Matt, the smell of the dead opossum filling my nostrils. I tried to shake it, then found his name in my address book when it hit me.

Tomorrow, we'll know if you're a real princess!

I stopped in my tracks, a strong unease spreading throughout my body. There was something off about that sentence.

Tomorrow, we'll know if you're a real princess.

Those had been his words. As a mother, I knew it was a line from the fairy tale, *The Princess and the Pea*. They were said by the old queen mother who put the pea underneath the princess's many mattresses because only a real princess would be able to feel it through all those mattresses and say she had slept terribly.

Why had the caller said that?

I smelled the air, uncomfortably, then got out of the bed and took a few steps away from it. My heart hammered in my chest as I found the courage to finally take a look. I grabbed the side of the mattress, then lifted it.

I took one glance at what was beneath it, then turned around and threw up on my brand-new carpet.

Chapter 48

THEN:
"Are you okay, Gary? You feeling okay?"

Peterson was speaking to Gary in his earpiece. They were staying far away, behind the row of trees, ready to jump out as soon as the kidnapper showed himself.

The drop-off area was a small park with picnic tables in the center of town. The kidnapper had called two days ago and told them exactly where to place the money. If any police showed up, Oliver was dead, he said. If they tried to trace his call, Oliver was dead. All they needed to do was to have Gary bring the money to the park, wrapped in a newspaper, and leave it there on the third picnic table. If the money was there, the child would be returned to them unharmed.

It was as easy as that.

"We'll get him, Gary; don't you worry," Peterson said like he had said so many times over the past seven days that Oliver had been missing. Every time he said it, Gary felt less and less convinced of the truth behind those words. He had hardly slept in almost seven nights, and he felt so exhausted. Iris was close to losing it, completely torn to pieces while they waited for the kidnapper to contact them. It tormented him to see her like this, but at the same time, a gap had grown between them. He felt like he should comfort her, but he didn't really want to. He hardly wanted to touch her anymore and could barely look at her.

"Okay, G, this is the spot. You place the money on the table, and then you leave. We'll take care of the rest."

Gary stopped at the third table, then looked down at the newspaper between his hands. He knew he was surrounded by FBI agents and that there would be no way for the kidnapper to escape from the park once he got there, but he wasn't so sure it was a clever move. Didn't he need to get back to Oliver in order to bring him back to them? If they took him down, would they ever find the child? Peterson believed so. There was no criminal that he hadn't been able to crack so far, he always said.

He knows what he's doing. You know he does.

Gary's partner, Agent Wilson, and several of his other colleagues were guarding his home and his wife. They had it all covered.

So why did it feel like they didn't? Why did it feel like everything was about to go wrong?

Gary shook the thought and focused on the task ahead. He took a glance around him, then sat down at the picnic table. Carefully, he placed the newspaper on the table, his fingers shaking when letting go of it.

"Okay, and now you go," Peterson said in his ear. "Just get up and walk away, leaving the package behind like you don't need it anymore."

Gary stood to his feet, abandoning the newspaper on the table like he was told. He looked around him and spotted a woman jogging by with her dog, panting rhythmically as she went. A man was sitting on a bench further down, reading a book. A younger man was drinking from his water bottle, sitting at another of the tables, looking at his cell phone. He glanced briefly at Gary, and their eyes met.

Is that him? Is that our guy?

The young man smiled, then looked back at his phone before he finished his water bottle, then rose to his feet and left, carrying his backpack over one shoulder.

Gary turned around to look in another direction. Two dogs were playing on the lawn. A mom walked with her kid by the hand, pushing a stroller with a sleeping baby. For a second, Gary thought he saw Oliver inside the stroller, but as the mom passed him, pulling her second kid along, he could see it wasn't his child.

"Gary. You need to leave now. Just walk away nice and slow like nothing happened. We'll keep an eye on the package. Come on, G. You gotta do your part."

"I'm walking away now," Gary said, his eyes letting go of the stroller. He turned around and let his eyes fall to the ground, focusing on his steps instead, trying to not look for suspects in the park. He took three steps toward the entrance when someone approached him, running up to him. Gary didn't see her till it was too late and she was standing right in front of him, high heels, short red skirt, and a jacket, holding out a microphone, a cameraman right behind her.

"Mr. Pierce. Have you placed the ransom? When do you expect to see your son again?"

Gary stared at the beautiful woman in front of him, then noticed more movement from behind her, more high heels, skirts, and more microphones. Before he could even protest, a crowd had gathered around him, questions being slung through the air from all sides.

Chapter 49

Olivia was the first to react. She stormed into my bedroom.

"What's wrong? Why are you screaming, Mom?"

"There's…don't come in here, baby."

She glanced at the vomit on the carpet, then at the bed. I could hear her whimper slightly.

"Call Matt, will you? Please? Use my phone. Tell him to come quickly. And keep the young ones out of here. I don't want them to see this."

Olivia stared at me, her eyes tormented. Then she nodded. "Okay."

I rushed to the bathroom and threw up again, then washed my face, taking in deep breaths to calm myself. A few seconds later, I heard Matt's steps on the stairs. I felt so relieved that he lived close to me. He had been my go-to guy ever since we were very young children and his house was the place I ran to when things got tough at home. His mom always had room for me and, even though we had been apart for twenty years, I had found that nothing had changed between us as soon as I moved back home. He was there for me, and always would be. I don't know why it had taken me so many years to realize he was the one for me, that he had been all along.

"What happened? What's going on?" Matt said as he stormed into my bedroom. "Olivia called?"

I turned to look at the bed. I had pulled the top mattress off, and Matt spotted the body inside the cut-open box spring below. He clasped his mouth, and his startled eyes landed on me. I swallowed.

"Oh, no," he said. "Is it...?"

"I believe it's Ava Morales," I said. "But she's so badly beaten up, it's hard to tell."

"And she's...?"

"Dead? I'm afraid so. Rigor Mortis has set in, and you can see the blood has gathered on the bottom part of her body. She's been dead a while. There's something else."

"Yes?"

"He called. He called me and told me, not in so many words, but he told me something that led me to her. If he hadn't, I might have slept on top of her all night."

The thought made me gag again. Maybe it was the smell, but I was feeling sick in every bone of my body. I could hear Olivia talking with Alex in the hallway outside the door. He wanted to see Mommy, *now*, but she wouldn't let him.

"Not now, Alex," I heard her yell, and then Alex burst into tears. Matt met my eyes.

"Go. Go take care of them. I'll call this in, and then we'll have someone trace that call. You should have called right away."

I exhaled. "I was about to when I found...her." I glanced once again at the young girl lying inside my mattress and felt tears pile up in my eyes. Her face was bruised terribly, as was her naked body.

"MOMMY!"

I swallowed the knot in my throat, grabbed the door handle, and walked out into the hallway while hearing Matt call it in as I closed the door behind me so my children wouldn't see anything. I wanted to protect them as much as I could against this. They had seen enough.

In the hallway, I grabbed my son in my arms and lifted him up. He was crying uncontrollably as I held him tight.

"I'm scared, Mommy; I'm so scared," he said, sniffling and rubbing his eyes. "I heard you scream."

"I'm scared too, buddy," I said and looked at Christine who was hiding in her doorway. I grabbed her hand in mine and pulled her into a hug as well, cursing this bastard far away. Who the heck did he think he was? Scaring my family like this? It almost brought me to tears to think about, tears of frustration and anger. I was going to get him for this. No one messed with my family.

No one.

I took all my kids downstairs where my mom was waiting, wearing a robe over her nightgown, a deeply concerned look in her eyes.

"What's going on, Eva Rae?" she asked. "I heard screaming? Is Matt here? I saw his cruiser in the driveway."

My eyes filled as they locked with hers, and she could see it. She could tell it was bad. Alex squirmed and wanted to get down, so I put him on the tiles, and he ran into the living room where he found his favorite teddy bear that Sydney had placed in the recliner. Christine sat down on the couch and looked at her phone.

"There was another one," I said to my mom, trying to whisper so the kids wouldn't hear. I didn't know how much Alex and Christine knew about what I had found, what Olivia had told them. "Here in the house. I found her body inside my box spring under my mattress."

"Oh, dear Lord," my mom said and clasped her chest. "How? Why? I don't understand? Someone has been in here? Inside the house? Why is this person doing this, Eva Rae?"

"I understand as little as you do," I said, tearing up. It was the honest truth. Why was I being targeted like this?

Why me?

"The sheriff's crime scene unit will be here any minute. I don't know what to do with the kids. They're scared. They need rest."

My mom nodded, a serious look in her eyes. "They shouldn't be here. I have an idea. I'll take them all to a hotel downtown. Just let me grab my purse and get dressed."

Olivia packed a bag for each of them with clothes and stuff they couldn't live without, like Alex's teddy bear and at least one of his firetrucks and Christine's favorite pillow. Soon after, they left in my mom's car, and I watched them as they disappeared down the street. It was a relief to get them all out of the house.

I didn't feel like any of us were safe there anymore.

Chapter 50

A tense night followed. The sheriff's crime scene unit arrived and parked their mobile lab in our driveway. They sent dogs out into the area and dusted for fingerprints all over my house. Matt sat with me in the living room while they combed through my house and yard, putting all the evidence in small bags as he took my statement for the report.

I went through it all with him, my afternoon with the kids and then the strange call in the middle of the night that led me to look under my mattress. When we were done, Matt then drove me to the hotel where I joined my family for the night, and the next day, I drove the kids to school. My mom asked if it wasn't better for them to stay home, but I felt like it was best for them to go. I wanted them to have as much normality as they could through this, and I sensed they felt relieved when I dropped them off. Tough as it was, I couldn't let this bastard destroy everything for us. I wasn't going to let him. He was in way too much control in all this so far, and I didn't like it one bit. This was also my way of showing him that he wasn't getting to me.

Afterward, I drove down to the station and rushed to my desk. Matt joined me about half an hour later when I was on my second coffee and had gone through the latest news from the lab.

When we realized we were alone, he leaned over and kissed me gently.

"That felt nice," I said.

He smiled and stroked my cheek, looking deeply into my eyes. "Are you okay?"

I exhaled. "Not really. I think I might need another one."

Matt chuckled and kissed me again; then Chief Annie approached us. Matt cleared his throat and went to his chair and sat down, blushing. Chief Annie chortled.

"It's not like it's a secret with you two."

She threw a file on Matt's desk, while Matt sent me a secretive smile.

"The forensics on the bomb are in. Apparently, it was a very simple pipe-bomb comprised of three devices, detonated with a timer, but only the main component exploded. The other two were found wired together in the back of the truck. The device was designed to be powerful enough that it could have caused serious injuries to a lot more people. The FBI's joint terrorism task force wants their fingers on it. I told them it's related to a murder case and that we already have one of their agents on it. So now, you better prove to be right. You catch this sick bastard before we have this entire town crawling with feds muddying the investigation."

I nodded, and Matt grabbed the file. "Thanks, Annie," I said. "I mean it. If they start screaming terrorism, then we will not be allowed anywhere near it. Then we'll never catch him."

"I put all my trust in you right now. Don't make me regret this, Eva Rae," she said and left.

I sure hope I won't.

Matt flipped through the file, then leaned back in his chair. "What are we looking at here? Who is this guy? Three teenage girls have been kidnapped; a fourth was strapped to a swing set, raped and blinded. A pipe bomb exploded and hurt a colleague, and now one of the girls has been found beaten to death. I don't get him. It makes no sense. I mean…think about it. He kidnaps three girls, he molests and rapes another, then he blows off a bomb before he beats another girl to death. There is absolutely no pattern. So, what is all this? Why is his MO changing constantly?"

I put down my coffee cup. I knew Matt was turning to me because of my background as an FBI profiler. I had years of experience with coming up with backgrounds, possible interests, and characterizations of suspects believed to be responsible in serial murders. I had written books on forensic psychology. But I had to admit, I was as dumbfounded as he was.

"I have to say I'm falling a little short here as well," I said. "Just when I think I have him figured out, he turns around and does something completely different. Up until now, I would have said with almost certainty that he was a white male, probably in his thirties, maybe forties, a loner, with military training as his background. But it doesn't fit with his profile of someone killing a young girl in anger, beating her to death. I just got off the phone with the medical examiner, Jamila, who told me they don't think he used a weapon to beat Ava Morales up; he did it with only his hands. They worked on her all morning because they knew we needed quick answers. But the thing is, someone capable of such a thing is an entirely different type of monster than one who sets up a bomb and blows it wanting to hurt a police officer. Is he targeting the police? Yes and no. Because he did place Molly in my backyard, and he did severely injure Cooper. But none of these girls that he has taken has anything to do with the police. Is he a sexual predator? Yes, in part since Molly was raped, but Ava wasn't. Is he a violent sadist who is turned on by torturing young, innocent girls? Yes, because he removed Molly's eyes with a scalpel."

"With a scalpel?" Matt asked, growing pale. He held hand up to his mouth, his eyes tormented.

I nodded. "Results from the ME's office were in this morning. I forgot to tell you," I said. "They're pretty sure the tool used to gouge her eyes out was a scalpel. The cuts were very professional, they said. We are possibly looking for someone with surgical experience, maybe even a surgeon, which is totally deviant from his profile so far…"

"Geez, that's awful."

"I know. It made me almost lose my morning coffee. The only comforting aspect is that they also believe she was sedated while he did it. They found large amounts of ketamine in her blood. With any luck, she didn't feel anything at all, maybe not even the rape," I said and exhaled, thinking about poor Melissa and Molly. Anger welled up inside me once again as I thought about this bastard. There was no telling what I might do to him once I got my hands on him.

"But my point is, he doesn't fit any profile."

"What do you mean?" Matt asked. "How can he not fit a profile? It makes no sense?"

I looked up at him, and our eyes met.

"He doesn't fit one profile," I said. "He fits them all."

Chapter 51

"It doesn't look good for you, Jordan."

Matt glared at the woman in front of us. She seemed to have become even smaller than the last time I saw her. Spending the night locked up could do that to you. She looked desperate and ready to chat.

Matt opened the file containing Ava Morales' case and pulled out the pictures of the girl that we had found under my mattress. Seeing them again made my stomach churn once more.

"Take a good look," he said. "We found her last night."

Jordan peeked at the pictures, at first seeming indifferent, but then as she realized who she was looking at, her face went pale.

"Ava Morales," I said. "The same girl we found pictures of in your house. The same girl you claimed you didn't know. Care to explain?"

"I didn't do that to her," she said, her eyes growing wider and wider. "I didn't. I swear."

I leaned forward. "Then, maybe you could tell us who did."

She shook her head. "How? How am I supposed to know?"

"Tell us how you got in contact with her," Matt said. "Did you write to her like you wrote to the others?"

Jordan looked at him, her nostrils flaring. "I wrote to her, yes. But only her, not the others."

"Okay. Let's start with that. So, you wrote to Ava; why?"

Jordan was scratching her arms. It was obviously a nervous reaction and something she had been doing all night. Her right arm was red and scratched up. She was ready to crack. This girl was hiding something, and I was going to get it out of her no matter how long we had to sit there till she broke down.

"She was pretty. I thought she could make some money. I told her she should consider having her pictures taken, but I was honest up front and said it costs money. I'm not a scammer like that. I gave her my number and then one day she called. She came to my studio, and we took her pictures, and that was it. She paid me, and I never saw her again."

"How much did she pay you for her pictures?" I asked.

"Two hundred bucks. I'm cheap. That's why so many girls come to me. I give them a good product for the money. Normally, they'd have to pay up to a thousand bucks, easily."

"And do they become models?" I asked. "After you've taken their pictures?"

She shrugged. "I don't know. That's not exactly my job here. I just take the pictures and give them a product they can send out to the agencies."

I flipped a few papers in Molly's file and found something.

"To Molly Carson, you said that you had contacts at agencies that she should meet with in Orlando. That was why she was supposed to spend the night at a hotel there with you."

"Can I see that?" Jordan asked.

I turned the paper so she could see the printout of the entire conversation from Amino. She shook her head.

"I never wrote that. I told you. The only one I contacted was Ava on Instagram. I only use Instagram. I never used that other site; what's its name?"

"Amino," I said. "It's a social media platform where you meet people who share the same interests as you, like arts and crafts, sports, anime, or even vegan food."

"Yeah, I don't even know that one. I'm telling you I didn't write any of that."

I exhaled, getting tired of this when there was a knock on the door to the interrogation room. Peter from the Sheriff's Forensic Computer Department peeked his head inside.

"Could I talk to one of you real quick?"

Chapter 52

THEN:

They waited for twenty-four hours, but the kidnapper never showed. The package with the fake ransom remained on the picnic table, but no one came to get it.

"It's the darn media," Peterson said back at the house. He lifted the curtain, and they could see their vans parked outside on the street.

They had kept quiet about the kidnapping so far, but somehow, the media had heard about the drop-off being made at the park, and now there was no stopping them.

"They scared him off."

"So, what do we do now?" Gary asked.

"We wait," Peterson said. "Hopefully, he'll call again with a new drop-off site."

"If he isn't so scared that he got rid of the kid," Gary mumbled.

"Don't say that," Iris said.

Gary peeked out behind the curtain and was blinded by the flashing lights.

"There he is. That's the father," someone yelled, and a photographer took pictures of him. One photographer ran into the yard but was stopped by Gary's partner and thrown back behind the fence.

"Get away from that window," Peterson said and pulled Gary by the shoulder. "You're giving them exactly what they want."

"I hate them," he said. "I freakin' hate those vultures!"

"I know; I know," Peterson said. "But they have every right to be there, unfortunately. We need to focus on getting Oliver back, okay? Now, I want you to get something to eat. You've barely had anything for days, and to be honest, you're looking like you could pass out. We can't have that. We need you to be at your best. Agent Wilson ordered pizza, and there's still a lot left in the kitchen. Go grab a piece, and then we'll talk, okay?"

Gary wasn't hungry at all, but he was feeling weak and feeble. He didn't like the sensation of being out of control. He walked to the kitchen and grabbed a piece of the pizza, then sunk his teeth into it. As he chewed through it, he realized Peterson was right. He did feel a lot better as soon as he got some food in his stomach. They had set up an office at his house, and a bunch of agents were working the case, chatting on phones, tapping on their computers. A couple of hand-writing experts had come down from the FBI laboratory to examine the ransom note left in the carriage. They had given the special agents a course in handwriting analysis, and now they were going over specimens maintained by the DMV, the federal and state probation officers, prisons, and other munic-ipalities, trying to figure out if this guy with this particular handwriting was in the system somewhere. It seemed like an impossible task.

Barely had Gary finished his piece and taken up a second one when his phone rang in the living room.

"Everyone, quiet now," Peterson said as Gary walked back inside and stared at the vibrating phone on the table.

"What do I do?"

"Pick it up," Peterson said.

He did, his hand shaking. "H-Hello?"

"The corner where Washington Boulevard meets

Sycamore Street at one o'clock sharp. There's a trash can. Put the package in there. No police or your son dies. No journalists or your son dies."

"So…you still have him? Is he all right?" Gary asked.

"Just be there, and I'll tell you where to find your son."

Chapter 53

The darkness was worse than anything. Carina fought not to panic. Tara hadn't been awake at all while she had been sitting there, and every now and then, Carina would reach over a hand to touch her skin to make sure she still felt warm. Sometimes, she'd even reach for her neck and feel for a pulse, just to be sure. Now and then, Carina would crawl to Tara and curl up close to her just to feel a human being close to her, just to feel something. All this nothingness surrounding her made her anxious, especially since she had no idea how long it was going to last. The masked man hadn't been down there since he turned the light off, and Carina had no idea how much time had passed, nor did she know if she would live to see daylight again. There was no more water in the bucket and no more food. Carina felt her tongue stick to the roof of her mouth, and her lips were cracked. With no light and no one to talk to, there was nothing for Carina to do but to wait, wait for him to return or wait for death to come.

Carina drifted away, thinking once again about the night she had been crowned prom queen at the school. It had been her dream ever since she started middle school to one day be up there on the stage, with everyone in the school looking at her, admiring her.

Carina's mother had been prom queen at Cocoa Beach

High back in the nineties, and she spoke about it often while Carina was growing up. Carina remembered playing with her mother's crown and sash in her bedroom as a child, when her mother didn't see it, dressing up in her high heels and putting them on, pretending to be crowned, holding pretend speeches and twirling in front of the mirror.

It hadn't exactly been in the cards for Carina to become prom queen. Growing up, she had been chubby...some would even call her fat. Her mom didn't know, but Carina saw the looks her mom would give her when getting her ready for her bath or when trying on new clothes and they almost never fit. Carina's mother was skinny and beautiful, whereas Carina was none of those things while growing up. Her mother kept telling her she would outgrow it, but as she hit middle school, she was still fat, and the more the other kids stared at her or teased her, the more she ate.

It wasn't until eighth grade when Tommy Cheatham asked her to the middle school dance that things changed. She was wearing a beautiful green dress that her mother had bought for her, sized XXL. When Tommy asked her to dance, she reluctantly accepted, but as he swung her around to the tunes from *Panic! at the Disco*, her dress ripped in the back, and she was suddenly standing in the middle of the dance floor, half naked. To this day, she still shivered when remembering that terrifying moment. She could recall everything. Every face, all the eyes staring at her, the pointing fingers, and sometimes she could even still hear them laughing.

It was at that moment that she decided enough was enough.

Carina started running the very next day, even if she only managed to walk in the beginning. She stopped eating completely for a few weeks, and after that, only ate vegetables and a little fruit and only meat once a week. It was a strict diet, and tough as heck, but it did the trick. A year after, she was suddenly a size medium, and the year after that, she could fit a size small. The eyes staring at her now weren't teasing or judging her; they were now admiring her. And she had kept it that way ever since. She had even kept the dress in her closet, and every now and then, she would take it out to remind her of how fat she had been back then, and that would keep her off the sweets.

Ironically, Carina could now feel the bones poking out on her shoulders and chest. She was skinnier than ever before, and it was threatening to kill her.

Carina closed her eyes and felt the hunger as it ate at her insides when she heard the familiar sound of the key being put in the metal door and the deadbolts being slid aside. Carina held her breath, listening, while anxiety rushed up inside of her. A moment later, the door was opened, and light flooded the room. It blinded her momentarily. Once her vision returned, she saw first his boots, then his doctor's scrubs as he was slowly making his way toward her.

"Please," she said, as the stabbing light hurt her eyes. She searched his hands for food or fresh water, but his hands were empty, except for a key in one of them.

"You're coming with me," he said. "It's your lucky day."

The masked man leaned over and freed her shackles from the wall. The man pulled the chain on Carina's neck, and she struggled to her feet. Rising from the mattress was difficult; standing was even worse, and she had to lean on the wall next to her. He pulled the chain again, and Carina was forcefully pulled forward toward the door. She staggered out the door, then glanced back at the sleeping Tara, wondering if she would ever see her again, and then questioning which one of them was the lucky one.

Chapter 54

I returned to the interrogation room. Jordan looked up as I walked to the table and threw a new file on the table. I had been talking to Peter from Computer Forensics for about fifteen minutes and, as I came back inside, both Matt and Jordan looked exhausted. My guess was they hadn't gotten anywhere while I was gone.

I had a pretty good hunch why.

"They're done combing through your house," I said and sat down. "They didn't find any evidence that suggested that any of the other girls have been there."

"I told you," Jordan said.

"But they did find something else," I said. "On your computer."

I opened the file that Peter had given me while Jordan went pale. I pulled out some photographs that Peter had printed out for me and placed them in front of Jordan.

"I think it is reasonable to say that these pictures are fairly different than the other ones we found at your place," I said. "What kind of agencies do you expect your clients to send these pictures to?"

Jordan stared at the naked girls but didn't say a word.

"So, here's how I think it played out. Feel free to correct me afterward if I'm wrong," I said. "You contacted these girls on Instagram, and don't tell me you didn't 'cause we found a lot of history of you doing this on your profile once we dug into it. We found hundreds of girls that you have been contacting, telling them they were gorgeous and that they should consider becoming models. A lot of them bit into it and contacted you, and then you set up a photo shoot at your house, giving them a fair price for a set of photographs, making it a lot cheaper than any other photographers around. Nothing wrong with that. The girls came to you and paid you to do a service. That's not illegal. But these pictures are." I placed a finger on one of the naked girls who shyly looked back at us. "These girls are underage, Jordan. And they trusted you. They came to you with their dreams and money, and they thought you were okay because you were a woman. And you exploited that fact to make them go further than they were comfortable. You told them to take off one piece of clothing then another till they were finally completely naked. And then you took a series of photographs of them completely naked while they thought it was okay because a woman wouldn't touch them and you said it was just for them to feel more comfortable in front of a camera, that it would help them loosen up, that no one would ever see these photos. But then you—and this is the part where it gets a little ugly— then you sold them to pornographic sites online. You sold these pictures to nasty pedophiles out there who would pay a lot of money to see young underage girls naked. Now, please tell me if I'm wrong because I have to say, I really want to be."

Jordan stared at the pictures, her hand shaking. Not a word left her mouth till she finally looked up and said, "I'd like to speak to my lawyer now."

I nodded and closed the files. "You're gonna need one. This is not looking good for you."

Matt held the door for me, and we walked back into the hallway where Chief Annie was waiting. I had asked her to listen in on the conversation from the observation room over-looking the interrogation room. She smiled and nodded.

"Good job, Detectives," she said. "I'll have Jamieson take her from here. You need to focus on your own case."

"So, just to get this straight," Matt said, "she had nothing to do with what happened to Ava Morales or any of the other girls?"

I shook my head. "Nope."

"But she sent those messages to Molly?"

"It wasn't her. Peter from Computer Forensics told me her account was hacked a few weeks ago. The messages weren't sent from her IP address and, when he tried to track them, the trail ended somewhere in Africa."

"So, we're looking for a skilled hacker and not a surgeon?"

"Possibly," I said. "Maybe he's both. One thing is certain; he's someone who knows a lot about how law enforcement works."

"The drawing is done," Chief Annie said and approached me holding out a hand-drawn picture. "This is what the man who delivered the package looked like, according to Jane Martin. This is your guy."

I stared at the picture of the man with the goatee in front of me, looking into his eyes. I couldn't escape the feeling that there was something familiar about him; I just didn't know what.

Chapter 55

When he arrived at the hospital, Boomer looked at his face in the rearview mirror of the car. He touched the fake goatee and made sure it was on straight and wouldn't fall off. He had sedated the girl and put her in the back seat, where she looked like she was sleeping underneath the blanket. His truck was big and the windows dark, so no one would be able to accidentally peek inside while he was gone and wonder about her. He had given her a dose of Ketamine. She was so skinny now that she didn't need much to knock her out cold.

Boomer smiled at his own reflection, then grabbed his ID badge and got out of the car. He approached the back entrance and let himself in, then walked to the elevator and pushed the button. A couple of nurses greeted him as they passed him with a nod before continuing down the hallway. Boomer smiled and greeted them back and, when the elevator arrived, he got inside.

A doctor was in the elevator already, and he nodded in greeting.

"In for the night shift today?" he asked.

Boomer nodded. "Yeah, it's gonna be a long one all right. And you?"

"Just coming off my shift in fifteen minutes. Then home

to spend the night with the wifey. The kids are with their grandmother, so we'll finally get some time alone. It's been awhile."

"That's what this job will do to you," Boomer said.

"I guess we knew what we got ourselves into when we signed up."

"I guess so."

The elevator dinged, and Boomer smiled. "This is my stop."

"See you around," the doctor said as the doors closed.

A nurse smiled at Boomer as he passed her, and he turned right and entered a room with the sign *Acute Renal Dialysis*. Seven patients with acute kidney failure were sitting in there, dialysis lines inserted into their veins. Some were reading, others napping.

"Hello there," he said, smiling from ear to ear. "And how are we feeling today?"

Chapter 56

Carina's head was pounding. She blinked her eyes to be able to see better, but the light was blinding.

Where am I?

She was shaking, her hands unable to remain still, her legs shivering, yet she wasn't cold.

What happened?

She felt confused, disoriented. She tried hard to remember but couldn't. The last thing she did recall was the door opening to the room and the masked man's eyes as he looked at her over the surgical mask.

Light hit her face, and she realized it wasn't from a lamp. It was real sunlight coming from outside. Carina blinked a few times, trying to get her eyes to cooperate, then sat up and stared out the window.

What the...am I...in a parking lot?

Expecting to see the masked man somewhere, she turned around with a gasp as she heard footsteps outside the car, but it wasn't him. It was an elderly couple getting into the car next to the one she was in.

Carina breathed. She looked around and spotted a canned soda by the front seat. It was open and someone – probably the masked man – had already been drinking from it, but it didn't matter. Right now was all about survival.

Carina reached between the seats and grabbed the can, then downed the entire Fanta. Never had anything tasted better.

She finished the can and waited for even the last few drops to get the most out of it, then tossed it onto the passenger seat. She looked at herself under the blanket, then realized she was naked. Covering herself up with the blanket, she grabbed the door handle and opened it, then slid out into the parking lot on her bare feet, the black asphalt burning the bottom of her soles. Holding her breath, constantly checking around her, Carina tiptoed across the parking lot, fear rushing through her veins when a voice spoke from behind her.

The sound of it made her shiver in terror.

"Where do you think you're going?"

Chapter 57

"Any news?"

I looked up from my computer screen. I could barely see Matt behind all the files and paperwork. I was tired and had run out of coffee. We had been going back to the beginning, looking through all the files on the three missing girls, then going through Molly's case files to see if there was anything that stood out, any detail we had missed that might be important. Earlier, we had also been to the hospital and talked to the Medical Director there, asking him questions about the procedure of removing eyes and how skilled a doctor should be to perform such a task. He had basically told us any type of surgeon could perform an enucleation, as it was called, to remove a damaged or diseased eyeball. It was a very common procedure that wasn't very difficult to perform. So that didn't get us any closer to finding our guy. There were hundreds of surgeons in Brevard County, and we didn't have time to visit them all. I had generated a list of the three surgeons living in Cocoa Beach and sent a couple of detectives to check them out. I instructed them to ask them about their whereabouts on the night when the girls disappeared and the night when Molly was taken, and also when Ava reappeared. I had also given them a copy of Jane Martin's drawing to take with them.

Now, I stared at the drawing of our guy on the white-board behind Matt, wondering who the heck he was and what his deal was.

"I can't help thinking," I said while Matt fetched me another cup of coffee. I stared at the girls and then at Molly and thought about the way she was found and Ava the way she was found.

Matt sipped his coffee. "Yes? Eva Rae?"

"What?"

"You drifted off just then," he continued. "Where did you go?"

I blinked and sipped my coffee. "I'm sorry. There's just something I can't let go. Remember how I told you that I once worked a case on a guy who removed the eyes of his victims? And how I couldn't believe he was back because he was dead?"

"Yeah, the guy who poked out the eyes of his victims before he raped them, so they wouldn't be able to recognize him in a line-up? I remember that. What about it?"

I stood to my feet and stared at Ava Morales. "There's something else."

I paused while a million thoughts rushed through my mind at once.

"Yes, Eva Rae? Eva Rae?"

My eyes were flickering across the board now, as my mind wouldn't keep still. Pictures of my old case and the victims with their missing eyes ran like an inner movie in my mind.

We'll see tomorrow if you're a real princess.

When the dime finally dropped, I turned to look at Matt, fear struck in my eyes.

"What's going on, Eva Rae? Are you okay? You look like you're about to get sick."

I grabbed my phone, badge, and jacket, then looked at Matt.

"We need to go. Right now."

"Where are we going?" Matt asked. "Could I get a hint, at least?"

But I was already out the door, running toward the cruisers parked in the back.

Chapter 58

He had felt tired for quite some time but kept thinking it was just his busy schedule and social life. At the age of twenty-nine, Brad Williams was at the prime of his life, and his business selling solar panels was booming. But then came the headaches, migraines so deep and invading they completely destroyed his life, making it impossible for him to be out of bed for more than a few hours at a time. But even then, Brad believed it was just a phase and that it would pass soon.

"Allergies," his mom told him over lunch at Grills River-side one day. "It's been a terrible season for allergies. It used to knock you out constantly when you were younger too."

So, Brad took a Claritin and went about his life, thinking it would all get better once this allergy season was over. As he realized the allergy pill didn't work, Brad went to his GP to ask for steroid injections like his neighbor had gotten, and *puff*, gone were his allergies. Just like that. It was no biggie, just one shot, and it would all be over.

At the GP office, after Brad was weighed, they took his blood pressure. Brad was joking and flirting with the nurse, ignoring the pounding headache and the itching skin that he had gotten used to. After all, they were nothing but allergy symptoms, and he wasn't going to let those stop him from enjoying his life.

As the nurse took his blood pressure, she went pale, and the flirting stopped abruptly.

"I need to get the doctor in here," she said and, seconds later, Brad's GP entered, a serious look on her face. She took his blood pressure once more, then looked at him.

"This is not good, Brad. We need to get you to the hospital right away. I am going to call an ambulance."

And so, she left, leaving Brad back in the room, scared senseless.

Now, as he sat in his wheelchair and a nurse hooked him up for his acute dialysis, he still remembered how it felt, the panic settling in when you see your own doctor get worried and then being rushed away on a stretcher, not knowing what is happening.

At the hospital, they took tests, and his potassium levels were so high he was about to have a heart attack, they said. He came in at the right time. A few hours more like that and it would have been too late.

His kidneys had failed completely, *Acute Renal Kidney Failure*, they called it, and he needed acute dialysis. He would have to prepare himself for living a life on dialysis.

Brad wasn't prepared for that at all. As he sat in his wheelchair, he wondered about how his life had been so normal and so on track just a few days ago, and now he was here, everything changed forever.

"Are you comfortable?" the nurse asked.

Brad stared at her. Comfortable? Comfortable? How could he be comfortable when his life was never going to be the same again?

Some annoyingly cheerful doctor entered and asked them how they were all doing today. Two other patients smiled and said they were just glad to be alive. Brad stared at them, feeling all kinds of anger and resentment. How could they sit there and be so happy to be alive? What kind of life was this anyway? Spending hours attached to a dialysis line three times a week?

It was only the second time Brad was in dialysis, and he had been told it would take some getting used to. So far, Brad had found it to be painful, and he dreaded the treatment. As the liquid ran into his veins and through his body, Brad leaned his head backward and dreamt of the ocean, of running on the beach as a child, feeling the freedom. He took a deep breath and was almost certain he could smell it. It brought him such calm.

About half an hour into the treatment, Brad suddenly opened his eyes with a gasp. A wave of agonizing pain shot forcefully through his chest and, seconds later, he went into cardiac arrest.

Chapter 59

Carina's heart was pounding so loud she could barely hear the sound of the feet running behind her. She was crossing the parking lot, the man right behind her. A couple drove past her and stared at her through their window.

"Help!" she screamed, but they didn't do anything.

Why don't they help me? Why don't they react? Why are they only staring at me?

Carina took a left turn and ran toward the hospital in front of her, forcing her skinny legs to carry her as fast as possible while scanning the area for anyone who could help her. Why couldn't there be a cop? Don't they usually hang out around hospitals? Why couldn't there be an ambulance or just someone for that matter, anyone who wasn't too scared to help? Someone who wouldn't just stay inside of their car, paralyzed in fear?

"You come back here," the man yelled behind her. "I'm gonna kill you when I get my hands on you."

Carina saw the entrance to the ER and managed to speed up, hope fueling the adrenalin pumping in her veins, providing her with the strength she needed right now to outrun this guy.

Please, don't let him get to me, God, please. I'm so close now. Just a few yards more. Just a few.

"Oh, no, you don't," the man yelled as he realized what her plan was. He sped up, and soon Carina sensed that he was right behind her, reaching out his hand to grab her.

Just a few feet, please.

Carina felt his fingers grasping for her hair and shrieked in fear.

I am not giving up. I refuse to give up.

The fingers grabbed her hair and pulled, but then her perpetrator suddenly screamed out in pain, and the hand in her hair disappeared. Carina didn't stop to look what had happened but continued toward the hospital's ER entrance.

Just as she was about to enter, she turned briefly to look anyway, like Lot's wife. And just like the woman she heard about in Bible camp, she was frozen in place. Not turning to a pillar of salt, and not paralyzed, but still, she stood there looking at the man who was screaming in pain as he lifted his foot, blood gushing from the wound where a metal spike had cut through his shoe and into his foot.

Carina now realized she had won, and she sent him a victorious smile, then walked toward the sliding doors.

But to her surprise, they didn't open.

An alarm sounded from the inside, and Carina tried the doors again, but they didn't budge. Desperate, she glanced at the man again and didn't see the gun in his hand till it was too late and the shot was fired.

Chapter 60

"Acute Dialysis?" I asked the woman at the front desk, showing her my badge.

I had parked the police cruiser outside of the front entrance of the hospital after running it through town with blaring lights and blasting sirens. I hadn't had time to explain to Matt in detail what my suspicion was since I was too focused on my driving, but I had told him what he needed to know, and most importantly that I feared many people might die if we didn't make it in time.

Matt had called it in, and officers from all surrounding areas had arrived to help. I had also tried to call the hospital to get them to stop the dialysis treatment, but they told me it was too late. Four out of seven patients had gone into cardiac arrest just a few minutes ago and were being treated elsewhere in the hospital.

"I need all the entrances blocked," I had told them. "No one leaves the building."

Chief Annie came up behind us, her eyes worried.

"I have men on all the exits. You think he's still in the building?" she asked.

"There's a chance he might still be here," I said.

Matt and I took the elevator up to the third floor, then rushed out. A nurse met us, her eyes bewildered.

"I don't know what happened," she said, crying. "I set them up as usual; nothing was different."

"Was anyone in here?" I asked, looking around the room where the patients had been. "Did anyone touch the dialysis lines?"

"No one who wasn't supposed to."

"But maybe someone who wouldn't cause suspicion. Like a surgeon or a doctor?"

She shook her head. "Only Clark."

My eyes grew wide, and my heart dropped. "Clark?"

She nodded. "Yes, he was here briefly, helping out. He's new around here, so I didn't really know him till he told me today."

"What was his name more than Clark?"

"I don't remember. I didn't get a good look at his ID badge. His last name was something with a T."

"Was he alone with the patients?" I asked. "Did you leave at any point?"

She shrugged. "I went out to get some more magazines for them. Some patients like to read while they wait for the treatment to be over. It's a long time that they sit there. There isn't much to do."

I turned around and scanned the area, then spotted the jug leaned up against the wall in the back, a syringe next to it. I literally felt the blood as it left my face.

"What's going on?" Matt asked.

I hurried to the jug and knelt next to it.

"Bleach?" Matt said. "Care to explain?"

"He injected it into the dialysis lines. That's what caused them to go into cardiac arrest."

"He did what?" he said. "But why?"

"Because he knew I would find out. He even left the jug of bleach like she did."

Matt gave me a look. "Like who did? I think this is the time when you fill me in."

"Back in two thousand and eight, there were nineteen deaths at a dialysis clinic in Texas in just four months. Most of them suffered cardiac arrest while still in dialysis. Two witnesses told the police they had seen a nurse inject bleach into the lines of those patients and an investigation was started, running across several state lines. This nurse had worked many places in the country over the previous ten years, and at all of them, there had been a spike in deaths while she was there."

"I think I heard about that," he said. "The killer nurse. She was sentenced to life with no parole; wasn't she?"

"She was only convicted of five deaths and five serious injuries, but we believed she had killed many more than that. I had at least ten cases that we just didn't have evidence enough to run with."

"So, the case was yours?" he asked.

"Yes, and the woman's name was Nancy Clark."

Matt stared at me. "Clark?"

"A fake name, I assume, but it's a message, as is all this. Our killer is trying to tell me something."

"How do you figure?" he asked.

"Well, there is the old case of the guy removing the girls' eyes, like Molly."

"Yes. We established that."

"And then Ava Morales was found in my mattress, beaten to death."

"Yes," he said. "And?"

"There was another case I worked on back early in my career. A woman had been attacked in her own home by someone ringing her doorbell, pretending to be from the local water company, there to check on her faucets. She let him in, and he attacked her, wanting probably to rape her, but she was strong. She knocked him out with a meat pounder. To her surprise, he was dead when she went to check on him. This woman panicked, thinking she was going to jail and hid the body inside of her mattress so her husband wouldn't find him. I know, it's crazy, but reality out there is often a lot crazier than you think. Anyway, the smell naturally stunk the house up, and she was discovered. But the point is that the finding of Ava Morales felt very familiar to me; it was also like a case I once worked. My first case was the kidnapping of three girls in Cleveland. You see a pattern yet?"

"I see what you're saying. The three girls, Molly, Ava Morales, the dialysis patients. This guy is making you relive all your old cases?" Matt asked. "He reenacts them."

I nodded. "And not only that. He's also using my theories. It's all from my book, the first one I wrote. This guy is toying with me and my knowledge of serial killers. He's following my theories and years of study leading to my book where I was examining the association among four serial killer typologies: lust, anger, power, and financial gain. Molly was raped; that's the first one. Ava Morales was beaten to death in anger; that's the second. And the third one is this here, the patients succumbing to a man with high authority and who holds the power of life and death, as doctors do. He is speaking to me through his choice of victims and how they're killed. Now, we haven't seen financial gain, but that would be his next move."

"So, you're saying that this guy read your book, and he's using it to send you a message?" Matt asked.

"Not only did he read the book. He knows me very, very well."

Chapter 61

THEN:

"I'm terrified. What if he doesn't show?"

Gary stared at his boss. Peterson was holding the package with the fake money inside the newspaper. This was their fourth try at handing the kidnapper the money. He hadn't shown up at any of the drop-off points so far. Every time, he had called afterward and given them new instructions. Gary and Iris's home had been turned into a war room, and they had a handful of agents constantly sitting in their living room. Some were sleeping on the couch, others tapping away on their computers, talking loudly on phones, eating their food in the kitchen, and drinking their coffee. All while trying to find the guy who had taken their son.

Meanwhile, Gary and Iris were barely sleeping or eating. Their son had been gone for fifteen days now, and they had no idea if they would ever see him again. Peterson kept reassuring them that they would, that all this guy wanted was the money, but Gary couldn't—for the life of him—figure out why it had to take so long. Why didn't the guy just show up and take the money so they could get this over with? All he wanted was for life to return to normal, or at least as close to normal as humanly possible. He wanted to spend Saturday mornings with the baby on his stomach, trying to give Iris some much-needed rest from being up all night breastfeeding. He wanted to be tired because he had been woken up by the baby's sounds and crying all night. He wanted to be annoyed because he was falling apart from having to take care of a family and a demanding job at the same time. He wanted all those things back. He didn't want to be exhausted because he didn't know where his child was. This was supposed to be the happiest time of his life. This was supposed to be the time that people told you to cherish because it would never come back.

It wasn't supposed to be like this.

"He will," Peterson said. "He needs money. That's why he took Oliver in the first place."

"But he didn't show up those other times."

"He's scared. He sees the press or even suspects that there might be police or reporters there, and he wets himself. You know these types."

Peterson was still insisting on this guy being some addict who accidentally passed on the street and saw an opportunity when Iris went in for her bag and left the baby alone. But Gary wasn't so sure anymore. Something told him that this guy was smarter than they gave him credit for. But what he couldn't quite figure out was why he had chosen to take the child of an FBI agent, if he was so bright.

"You've got this," Peterson said and put his hand on Gary's shoulder when someone entered the room.

"Peterson, you need to take a look at this."

"Give me a sec," he said to Gary. "I'll be right back. You just keep practicing how to hold your son 'cause you will in a very short while; you hear me?"

Gary exhaled tiredly as Peterson left. He sat down in his recliner and studied a picture of his son on his phone, trying hard to remember what he smelled like. He had loved that smell more than anything in the world.

Soon, Peterson came back in and closed the door, a serious look on his face.

"We have an ID on our guy. It was the handwriting that

helped us. The handwriting on the ransom note is very similar to that of a guy in a probation file."

Peterson's eyes lit up as he looked at Gary.

"We've got him."

Chapter 62

"We've searched the entire area. No sign of our guy."
Chief Annie gave me a disappointed look that mirrored exactly how I felt. I had a feeling he wouldn't be there, that he would have taken off from the hospital grounds, but a girl is allowed to hope, right? I desperately wanted us to find him and get this over with. But of course, it wasn't going to be that easy.

"We should keep the hospital on lockdown for a little while longer, just in case he's hiding somewhere in the building," I said.

"How about surveillance cameras?" Matt asked.

"I have a couple of officers going through them in the basement," Annie said. "But there is something else that you need to take a look at. A nurse came to me and said they had taken in a girl at the ER. She claims to be one of the three that were kidnapped. It might just be a hoax since it has been all over the news, and you know how weird people get, but could you check it out?"

"Sure."

Matt and I took the elevator down to the first floor that held the ER ward and then found the front desk.

"Detectives Thomas and Miller here to see about a girl who claims to have been kidnapped?"

"One minute," the woman said and grabbed the phone. She spoke in it for a few seconds and then looked at us.

"The nurse who spoke to her will be right out."

A few minutes later, a small woman in scrubs came out to us. She looked terrified.

"What can you tell us about the girl, ma'am?" I asked.

"She was outside when the alarm went off. The doors were locked, and the alarm was blasting so loud that I think I was the only one who heard it."

"Heard what?"

"The shot being fired. I'm pretty sure she was shot right out there on our front step. I didn't see her till it was too late, but I heard the shot. I talked to my colleagues, and they say they didn't hear anything, but I went there to look, and then I saw her. She was in a pool of blood. I know I'm not supposed to since we were on lockdown, but I opened the sliding doors and rushed to her. I dragged her inside and locked the doors once again. I know I'm not supposed to do that, but I could hardly leave a poor girl out there bleeding to death."

"Did you see anything?" I asked. "Anyone run away from the scene?"

She shook her head. "I focused on the girl and getting her inside. Then I called for assistance, and they came with the stretcher. Right before she was rushed down the hallway, she told me to call the police and said that she was one of the kidnapped girls."

"Where is she now?" I asked. "Can we talk to her?"

"She's in surgery. She was shot in the stomach. She'll be lucky if she survives."

"Did she tell you her name?" I asked.

"Carina I believe she said her name was. Carina Martin, yes, that was it."

Chapter 63

"**A**nything on the surveillance cameras?"

I walked up behind the two colleagues sitting by the computers in the security room of the hospital. The hospital's own guard was helping them. Chief Annie was sitting with them. She nodded.

"We found the girl," she said and pointed at the screen. "There she is running toward the back ramp behind the ER where the ambulances usually come in. You can see she is running up the ramp and there is someone behind her. There, can you stop it, please?"

The officer clicked the mouse, and the footage stopped. I stared at the screen, getting really close, but it was so grainy and murky I couldn't make out a face.

We can get video of the birth of a star in outer space, but see if we can make a decent surveillance photo that isn't grainy? It makes no sense.

"Is this the best you've got?" I asked.

Chief Annie ran a hand through her bangs. It was hot in the security room with all the electronic gear, and the AC seemed to have trouble keeping up. "He does come a little closer if we run it for a frame or two more."

The officer did, and the man moved closer, but still not much. Now the girl was trying to get inside, walking up to the sliding doors. But they didn't open. My heart dropped as I saw this. Next thing, the girl turned to look at the man again, and that was when the shot was fired, and the girl fell to the ground, rag-doll limp.

"Geez," I said and turned away, clasping my mouth. "She tried to get in but couldn't. Because of the lockdown."

I lifted my glance and met Matt's eyes. He pulled me into a hug. "You can't beat yourself up over this."

"Why not?" I said. "I ordered the lockdown, didn't I?"

"Thinking you were protecting more people from getting hurt by stopping a killer. Don't be so hard on yourself."

"It's all my fault," I said, pressing back tears. "All of it. Don't you see? He's doing this to get back at me. He's hurting all these people to get to me."

"Because he knows you're the type of person who would give her life if it meant saving someone else," Matt said and looked into my eyes. He touched my cheek gently. "He knows this will hurt you terribly. But you can't let him win, Eva Rae. It can never be your fault that he's a sick bastard. Just like it can't be your fault that someone gets cancer and dies."

I sent him a smile, knowing he was talking from personal experience. Matt's dad had died from cancer when we were teenagers. It had taken him years to realize there was nothing he could have done to change it. He kept telling me he knew his dad wasn't well, that he knew it was too long before he even went to the doctor and that if only he had encouraged him to see a doctor sooner, then maybe they would have caught it and maybe his chances would have been better.

"Why didn't people react?" Chief Annie asked, staring at the screen. "A naked girl wrapped in a blanket runs across the parking lot, chased by a man. It's a pretty well-trafficked parking lot. Someone ought to have seen them. Why didn't anyone call for help or run inside to get the guard?"

Matt let go of me, and I approached the screen. "For the same reason that no one reacted when he walked into the dialysis room and injected the lines with bleach. He's wearing scrubs and a doctor's coat. He looks like he is the one who belongs here. It's the power of the role he is playing. But you are onto something," I said. "There have to have been witnesses. Someone must have seen him. Maybe we could find them. We also need to have a list of newly hired doctors, especially surgeons at this hospital."

There was a knock on the door, and an officer entered. He spoke quietly with Chief Annie for a few minutes, then left. Annie approached us.

"I have news," she said. "They believe he came in through the back entrance, the one that the employees use, and on the list of people that have entered through there today is a name that we know."

"Who?" Matt asked.

"Charles Turner."

"Mr. Turner? Leanne's dad?" I asked. "But he's not a doctor? I checked everyone in the families of the kids involved, including Leanne's family. No one had a doctor's degree."

Chief Annie shook her head and put both hands on her hips. "Nope, but he does work here as a Registered Nurse. And according to this, he entered the hospital today at ten forty-five a.m. using his ID card."

"Well, I'll be…Let's bring him in," I said addressed to Matt. He nodded in agreement.

"How are the patients?" I asked Annie as we were about to leave, and she walked with us toward the exit.

"One has died," she said. "A Brad Williams, age twenty-nine. The three others, they were able to revive. Two more have fallen ill, but not gone into cardiac arrest."

"And Cooper? How's he holding up?"

"He's hanging in there," she said. "He had the skin transplant, so now we're just waiting. It's gonna take some time. He's also looking at having his leg amputated from the knee down. I don't know when."

I swallowed the guilt and anger that were rising up in me,

seeing the trail of death and destruction this guy was leaving behind, all because of me. What I just couldn't figure out yet was the reason why.

I hoped Charles Turner would be able to give me some clarification on that.

Chapter 64

Charles Turner was in the back, working on his boat when we pulled up. Besides Matt and I, we had brought two other patrol cars just in case this situation escalated. We walked around the house and approached him, hands on our weapons. He was sitting in his boat on the canal and looked up as he spotted us.

"Mr. Turner?" I said.

It is often stated that cops have instincts, that we somehow know that people are up to no good or that something is off when we enter a situation. This was one of those times. I can't explain what it was; it might have been in his eyes, but I just knew this guy would make a run for it.

And I was right.

Charles Turner gave us one quick glance, then made his decision. His eyes scanned the area for possible ways out, and then fired the engine up and took off.

"Darn it," Matt said and pulled his weapon.

As Charles roared down the canal, he pointed it at him. "Get back here, Mr. Turner," he yelled. "Or I'll have to shoot."

But Charles Turner didn't. He was already long gone, exiting the canal and driving the boat into the intracoastal waters.

"He's getting away!" I yelled. The two other officers we had brought with us came running down to the canal.

"I can barely see him anymore. We need boats in the water," Matt said. "And choppers in the air."

"I'll call it in," one of the officers said.

"Is he armed?" the other asked.

I shook my head. "We didn't see any weapons."

"He could have a gun on the boat," Matt said.

My heart pounding, I looked toward the area where Charles Turner had disappeared. I then laid eyes on the neighbor's boat that was docked there, then looked back at Matt.

"That one has two three-fifty outboard engines. That's a lot more horsepower than his. We could catch up to him easily," I said.

Matt knew where I was going and nodded. We ran into the neighboring yard and got the boat lowered into the water, then jumped in. Like most people in Cocoa Beach, this boat owner had left the key in the boat, in a small compartment next to the steering wheel. I grabbed it and dangled it in front of Matt.

"Nothing really changes around here, does it?" he said with an exhale. "We've told people at town hall meetings so many times to never leave their boat keys and car keys in their vehicles if they don't want them stolen. Yet, they still do."

I put the key in the ignition, and the engines roared to life. As I drove the boat out of the canal, and as soon as we were out of the manatee zone, where we could accelerate to top speed, I said:

"I, for one, am thrilled that nothing changes around here. Now, let's get this bastard before he leaves the county."

Chapter 65

THEN:

The most important part was to make sure that Oliver's life wasn't endangered when they raided the house. Peterson had made sure to determine where all the suspect's family members lived, and they were going to hit all of the houses simultaneously. On October 22nd, six weeks after Oliver had disappeared from his home, teams of fifty-five FBI agents and detectives took up positions outside Diego Sánchez's home in Brentwood, one of the tough neighborhoods in the D.C. area. Sánchez was on probation for drug possession and was known by the police as part of one of the well-known Mexican gangs in Washington.

They struck the moment Sánchez came home with his wife, driving into the street and up their driveway, with their two children in the back seat. They had been visiting his parents on the outskirts of town. A patrol car had followed them as they drove home, and Gary watched with his heart in his throat as they parked in the driveway.

"The package is in. Let's rock and roll," Peterson said on the radio. He gave Gary one short glance of reassurance, then left the car.

They had agreed that Gary would stay behind since he was too emotionally wrapped up in this and they couldn't risk him ruining the mission, which was to get the kidnapper and bring back his son safely. One wrong move or emotional decision could put his child's life in danger. This man was dangerous, and there was no saying what he might do under pressure.

Gary held his breath as he watched the team approach from all sides, guns ready. A big part of him regretted having listened to Peterson. He really wanted to be one of them—to be the one to press that gun to the kidnapper's head and ask Sánchez where the child was. Sitting out there all alone in the car made him feel so helpless, so frustrated. Yet he knew Peterson was right. He would only end up killing Sánchez if he got the chance.

Still, it was hard just to sit there and watch, wondering about all the things that might go wrong. Was Oliver with them in the car? Was he in the house? Or had they left him with one of the relatives? If so, then one of the other teams would find him, wouldn't they? Or would they be able to get away with him?

Gary sighed deeply as he watched out the window how Sánchez was pressed up against the front of his car and patted down, his legs spread out, his hands behind his back, then cuffed. There was a lot of yelling, and his wife screamed and took her children in her arms. But the children were taken from her, and she too was put in handcuffs, while she was screaming, and her children taken away in another car. They would be put in the hands of the DCF and probably be taken to another family member to be taken care of while it was determined who was involved in this kidnapping and who wasn't…whether they were in it together. It was probably going to be a mess to figure out, but Gary couldn't really think about that right now. He was staring at Peterson and the agents searching the car and then going into the house, his hands beginning to shake.

Would the child be in there all alone? Had they left Oliver in there while they went out? Was there someone to take care of him? Would they find him alive? Had they fed him?

An agent came out holding something in his hand, and Peterson immediately turned around to face Gary in the car, a serious look on his face. He signaled Gary to approach, while Sánchez and his wife were being held down, the woman crying helplessly for her children.

Gary got out and rushed toward the agent holding the light blue teddy bear in his hand, Oliver's favorite bear, the one he got from his grandmother when he was just born. It was the same one that always made him calm down when he woke up in the middle of the night crying helplessly.

"The boy is not inside," the agent holding the bear said. "He's not in the car either. And Sánchez won't speak."

"You recognize this?" Peterson asked.

Gary swallowed and tried not to look at Sánchez, who was still pressed down on the front of his car while being searched. Still, Gary couldn't help himself; his eyes met Sánchez's, and he sensed he was about to lose it. He clenched his fists and tried to calm himself, but he couldn't. Instead, it was like everything exploded inside him. Weeks of frustration and helplessness erupted inside of him, and he rushed toward Sánchez before anyone could stop him. He placed his face close to his and pressed his gun against the man's head, yelling: "Where is my son? Where is he?"

Chapter 66

I t really was a fast boat. As soon as Matt and I entered the Banana River and I pushed it to its max, we spotted Charles Turner on the horizon. He was flying down the river toward Satellite Beach south of us, but we were going a lot faster. It didn't take us long to gain on him. Meanwhile, Matt was on the phone, talking to the sheriff's office. They had gotten the chopper in the air, and he was keeping them updated on where the suspect was and where he was heading.

"We're catching up to him," I yelled through the loud noise. "Almost there."

Charles Turner realized how close we were and turned to look at us. Then—as we were almost to the side of his boat— he pulled something out and pointed it at us.

"It's a gun," Matt said. He immediately went in front of me to protect me. Then he spoke into the radio. "He's got a weapon. I repeat suspect is armed and dangerous."

Matt pulled his gun too and, as I steered closer, he held it up so Charles Turner could see it.

"Stop the boat," Matt yelled, "and put down your weapon. Put down your weapon now!"

We could hear more boats approaching from the sides, and the chopper was soon hovering not far from us.

"Stop the boat!" Matt repeated.

In return, Charles Turner fired a shot at him.

"Get down," Matt yelled and jumped on top of me, pulling me to the bottom of the boat. I landed on my back, Matt on top of me. I felt something wet hit my face, and I wiped it away, only to realize it was blood.

Matt's blood.

The blood of the man I loved.

"Matt?" I screamed hysterically. "Matt? You're bleeding. You're hurt. You've been hit!"

Crying, I pushed him away from me and sat up. I then turned the unconscious Matt around, searching for an exit wound. The blood seemed to be coming from the back of his head.

Oh, dear God. He's been shot in the head!

Frantically, I grabbed the radio on his shoulder and pressed the button. It was hard for me to get the words across my lips as everything inside of me was screaming.

Not Matt. Not Matt of all the people in the world.

"Officer down. I repeat. Officer down!"

I didn't wait for the response as I realized the bastard was getting away. I rushed to the steering wheel and got the boat back on track and pressed it to its maximum. Crying in anger, I screamed at Turner to stop. Turner sped up and looked back at me when a police boat coming from the other side made him make a sudden turn and, as he did, my boat rammed into the side of his. I felt the impact the moment it happened, but that is all I remember.

Chapter 67

"Eva Rae? Eva Rae?"

I blinked my eyes and slowly regained consciousness. In front of me, bent down over me, stood Matt. His beautiful blue eyes gleamed as he saw that I had opened mine.

"She's waking up. She's awake," he said with a relieved exhale. "God, you had me worried there, Eva Rae."

I stared at him, blinking. "I had *you* worried? What the heck do you mean? You were shot?"

He shook his head. "No. I hurt the back of my head as I jumped to protect you. Some metal pipe that stuck out, I didn't see it myself. But I have a wound in the back of my head from it."

"You weren't shot? But I was so sure…?"

"I'm fine. I'm still bleeding, though," he said and held a towel to the back of his head. That was when I realized we were still on a boat, but a different one. An officer in uniform was steering it.

"Turner?" I asked and sat up, then got dizzy.

"Whoa, whoa," Matt said and put me back on the deck. "You've been out for a little while there, Eva Rae. Too early to start sitting up."

I felt my head. It was pounding. The blue sky above me was moving slowly. The boat wasn't going very fast.

"What happened?"

"Our boat slammed into his, and you were slung through the air. You landed in the water, where a police boat pulled you out. Same thing happened to me. I woke up the moment my face hit the water."

"Detective Miller is being modest," a man in a uniform from the sheriff's office said. "He was the one who swam to your rescue and made sure to keep you out of the water till we could pick you up."

"I'm just glad you're okay," Matt said. "I feared that I might lose you for a second there."

"Same," I said and looked into his eyes. Then reality hit me again as another wave of pain rushed through my head. Matt handed me a bottle of water, and I drank greedily.

"What happened to Turner?" I asked when the bottle was empty, and my headache eased up on me.

Matt's eyes grew serious. "He was killed in the crash, I'm afraid."

That made me ignore all the pain and dizziness and sit up straight.

"No!"

"They airlifted him to the hospital, but he died in the chopper. That was the latest I heard right before you woke up."

"But…how are we supposed to find the last girl? How are we going to find Tara Owens?"

Matt put his hand on my chest and helped me lay down again. "We'll worry about that later. Right now, we need to get you to the shore and have the paramedics check you. You might have suffered a concussion from the crash."

I sighed. "I'm fine. I promise, Matt. Don't worry about me."

He gave me a look. "I'm not taking any chances here. Not with the woman I love."

That shut me up.

The woman he loves? Matt loves me?

I guess I knew this, deep down, and also that I loved him. We just hadn't said it to one another yet. He picked a heck of a time to do so, but I wasn't complaining. But I didn't say anything back. The moment had passed, and it wasn't the right time for me to tell him I loved him yet. It was a little early for me still.

I hoped he understood.

Chapter 68

Three days later, we still hadn't found Tara Owens or any sign of her. We had raided Turner's house and, together with the techs, we had combed through it over and over again, looking for secret attics or basements or just small rooms. We had torn up all the carpet in the house and dug up most of the yard.

Still nothing.

Matt and I were sitting at our desk, staring at the whiteboard after going through the latest in the case.

"And we're sure that Turner is our man?" I asked.

"I'm pretty convinced," he said. "He worked at the hospital. He entered the hospital that morning, even though he wasn't scheduled for work that day."

"The nurse at the dialysis area wasn't sure it was him," I said. "She said she didn't know Turner since he worked in another department, but when we showed her the picture of Turner, she wasn't completely sure it was him she had seen that day."

"He has the goatee," Matt said. "He looks like the drawing, and when we showed the picture to Jane Martin, she said it looked like the guy who had given her the package with the sash in it. Plus, he tried to shoot me when we approached him. He had guilty written all over him. You don't run from the police unless you have something to hide."

"But he's not a surgeon," I said. "And Jamila at the ME's office specifically said the eyes had been surgically removed. Enucleation, she called it."

Matt sighed tiredly and sipped his coffee cup. "True. But he could have seen it done or maybe read about it somewhere. Heck, I bet there might even be tutorials online on how to do this stuff."

Matt was right. I did one quick search on Google and found both an article in the American Academy of Ophthalmology that described every step of an enucleation in gut-wrenching detail, and several videos showing exactly how it is done.

I stood to my feet. I had gotten a clean bill of health from the doctors at the hospital. After that, I had gone back to my house, removed the crime scene tape, and cleaned out all the signs of there having been crime scene techs, especially the fingerprint powder that seemed to be everywhere. The techs had found several cameras the size of a screw installed in my house, and the thought of this perp watching me gave me the creeps. Still, I loved my house, and I wasn't going to let this guy ruin it for me. When I was finally done after an entire day of cleaning, I had let my children and mother come back inside. We were all happy to be home again, especially the girls were glad to be able to hide in their rooms, able to close the door against Alex, who—according to them—ruined everything.

My mother was happy to be back in the kitchen and cooking again, and for once, no one said anything about her Coconut Chickpea Curry dish. We all ate it with delight and told her it tasted great, even though I found it terrible.

Now that I was back to work, Matt wanted me to accept the fact that we had gotten our guy, but just not found the girl yet, and that was our task. I agreed that Tara was our task right now, but I wasn't as convinced that Turner was our man, and it annoyed Matt. He wanted this to be over soon, so everything could go back to normal. I couldn't agree with him more on that part, but I wasn't sure we were going to achieve that if we kept looking at Turner as our main suspect.

I sighed and rubbed my face.

"What's with you today?" Matt asked.

"He had no motive," I said. "For doing the things he did. There, I said it. I know that you and Chief Annie are all excited because we found our man, but we can't answer why he did it, and that, to me, isn't solving anything. Why did he do the things he did? Why did he recreate all my old cases, huh? Why did he target me?"

"We found your book at his house," Matt said. "The one you spoke about with the many serial killer typologies. Isn't that enough? He was obsessed with your work."

"But it still doesn't answer my question. Why? This killer went to such extremes to get my attention; why did he do that, Matt? This guy didn't even know me."

Matt sighed again. I was waiting for him to roll his eyes at me too, just like my kids.

"Maybe he read about you in the paper. There was a story about you when you solved the last case, remember? They did this entire piece just about you and who you are. He could have seen it, then read your book. It doesn't take a genius to find out what cases you solved while working at the FBI, and some of them were mentioned in the article as well."

I sat back down with an exhale, then finished my coffee.

"Maybe you're right," I said, putting the empty cup down. "It just doesn't feel like it's good enough. It doesn't feel right."

I stared at Matt, feeling hopeless, thinking about Tara Owens and how to find her when the phone rang, and Matt picked it up. He spoke for a few seconds, then put it down, smiling.

"What?"

"That was the hospital. Carina Martin is awake and ready to talk."

Chapter 69

B oomer paced the living room. Back and forth he went, biting his nails while watching the news. They were telling the story of the girl who had returned from being kidnapped, a reporter standing outside of Cape Canaveral Hospital, reporting live from the parking lot.

"Well, Greg, we just spoke to one of the doctors here, and he told us that the girl, Carina Martin, has just woken up, but hasn't spoken to the police yet," the reporter said. "They hope, naturally, that she will be able to confirm that her kidnapper was, in fact, Charles Turner, the man who died while trying to run away from the police in his boat. It is believed that he was the one responsible for kidnapping the three girls weeks ago, but also for having kidnapped a fourth girl, one of their friends, blinded her, and raped her. Earlier in the week, the police released this sketch of the kidnapper along with a very grainy picture taken by a surveillance camera outside of the hospital, allegedly showing Charles Turner. The police say they are also working the theory that he was the same man who booby-trapped a FedEx truck and blew it up in the main intersection of Cocoa Beach last week, injuring a local police officer. This is what they hope that Carina Martin will confirm later today when she speaks to the police. Back to you, Greg."

The camera cut to the studio and Boomer turned off the TV. Things weren't going the way he had planned them, but all wasn't lost yet. Even if he had to abandon his initial ideas, there was still a way to end this in a manner that would satisfy him. There was still the last girl, and she would get to serve her purpose.

Boomer still had a couple of aces up his sleeve.

Chapter 70

THEN:
"I'll tell you where the baby is if you release me."

Gary stared at Sánchez through the glass overlooking the interrogation room, clenching his fists. They had been at it for more than forty hours now, and still, the man hadn't said a word that could lead them to Gary's son.

It almost tore him to pieces.

Who was feeding Oliver? Who was changing his diaper? Who took care of him?

They had kept both Sánchez and his wife María and were questioning them both in each of their rooms. Still nothing. Not even a hint.

The agents had raided all of their relatives' houses but found no baby there either and no sign of him. All they had was the teddy bear. That was the only clue they had that the boy had been at their house at one point.

But where was he now?

The boy had been gone for longer than he had been alive when he disappeared now. They had known more time without him than with him. It was unbearable to think about.

"You're not being released. You kidnapped a baby, Sánchez," Peterson said. "You're the one in trouble here, buddy. You don't get to make demands. And you definitely don't get to go free. You tell us where the baby is, and then maybe we'll feed you, how about that? Maybe we won't stick your head into the toilet bowl."

Sánchez looked up at Peterson. His eyes were exhausted. He hadn't slept, shaved, or showered in forty hours. They had given him water to drink but nothing else.

"Where's the kid, Sánchez?" Peterson repeated.

"Let me and María go, and I'll show you to him," he said like he had said maybe a hundred times earlier. If Gary had to hear that answer once more, he would throw up.

They were getting nowhere, and in the meantime, Oliver was somewhere, alone and scared. He was nothing but an infant, for crying out loud. Completely helpless, completely dependent on his surroundings.

Peterson got up, his chair screeching across the floor. He came out to Gary. Gary ran a hand across his sweaty forehead.

"I can't take it anymore," he said. "Why won't the bastard speak? Not even when I pressed that darn gun to his face did he say anything."

"He's a tough one; I admit to that," Peterson said. "But I still haven't met the criminal that I couldn't break. He's gonna spill. Look at his eyes; he's getting close now, just you wait and see. Give it time."

Gary scoffed. "I don't have time. That's the one thing I don't have to give."

Peterson nodded, then looked briefly at his shoes. "I might have an idea," he said. "Actually, it was Agent Wilson who told me it might work."

"Anything at this point. You know that," Gary said. "What is it?"

"The wife," Peterson said. "We bring her into the interrogation room. See if she can get him to talk."

Chapter 71

"Can you describe the man who kidnapped you?"

Carina looked at the two detectives that had entered her room. She had explained everything she remembered from the night she was attacked to them and told them as much as she remembered from their time in the room underground. Talking about it made her tear up, even though she tried to stifle it. She was still feeling dizzy and couldn't find rest. Everything felt so confusing to her, almost surreal.

The doctor, a small woman with blonde hair, had told her she had been lucky, that they had performed surgery on her for almost twelve hours to save her life. She had also told her she was malnourished and that all her levels were alarmingly low. Furthermore, they had found traces of a date rape drug in her blood. It could affect her memory, she had been told. And now that the female detective, a small chubby-cheeked redhead with her hair in a ponytail, asked her for details about the man who had tormented her and kept her prisoner, it was hard for her to picture him.

"He was…h-he…"

"Take your time," the redhead, said, sounding sympathetic. "Make sure the details are correct."

"He wore a mask when he came to the room where we were kept—a surgical mask. I can remember the eyes; they were grey. Maybe it was the light or the lack of light in the small room, but they looked grey. Could have been bluer."

"And the hair?" the male detective said. He was quite handsome and looked like he enjoyed surfing, judging from the blond strands of hair in between the brown ones.

"I wanna say blond," she said. "But I'm not completely sure. It could have been a light brown."

The female detective showed her a sketch.

"Is this him?"

She looked at it, then nodded. "Could be."

She showed her a grainy surveillance photo. "And this is the same guy?"

Carina nodded and remembered vaguely running across the parking lot, her heart racing in her chest, fear fueling her, giving her almost superhuman strength. She couldn't believe she had made it out, that she had actually escaped.

The female detective showed her another picture.

"This man," she said. "Do you recognize him?"

Carina looked at the photo. "I think so. He's...he's Leanne's dad, isn't he? She lives not that far from me?"

"Is that the man who kidnapped you?" the female asked.

Carina looked at the picture, then shook her head. "No."

The two detectives exchanged a glance. The female addressed her again, leaning closer with the picture.

"Look at it again, Carina, please. Are you sure this is not the same man?"

Carina looked at Leanne's dad again, then nodded. "Positive. The goatee is fake. I saw him put it on in the car while he thought I was out. He thought he had sedated me, but the syringe fell out while he did it back at the house and the contents were emptied inside my dress instead. I felt it happen but pretended it didn't. I felt the sedation at first, but it was quickly out of my system, so I just laid there while he undressed me and carried me to the car. Then I waited for him to leave the car. But I saw him put on the fake goatee and glue it to his face."

"Are you sure about this?" the male detective said. "He was wearing a mask for most of the time you saw him."

"I am certain. This is not the same guy. I would have known. I used to play with Leanne when we were younger before we drifted apart, and I know her dad very well. I would have recognized his eyes. It's not him."

Chapter 72

"So, he is still out there," I said and looked at Matt, feeling the adrenalin begin to rush through my body. We had killed the wrong man. I know Matt would say we didn't exactly kill him and that he did shoot at the police, so he knew how it would end, but still. A man, a father was dead, and he wasn't even our guy.

This didn't feel right.

I leaned over and whispered to Matt. "We need a guard by her door twenty-four-seven. He's gonna come for her."

"I'll take care of that," he said and left.

I turned to face Carina again, suddenly worried about her and if she would be safe. This guy knew his way around this hospital, and we didn't even know his name.

"Did you know this man from anywhere else?" I asked.

Carina closed her eyes and nodded.

"You did?" I asked hopefully.

"He's a friend of my dad's. Not a very close friend since he only moved here a little while ago, I think."

"Okay, now we're getting somewhere. So, your dad knows him too, where from?"

"He's...He's..." Carina spoke through tears now. "He lives down the street. He kept us at his house in a bunker underground in his yard."

I could barely breathe. "He's someone from the neighborhood? You were kept that close all this time?"

She nodded, biting her lip. "I know this because we helped him build the bunker."

What?

"Excuse me? I'm not sure I understand?" I said.

Tears were running quickly down her cheeks now, and I could tell she was bravely trying to focus and not break down. She knew as well as I did how important it was that she told us everything. Even if it meant she had to force herself to speak.

"I'm sorry if I'm a little all over the place. I should have told you this first when you came in, but I was just…well, I can't seem to focus properly."

"The doctor said this could happen," her mom, Jane Martin said. She was sitting by her bedside, holding Carina's hand. "She's been drugged, and it can affect her memory."

I nodded. "Okay, Carina. So, he lives in the neighborhood, and you helped him build the bunker? Can you explain that?"

"His house is kind of set back on the lot and covered by sea grapes and trees, so you can't really see it that well. One time, some months ago, he paid all the kids in the neighborhood to come and help dig out his back yard. He said it was for a pool, and we believed him. It wasn't until I was sitting down in that hell-hole that I realized I had helped dig my own grave."

Jane Martin clasped her mouth and was about to break into tears. She held her daughter's hand tightly.

"Maybe we should stop for now," she said. "Carina is tired."

"No, Mom," Carina said between sobs. "I want this guy caught; don't you understand? I want him in prison like he put me in prison. And I want them to find Tara before it's too late. When I was taken out, she was still down there. There's an opening under the carpet in the hallway that leads down to it. You need to remove a bookshelf on top first, then you'll see it. Please, hurry. Tara wasn't well when I was taken out. Please, get her out of there before it's too late."

Chapter 73

There was no time to waste. We couldn't wait for the sheriff's office to get there with a team from the mainland. Every minute counted, so we decided to go in on our own. Matt drove the cruiser up in front of the house on Country Club Road and parked it on the front lawn. Two patrols came up behind us, on Chief Annie's orders after I spoke to her on the phone, letting her in on what Carina had told us.

Matt and I both put on our vests and drew our weapons.

"We're looking for a female, sixteen years of age, light brown shoulder-length hair and green eyes," I told Sgt. Mason as he approached us, the other officers following closely behind him. I had only known Mason for a short while, but Matt told me he was the man you'd want having your back.

"Got it," Mason said and nodded.

"The suspect might be in the house, so be careful," I said. "Suspect is extremely dangerous."

I met the eyes of Sgt. Mason and felt a connection. It was important in situations like these that we operated on the same page.

I cocked my weapon and nodded.

Matt was the one who knocked on the door. "COCOA

BEACH POLICE DEPARTMENT. OPEN UP, OR WE'RE COMING IN."

No response. That was expected.

I nodded again, and Matt grabbed the door handle. It was locked. This was also expected.

I signaled for him to walk with me into the back. The fence leading to the yard wasn't locked, and we walked inside, then up to the porch. I looked at the grass area wondering if the bunker was beneath it, then shivered at the thought.

It's open, Matt mouthed as he grabbed the sliding doors. I nodded, and we rushed inside the living room, holding our guns up in front of us, heart hammering in my chest.

I moved along the wall of the living room. It was sparsely furnished with only a recliner in front of an old TV and nothing else. The carpet was old and had stains from where the previous owner had furniture.

I moved into the kitchen.

It was empty. Extremely empty. Only a big bag of dog food on the counter. That was it.

I moved down the hallway to the first bedroom. Empty. Second bedroom, also empty, not even carpet on the floors. The third bedroom actually had a bed in it. Chains were hanging from a pipe under the ceiling. There was blood on the bed.

Whose blood is that? Molly's? Carina's? Ava's? Or Tara's?

"Clear," I said.

I returned to the hallway and met Matt's glare. We both saw it at the same time…the bookshelf in the middle of the hallway. It looked awkward and out of place. Seemed to be the only bookshelf in the entire house.

Matt grabbed the top while I pulled at the bottom, and soon, the bookshelf was removed. The carpet was loose underneath just like Carina had told us. As we pulled it off, a concrete block was revealed underneath. Sgt. Mason came up behind us. He was a big guy.

"Let's get that for you," he said.

Sgt. Mason ran for a crowbar, then cranked it open, lifting the block so we could pull it aside.

I stared into the black hole as it was revealed underneath, my heart crying for those poor girls who had been hidden down here all this time, while the entire town searched for them.

In the neighbor's house of all places.

In plain sight.

Chapter 74

Using flashlights to lead the way, we walked through a small tunnel that led to a metal door with deadbolts on it. Pressing back my tears, I opened them and entered a room the size of a closet with three mattresses on the floor. On top of one of those mattresses laid a girl. She was on her side, curled up in the fetal position.

Tara.

I went inside and was met by a wall of bad smell that almost made me throw up. I held a sleeve to my mouth and knelt next to her. Flies were swarming the room, and I worried that the girl had died. I put a hand on her shoulder, then pulled gently till her body turned to its back. I gasped, startled, and turned my head away for a second. Tara's lips were white and cracked, her eyes were sunken, and her skin dried up, making it look paper-thin.

"She's alive," I said as I put my finger on her throat and felt the weak pulse. "But not responsive."

Matt was right next to me.

"Do you think he forgot her?"

I scanned the room. By the door, I spotted three buckets. Two were empty; the last one was filled with old human excrement, and flies were swarming it. How flies always found a way, even into a room with no windows and a door that thick that hadn't been opened in a while, remained a mystery to me.

"It's hard to say," I said. "There's no fresh water or food."

"We need to get her to the hospital right away," Matt said and rose to his feet.

I sniffled, looking at the poor girl who was barely alive. I took her in my arms and lifted her with no effort whatsoever. She couldn't weigh more than eighty or ninety pounds. As I looked down at Tara in my arms, spotting a big wound on her abdomen that had been recently stitched together, I suddenly remembered something. It was like I had been here before.

In a situation just like it.

"Matt. Stop."

He turned around and shone his light at my face. "What's wrong? Eva Rae? What's going on?"

I lifted my glance and met his eyes. "I don't know. There's something... something familiar about this."

Matt wrinkled his forehead. "What do you mean, familiar?"

"There was a case I worked. Four bodies were found in a basement in Chicago. All illegal immigrants. The FBI was sent there to assist, but as we retrieved the bodies..."

I stopped and looked at Matt, fear rippling through every cell in my body.

"We need to get out of here. Now!"

"But..."

"Matt, get out of here."

"I'm not leaving you here if that's what you mean."

"Matt, if I'm right, then you have to save yourself."

"Save myself? What do you mean? Explain, Eva Rae."

I swallowed, sweat prickling on my forehead. "The bomb is inside of her. If I'm right, the bomb is inside of Tara. Bombs were in the bodies in Chicago. All four of them had bombs surgically inserted into their bodies."

Chapter 75

I held Tara close while crying helplessly.

"I don't know what to do, Matt. I can't just leave her here. I can't; I simply refuse to!"

"You have to, Eva Rae. You must. If she explodes, she'll take all of us with her. You have to leave her, and then we'll send down a bomb squad. We need to get away from here. Now!"

"They'll be too late. He wants her to explode with us close to her like it happened back then. We lost fifteen forensic techs, Matt. My partner and I were outside in the yard when it happened. The bombs went off simultaneously, and the house crashed on top of them. They all died. Each and every one of them!"

"You can't save her, Eva Rae. You can save yourself, but you can't save her if it explodes anyway."

I stared at the stitches on Tara's abdomen. "She's someone's daughter, Matt. Somewhere, her mother is waiting for her to come home. I have to save her. I simply have to!"

"You can't. Don't you understand, Eva Rae?"

I held the girl closer still, sobbing helplessly, then made my decision. I was about to put her down but then ran for the door instead.

"Eva Rae!"

I didn't listen. I carried the girl through the metal door, crying like crazy, Matt following behind me.

"COMING THROUGH!" I yelled up toward the entrance to the bunker, then climbed up the steps, holding her tightly, shaking violently in fear.

Please, don't explode. Please, don't go off now. Not now.

I reached the last step and could hear Matt panting agitatedly behind me. Sgt. Mason reached down to help me, to grab the girl from my arms, but I yelled at him to get away.

"STAND BACK!"

Sgt. Mason obeyed and got out of my way while I reached the main floor, then ran through the house, the girl tightly clutched in my arms. I was screaming violently in fear and to get people to move out of my way. I stormed into the yard and, just as I was about to put her down on the grass, I heard a sound come from inside of her abdomen.

In that second, I knew it was too late.

Chapter 76

I woke up to the delightful sound of my children fighting. Usually, it wouldn't make me smile, but on this day, it did.

"You're such a moron, Alex."

"You're a moron."

"Stop copying me."

"Stop copying me."

"Grandma? Alex is being annoying…again."

I blinked my eyes to make sure I was seeing things right. I was. Christine and Alex were standing right next to my bed, engaged in a heated quarrel.

"I think Mom's awake," I heard Olivia say. Then she approached me, and I saw her pretty face. "Mom? Are you awake? Mom?"

I smiled, but it hurt, so I stopped. "Where am I?"

The children surrounded me, their beautiful faces staring at me. My mother came up behind them.

"Ah, thank God, Eva Rae. We were so worried. The doctor said you'd wake up, but it took forever."

Is she seriously blaming me for being unconscious too long?

"I'm so glad you're awake, Mommy," Alex said.

"Me too," Christine said as the two of them fought about the space and who stood in front. Alex elbowed his way in front of her, and she pushed him back. Olivia rolled her eyes at them.

"Could you two lay off it for at least one second so Mom can wake up? She almost died. Geez."

"Where's Matt?" I asked, slowly remembering what had happened. Anxiety spread quickly through my veins. "Why isn't he here?"

My mom came closer. Her eyes looked sad and, in the few seconds before she spoke, I imagined a thousand scenarios, and none of them had Matt being alive.

"Mom?"

"Easy there," she said when I tried to sit up. "Don't get agitated. Christ, you were in an explosion, for crying out loud."

"Where is Matt? Please, tell me."

"Matt is fine. He just went out for coffee. He's been here the past twenty-four hours while you were out."

"And, of course, you wake up the moment I leave my post to get some coffee."

Matt's soft voice filled the room, and I felt myself relax again. He handed my mom a cup and kept the other one to himself, then sat on the edge of my bed. Christine and Alex started fighting again, and my mom told them that she'd take them to the vending machines to get some of that *junk-food you seem to enjoy so much*. The kids forgot their quarrels, cheered, and left with her.

Matt smiled and held my hand in his, then kissed the top of it. "Boy, am I glad to see those eyes again. How are you feeling?"

"My vision is a little blurry, and I have this ringing in my ears," I said. "I'm not in any pain, though, but I assume that has to do with the number of painkillers I'm on right now, am I right?"

Matt nodded. "The doctor said your vision and hearing might be affected for a little while, but it should normalize. You also have a concussion and burn marks on your legs and abdomen. Because of the blast and the pressure that your body endured, you might experience chest pain, and it might have damaged your lungs and central nervous system, but it's too early to tell, they say."

I smiled, then grew serious again. "What happened, Matt?"

"It went off. The bomb went off inside of her," he said. "Luckily, it seemed that the fact that it was inside of the girl sheltered you a little, but you were pretty terribly hurt; luckily, it was mostly superficial. It was an improvised bomb and a low-order explosive, they say. It would have been a lot worse if it had gone off inside the small bunker, though, and we would probably both have been dead. I was right behind you when it happened and I just…saw you be slung through the air. There was blood and tissue everywhere; I'll spare you the details, but luckily, it was mostly hers."

"So…she died?"

Matt nodded. He sent me a caring smile as I felt the tears fill up my eyes again. I couldn't hold them back, and soon they ran down my cheeks so fast I began to hyperventilate.

This was just too cruel.

Matt squeezed my hand tightly, stifling tears of his own. "You did your best. I know you wanted to save her; we both did, but it was impossible. You must understand this, Eva Rae. There was nothing you could have done differently. She would have died anyway. I spoke to a doctor about it, and he said she wouldn't have survived even if it hadn't gone off."

"I had her, Matt. I had her in my arms. We made it outside. We were so close."

"There was nothing you could have done differently," he said again and touched my hair gently. "Nothing."

"This is just too much."

He sighed. "I know; I know."

"Are we at least anywhere closer to finding this guy?" I asked, pressing back tears while beginning to feel tired, but staying awake due to the anger rising in me. I hated this guy. I truly hated this person. I wanted him dead for what he had done. I wanted him to be in pain just like I was in such deep pain right now.

"As a matter of fact, yes. The house is registered in the name of an Anthony Piatkowski. We haven't been able to locate him and believe he is in hiding. But we are pulling his driver's license from the DMV and are going to send the picture out to the press as soon as we have it. We found all his explosives in the garage, where we assume he made the bombs."

"Piatkowski, huh? I feel like I've heard that name before."

"He's new to the area. Bought the house five months ago. But get this, he's military. Two trips to Camp Marmal, Afghanistan. Enlisted in the navy right after high school and became an EOD. He was one of the most skilled recruits they ever had, they said when we spoke to them at Eglin Air Force Base, which hosts the Naval Explosive Ordnance Disposal School. His engineering skills were out of this world, they said."

"EOD, huh? An Explosive Ordnance Disposal technician," I said. "The people trained to safely disable explosive ordnance, improvised explosives, and weapons of mass destruction. That makes sense. He knows everything there is to know about explosives. But that name, though. It's not an ordinary name."

"Do you make a connection?" Matt said.

"I thought I did, but then I lost it. I can't think," I said. "I'm too tired and too sedated."

I closed my eyes, thinking about Tara's poor mother and what she had to go through now when my kids returned, and I bit back my tears.

"It is," Olivia said, addressed to Christine.

"Is not," Christine said.

They were holding candy bars from the vending machine. Alex had already opened his and had chocolate smeared on all his fingers and cheeks. Olivia had chosen a granola bar.

"Isn't it true that a granola bar is healthier than a chocolate bar?" Olivia asked me. "Christine says it is the same."

I felt so tired; I could only muster a weak smile. I didn't care that they were constantly fighting. These kids were mine, and they were all still alive. That was all that counted right now.

"It is not. There is just as much sugar in a granola bar as in a chocolate bar. Look for yourself. Tell her, Mom," Christine said.

"I don't know anything about it. Why is this so important right now?" I asked, almost dozing off, but fighting it. I wanted to be with my loved ones for a little while longer.

"Because Olivia wants to be skinny, so she can be a model," Christine said, dragging the word out in the end.

"Okay," I said, my eyelids growing heavier still.

"But, *Mo-om*, she's not even tall enough. Tell her she isn't tall enough. You have to be like five-ten at least."

"That's not true," Olivia complained. "Ugh, why do you keep saying that? Why do you even care, you little twit?"

I wasn't listening anymore; I was simply dozing off to the sweet sound of my beloved family, and soon, I was completely lost in the land of my dreams.

THEN:

"What is she doing here?"

Sánchez looked at his wife, María, a surprised look on his face as she entered the interrogation room, followed by Gary's supervisor, Peterson.

"Why did you bring her in here?"

María sat down and reached her hands across the metal table. Sánchez's handcuffs clanked against the tabletop where they were strapped down.

"Honey, sweetie," María said, tilting her head with a sniffle.

Sánchez became stiff. The smile on his face froze.

"Why is she here?" he repeated, even angrier than the first time.

"Diego," she said. "Look at me."

He did as she told him to.

"Did you kidnap that baby?"

He pulled his hands out of hers.

"Why do you ask me this?"

María sobbed, then wiped her eyes on her sleeve before she continued. "If you took the baby, you need to tell them where he is. This is an infant who needs to be with his mother. He needs to be fed; he needs care all hours of the day and night. You are a father; you know this. Think if it was Miguel or Juana this happened to."

Sánchez stared at her, his eyes flickering back and forth.

"Get her out of here," he said. "I don't want her here."

"Please, Diego. You have to tell them where he is."

"I don't know what you're talking about."

"Please."

Sánchez slammed his fists onto the metal table. "Shut up. Just shut up, will you?"

"There's a mother out there, Diego. And she is missing her child. If you did this and I was the mother, I would want to know where that child was. Please, tell them."

It was working. They could tell it was. His wife María could get to him like no one else. For the first time, he felt pushed up against the wall; for the first time, he seemed stressed out. Just the way you want him to be, just the way they usually are right before they break down and spill.

Sánchez's nostrils were flaring. He was getting upset now. This was a good sign.

"Diego, please."

"GET HER OUT!"

He rose to his feet, the chains restraining him, growling in anger. María started to cry, and Peterson put a hand on her shoulder. And that was when it happened.

Sánchez finally broke down.

"I'll tell. I'll tell you everything. I'll even take you to find the boy. But get her out of here. I don't want her to hear. Get her OUT!"

Chapter 77

It was in the late afternoon the next day. I opened my eyes with a loud gasp. The room was empty; everyone was gone, the blinds closed, leaving the room in darkness.

"Olivia," I said, feeling out of breath.

I lay still in the darkness, staring at the ceiling above, a million thoughts rushing through my head. Was it something I had dreamt? Where did this sensation come from? This feeling that something was terribly wrong?

It was something she said.

I sat up, thinking about what the girls had talked about when visiting. Olivia spoke about becoming a model. She had never talked about that before, ever.

Why now?

I grabbed my phone and called her.

She didn't pick up.

I put the phone down on the table next to me with a sigh.

She's busy—probably volleyball practice or maybe hanging out with her friends. Not everything is a disaster waiting to happen.

Yet, that was how I felt. Like a catastrophe was right around the corner, just waiting for me to discover it.

I couldn't leave it alone. The feeling was eating me up. I grabbed my phone again and called Matt. I got his voicemail.

Angry, I put the phone down again, then lay still in my bed, wondering.

Why now suddenly? Why all the talk about becoming a model?

I exhaled, telling myself I needed to relax, that I couldn't do anything about it now, that Olivia was fine. She had probably been in school all day, and now she was hanging out with her friends. This was perfectly normal.

I grabbed the phone again, then looked at Mappen, the tracking app I used to keep an eye on my kids. The map showed that she was at Marylin's, the new diner downtown that served milkshakes and burgers. There was nothing odd about that. That was a usual hangout for the teenagers of Cocoa Beach.

But today is Thursday. She has FSA-testing tomorrow and should be at home studying.

The thought made me sit up and sling my legs over the side of the bed. I stared at the map for a few more seconds and realized it wasn't moving at all.

Had she gone there with some friends? Were they eating and maybe studying together?

Yes, that had to be it. Olivia was very determined to do well in school. She would never put her friends above an important test.

I lay my head back down and relaxed. Olivia was fine. I closed my eyes, trying to get some more sleep, but after fifteen minutes or so, I sat back up and tried to call her again.

Still, no answer.

I tried once more, and suddenly someone picked up.

Oh, thank God.

"Olivia? Olivia?"

"Who's this?" an unknown voice said.

My heart dropped.

"Who is this?" I asked.

"I'm Martha. I found this phone. I work at the diner and was taking out the trash when I heard it ring."

My eyes grew wide, and my heart started to pound. "The trash?"

"Yeah, the dumpster behind Marylin's. It was right on top. Is it your phone?"

"It's my daughter's. Please, hold onto it. I'll send someone to pick it up."

Chapter 78

Boomer looked at the girl on the bed. She was completely out, heavily sedated, and wouldn't move a muscle for the next several hours. He felt satisfied with this. Taking her had been one of the easiest tasks he had ever performed. She was the one who had contacted him. He didn't even have to write to her like he did those other girls using the photographer's account. He had told her to meet him after school in the parking lot by the new diner, Marylin's, and to bring six sets of clothes for the photoshoot. That last part was just to make it sound legit. As soon as she had approached him in the parking lot behind the diner and hugged him, he had told her to get into the car, and he'd drive her to the photographer that he knew, who would take the photos. Believing him—*yes, she was that gullible*—she had gotten in, and he had placed the syringe in her thigh and emptied its contents while holding her mouth so she couldn't scream. Minutes later, she was out, and he could grab her phone and throw it in the trash, knowing how easy those things were to track, just like he was very good at hiding his tracks online.

Boomer was self-taught at hacking but had been helped on his way when hanging out with one of his buddies in Afghanistan. The many long hours at the camp, waiting for a job, they had spent on computers, learning how to hack into any secure system and how to hide their tracks. It was a skill he believed he would get a lot of use out of later, and he had been right.

He had gotten the name Boomer because of the mushrooms he liked to eat that were also called boomers while hanging out under the trees at the camp. They helped him endure those long hours of nothing to do while waiting to be called out to disarming the next IED. It was a job not just anyone could do.

In a combat zone such as Afghanistan, EODs are everyone's friend. They were the ones to call when an explosive threat was found, and Boomer was an expert at eliminating that danger.

But some guys that Boomer went to school with got hurt while out there. And that hit him hard. It was tough not to think, *That could have been me. I could have been that person out there.* Doing what he did kept him constantly close to that threat. It didn't make for an easy return to the civilized world.

He had dreamt of becoming an EOD since he was just a child because his father had been one too. Once he joined the Navy, that was all that was on his mind—making his dad proud.

Chapter 79

M att still didn't pick up the phone, and I was getting more and more anxious. I even called the station and told them to have Matt or Chief Annie call me back as soon as possible.

Then I decided I couldn't just lie there in my bed and do nothing. Something was wrong with my daughter, and I had to act. Now.

So, I rushed out of my room without being seen and asked for an Uber to pick me up at the hospital entrance. I asked the driver to take me home and ran up to the entrance and walked inside.

"Olivia?"

My mom came out of the kitchen, wearing an apron, wiping her hands on it.

"Eva Rae? What on Earth…?"

"Mom, where's Olivia?"

My mother looked confused. "She said she was going out with her friends after school. They were going to Marilyn's, that new place. I told her I hoped she wouldn't eat any of the greasy food they have there, but…"

"Mom, I think something terrible happened to her."

"Why…why…I took her to school. She's been absent for

two days, so I figured it was best she at least showed her face today. Finals are coming up and…"

"Someone threw her phone in the trash behind Marylin's," I said. "When I called it, a woman who worked there picked up."

"But…surely…Are you sure she's not…I mean…listen, Eva Rae. You're on a lot of drugs right now; you're not thinking clearly. Maybe you're hallucinating. Could it have been a dream?"

"No, Mom. I am not hallucinating. I know something happened to my daughter," I said and rushed up the stairs to her room.

I rushed inside, calling her name, but as expected, her room was empty. I sat at her computer and opened her social media accounts, beginning with Instagram, which she used the most. Not finding anything, I went through her Snapchat account, then WhatsApp, Amino, Twitter, and even her Facebook, which I knew she never used.

Nothing. I found nothing suspicious. No creepy photographer, no strangers contacting her.

How did she get this idea into her head?

Frantically, I kept going through all her emails, all her messages on Instagram, when my phone rang. I looked at the display. Since the killer had called me the last time and told me where to find Ava Morales, the sheriff's office had been monitoring my calls. The first one they had only been able to locate within a ten miles radius of Cocoa Beach, which didn't give us much to go after. The phone was a burner. As I saw the *unknown caller* on the display again, my heart literally stopped.

What if it was him? What if he was calling me to let me know that he had my daughter?

My hand shook as I pressed the button.

"H-hello?"

Chapter 80

It was Chad. I gasped for air while trying to calm my poor hammering heart.

"Always had impeccable timing, Chad," I said and sat down on Olivia's bed.

"Is this a bad time?" he asked. "I can call again later. I was actually looking for Olivia, but she's not picking up her phone. I wanted to know if she received the money."

Money?

"You gave her money, Chad? How much?"

"A thousand dollars. It was for some photo shoot."

"A photo shoot? You gave her money for that? Did she mention when or where she was going for it?" I asked.

"No. She just said she needed the money and that it was a big deal for her, that it was her dream coming true. Are you telling me that you didn't know about this, about her asking me for it? I thought she ran this by you and figured you just didn't want anything to do with me after last time we spoke. You made me feel really awful. I thought giving her the money was a way for me to make it up to her. I wired it to her this morning."

No. No. No!

I rubbed my forehead. "Of course, you did. Listen…Olivia…"

For a second, I was about to tell him that I believed Olivia was in trouble but then decided against it. There was still a chance she was just out with her friends and that she had forgotten her phone at the diner before they left to go somewhere else. Or someone might have stolen it and thrown it in the trash when they realized they couldn't open it. If she was, in fact, missing, I'd have to tell him when I was certain.

"I gotta go."

"Wait; there was something else," he said.

Of course, there was.

"What? I'm kind of in a rush here, Chad, could you get to the point a little faster?"

"I eh…figured out how to be with the kids more."

"Yeah? That's great, Chad," I sighed while my mind worked overtime trying to figure out where my daughter could be. "How so?"

"Well. The thing is, Kimmie left. Or rather, she threw me out. We're splitting up. She gave me two weeks to find something else. I could get a new job closer to you guys. I was actually thinking about coming to Cocoa Beach. Maybe coming…home?" he paused, probably waiting for my reaction, but I had no words yet. It was a lot to take in right now.

"It's always been you and me, Eva Rae," he continued. "I realized this recently. I don't know what I was thinking when I left you. We're a family."

Are you freaking kidding me?

"You wanna come…home?" I asked, not quite grasping this. Things were moving a little too fast for my liking right now.

"So…what do you say?" he asked.

What do I say? What do I say? I say you cheated on me and left the children and me without a word. I say I will never be able to trust you again. I say I am deeply, madly in love with someone else and we're doing fine without you. That's what I say.

But, of course, those weren't the words leaving my lips. Instead, I said, right before I hung up: "Like I said. You have impeccable timing. I can't deal with this right now. I gotta go."

Chapter 81

"Who was that?"

My mom stood in the doorway of Olivia's room. I rubbed my forehead. "That was Chad," I said.

"What did he want? It sounded like he wanted to come home?" she said and stepped closer.

I put my hands up. "Not now, Mom. I don't have time for this. I need to find my daughter, remember?"

"Don't shut him out just because of what he did. He is still the children's father. You didn't even tell him you didn't know where Olivia was. Why didn't you tell him? He deserves to know."

I lifted my eyes and met hers, then sent her a look to make her back off. "I don't owe Chad anything. He left us. Besides, I don't see how this is any of your business. I need to find my daughter now. So, Mom, please forget about Chad for a little while, even if you love him, and try to help me think. Now, Olivia never spoke about becoming a model before, how did she get this idea in her head? Could she have spoken to someone? I checked online, and there doesn't seem to be anything there. Could she have met someone at the diner? At school maybe?"

My mom shook her head. "I…I don't know, Eva Rae. She seemed perfectly normal to me this morning. Are you sure she's not just out with her friends and forgot her phone at the diner?"

Was it me? Was I overreacting? Maybe because of the drugs? I thought it over, then felt this pinch in the bottom of my stomach again.

No, something is wrong. I just know it is. Call it a mother's instinct; call it a cop's instinct, or maybe both. You can call it what you want. I just know this.

I rose from the chair and stood in my daughter's room, looking at the magazines next to her bed. There were all the big ones, *Elle, Cosmo,* and *Vogue.* I flipped the top one and stared at the super skinny models featuring strange clothes that I couldn't believe anyone would ever wear.

Maybe Olivia had been into this for longer than I thought?

"I need to find the list of numbers for her best friends," I said. "I keep it in the kitchen. I'm gonna start calling them."

My mom sighed as I walked past her, then followed me down the stairs.

"I'll help."

I found the list in my drawer, then stared at the white-board I had put up to organize our lives. Alex had a TAG— Talented and Gifted—trip today where they went to Kennedy Space Center, so he wouldn't be home till late, and Christine was at Orchestra. She had recently begun playing the double bass at school and rehearsed with the orchestra twice a week. Both of them were out, and that was good. I didn't want them to know what was going on or to worry about their older sister. They had enough with me being in the hospital and everything else that had been going on the past several days.

"I'll take the first one," my mom said. "Vivian, is that her name?"

I nodded. Vivian was one of Olivia's best friends that she had made since she moved here. I wouldn't say she had made any really close friends yet, but she had found a couple of girls from the volleyball team that she liked to hang out with after school from time to time. Vivian was the one she liked best.

"I'll try Shelly," I said.

As I said the words, my eyes fell on something on the floor by the front door. I walked to pick it up, then turned the object in the light, recognizing it.

"What's this?" I asked

My mom approached me, squinting her eyes to see better. "Let me see," she said and took it out of my hand.

"This doesn't belong to anyone who lives in this house," I said. "Someone was here, Mom. While I was in the hospital. Who was it? Who was here, Mom?"

Chapter 82

The gate was open when I drove up. The entrance was packed with cars, big limos, Teslas, and Maseratis. A young man in a suit asked me if I wanted to use valet parking, so I got out and let him park my car in the garage underneath the house.

It was Friday night, and they were having a party.

Someone held the front door open for the couple in front of me, who slid inside, the woman wearing a long blue sparkling dress. Me, I was in shorts and flip flops. Still, I managed to sneak in with the couple, and soon I entered the big hall where people were mingling. I recognized a couple of local politicians, some Hollywood starlets, a famous rapper that I only knew of because of my children, and I was pretty sure I spotted Tom Hanks by one of the big windows leading to the yard and ocean behind it. But I could be wrong. I never was good with famous people and recognizing them, much to my children's annoyance.

There was champagne in every partygoer's hand, along with caviar, and lobster canapés. I realized I hadn't eaten at all today. Not since the mushy breakfast at the hospital that contained pineapple juice, an orange, and something I couldn't identify but probably was supposed to be an omelet. I had barely eaten any of it, and now my stomach was grumbling angrily at me.

But there was no time.

I spotted Sydney—or Kelly Stone—standing between two well-dressed men, a glass of champagne held lightly between her fingers. Her eyes met mine, and she excused herself to them, then approached me.

"Eva Rae?" She looked nervously around her. "I thought you were in the hospital?"

"Save it. Where is she?"

She gave me a strange look. "What are you talking about? Listen, this isn't such a great time. I'm having a small party. You're welcome to stay, but…"

I held up her bracelet. "I found this in my house. Explain, please."

"I…I'm not sure I follow you here, Eva Rae."

"Cut the crap, Sydney."

"Maybe we should take this elsewhere," she said and looked nervously around her. A woman passed her, and she smiled politely at her while escorting me through a door into what looked like a big library. Thousands of books decorated the walls from top to bottom.

Sydney closed the door.

"Please don't call me that name," she said as she faced me again. "That is not my name."

"Okay, Mallory Stevens or Kelly Stone or whatever the heck your name is. Where is my daughter? I know you came to my house and spoke to her. My mom told me."

My sister sent me a wry smile.

"*Our* mother, if I recall," she said. "And, yes, that's true. When I heard what happened to you on the news, I went to your house. I was there to bring a peace offering. I spoke to our mother. I realized I was angry at her because I had been told my entire life that she didn't want me. That was why I told you I couldn't see you anymore. But as the days passed…and then you were hurt, well, I soon realized that I risked losing you again and that I had been silly. This was my family, and if you were reaching out to me, then I at least owed it to myself to take the chance. That was why I came back here in the first place. To find my family, that my dad—our dad—told me didn't want me. I wanted to find my roots, but gave up, thinking you would have looked for me if you wanted to see me again. But now, Mom told me everything. She told me about how I was taken, and that they didn't know where I was, how you all thought I was dead and gone for all these years. I never knew this. My dad, well our dad, told me she had thrown us out, that she never wanted to see either of us again and that was why we moved so far away and had no contact with her…or you. All those years, I thought our mother had chosen you over me, and that made me resent you. As I listened to her story, I began the process of forgiveness. But it's a journey. Wait. Are you mad about that? About me wanting to talk to Mom? To want to get to know you?"

I shook my head, tears springing to my eyes. "No, of course not. That's what I want too; believe me. It's my daughter. It's Olivia. She's been missing since after school today and I…well…"

Sydney looked surprised, angry even. "You thought I had taken her? Me who had recently learned that I was a victim of kidnapping myself?"

"I don't know what I thought. Maybe I hoped she was here and not taken by some sicko. You were at my house, and I was desperate. I thought maybe she had come to you." I turned around and found a leather chair, then sank into it, feeling hopeless. We called everyone that Olivia knew, and no one had seen her since school ended. She hadn't told anyone where she was going or who she was meeting. I even called the diner, and they hadn't seen her either. I had felt so certain it had something to do with my sister and the fact that she had been at my house two days earlier.

"I wish I could be of more help, Eva Rae," she said. "I really do."

"Yeah, me too, well…I should be…" I rose to my feet

when my phone vibrated in my pocket, and I pulled it out. It was a text from Matt.

GOT YOUR MESSAGE. PICKED UP HER PHONE AT THE DINER. HAVE ALERTED ALL PATROLS AND WILL ISSUE AN AMBER ALERT ASAP.

I exhaled, almost in tears. It was the right thing to do, but it suddenly felt so darn real. My daughter was gone. No one knew where she was.

"I have to go," I said and was about to leave when I stopped. "Didn't you say that your boyfriend Noah recently moved in with you?"

I turned to face her. She nodded.

"Yes, he's my fiancée. We're going to marry this summer. I will invite you and Mother, naturally."

"How much do you know about this guy?" I asked.

As I spoke, I received another text from Matt and opened it. It was a picture with the caption:

JUST RECEIVED THIS FROM DMV. THIS IS OUR GUY. THIS IS ANTHONY PIATKOWSKI. SENDING IT TO THE MEDIA ASAP.

I looked at the picture, then felt my heart drop. I showed it to Sydney.

"That's Noah; why?"

I swallowed. "This is our suspect. This is the guy we believe kidnapped three teenage girls from the school on prom night. This is the guy we believe kidnapped Molly Carson after promising to make her a model," I said, cursing myself for not having told Olivia what happened to Molly. I didn't want to scare her, so I had withheld all the details, but now I realized it was the worst thing I could have done. I should have warned her, and now she had fallen victim to the exact same trick.

"He raped and blinded Molly before placing her in my yard, chained to a swing set. He also killed one person at the hospital, severely hurt several others, and shot Carina Martin as she tried to escape. He killed Ava Morales and Tara Owens and put me in the hospital. It is also the guy I suspect has taken my Olivia."

Sydney looked at the picture on the phone, then shook her head. I could tell she was in shock.

"No. That's not the same person. You must have the wrong guy. That's not my Noah."

"Look at the picture, dang it. Is this your fiancée?"

Sydney's nostrils were flaring, and her eyes were flickering back and forth. She fixed her glare on the photo, then nodded with a sniffle.

"Yes…yes, that's him."

Chapter 83

"What do you know about him?" I asked when sensing Sydney still didn't fully believe me. I couldn't blame her. If she had been living with the guy and they were planning to marry soon, then this had to be quite a shock.

"His name is Noah Greenwald."

"Have you met any of his family?"

"No…well, he doesn't get along with them, he said. It's not like he's met mine either."

"I am so sorry for this, but he has been lying to you. His real name is Anthony Piatkowski. Five months ago, he bought a house on Country Club Road where he built a bunker… where he later kept the three girls."

Tears were in her eyes now as she shook her head. "No, Noah is a surgeon. He works at Cape Canaveral Hospital. He is very skilled and has earned many awards. Hasn't he?"

"Give me a sec," I said, then texted Matt back and asked him to look up Noah Greenwald. A few minutes later, he texted me back.

"I am sorry, sweetie," I said. "Noah Greenwald is a surgeon, or rather he was. He died in Afghanistan in 2017."

Sydney clasped her mouth and fought to stay calm. I placed a hand on her shoulder and looked into her eyes.

"Where is he now? Where is Noah?"

She swallowed. "In there," she said. "With the guests."

I felt my badge in my pocket and pulled it out. I had also brought my gun strapped underneath my CBPD jacket.

"You should probably stay in here," I said and grabbed my phone to call Matt.

"O-okay."

"He's here," I said into the phone. "I'm gonna take him in. I can't wait for backup. I'll risk him making a run for it. I don't care that it's dangerous. He has my daughter, Matt. I am not taking any chances."

Chapter 84

I walked back out into the big living room where the many people were gathered. No one seemed to notice me, so I continued through the crowd until I spotted him. He was standing by the grand piano in a corner of the living room, in deep conversation with a woman that I was certain I had seen before in some movie but didn't recall the name.

As my eyes landed on him, my blood froze. This was him; this was the guy who had been toying with me for weeks, who had been torturing me and this entire town. He had been here all along? Hiding in plain sight in my sister's house?

I couldn't wait to take him in and have him taste some of his own medicine. He was going to be locked away for a very long time. It was satisfying to know, even though I most of all wanted to kill him right there. I felt such deep anger toward this man, and yet, I hardly even knew him. My question was, why he had felt such resentment toward me that he wanted to put me through all of this.

What was his motive?

As he lifted his glance from the woman in front of me and our eyes met across the room that was humming with chitchat, it hit me.

I knew exactly why he was out to get me, and the realization struck me like a punch in the stomach. It almost knocked me out.

Anthony Piatkowski grinned when he saw me, then asked his company to excuse him, and left. He walked toward the backyard, and I followed him, hand on my gun. I wanted him away from all these people, in case I needed to pull the gun, so I let him rush into the yard and followed him just a few steps behind. Outside, he disappeared behind a corner, and I rushed after him. Barely had I reached the corner before a shovel was swung through the air and slammed right into my face, causing me to drop the gun in the grass. I fell backward up against the wall, a ringing in my ears, barely conscious, sliding down the wall, my back against it until I hit the gravel below. Above me, holding the shovel and seconds later my gun, was Anthony Piatkowski.

Chapter 85

"Okay, you were smarter than I expected," he said through the fog that was my brain right now. I tried to focus on him. He held the gun against my forehead.

"If you're so smart, I take it you also know who I am?"

I tried to nod, but my head was hurting. "Yes. It took me awhile, too long to realize who you were. It was the name that threw me off. You grew up with your mother; that's why you have a different last name than your dad."

Anthony nodded. "Very good, Detective."

"It was never on the news," I said. "It was never revealed to the public that those bodies we found in Chicago were filled with explosives. It was a terrorist nest, and they were experimenting with implanting bombs into bodies, using illegal immigrants that no one would miss as tests subjects. But all of them died in the process before they could be tested. It would be a gamechanger if they had succeeded. We didn't want to give anyone else that same idea, so it was kept quiet. The entire basement exploded when they discovered the bodies, and many died. My partner and I were outside, luckily. But that was how I knew. After you did the same thing to Tara. I knew it had to have been someone close to the investigation back then. I realized that while in the hospital.

How did you get the magnetic ID card from Turner? Did you steal it?"

"He sold it to me along with scrubs and surgical masks. I paid him fifty thousand dollars so he could buy the boat he always wanted."

"And that was why he ran," I said. "He thought we were there because of that."

"What a shame," he said.

"Turner's ID card gave you access to the hospital on the day you went in to poison the dialysis patients. You looked like him in the picture if you put on your fake goatee. You pretended like you belonged, but you never worked there. We checked their records. People just assumed you did. But you're no doctor. Noah Greenwald was. And he was in your battalion in Camp Marmal, right? And then he died."

"We were together on that day. I don't remember much except the birds singing and the blue sky above. We were driving toward Mazar-i-Sharif, the largest city close by when the IED went off on the side of the road. I was trapped underneath our car for almost twenty hours while trying to keep Noah alive. When help finally came along, he was no longer breathing."

"And you took his identity?"

"We were as close as brothers, maybe even closer. I was him; he was me. Sometimes, I'm still him. He lives in me."

This guy is crazy.

"Was he the one who taught you to perform enucleation? Like you did to Molly Carson?"

He nodded. "He showed it to me. One of our colleagues was hit by friendly fire, and the bullet went through his eye. Noah performed the surgery and let me watch. He took me through it step-by-step. I remembered everything he taught me while taking her eyes."

"I bet," I grumbled sarcastically while slowly regaining my strength. Piatkowski seemed lost in his memories for a few seconds. The shovel had cracked my lip, and blood was running down my chin. My face pounded like someone was playing drums on it. I was stalling, hoping to keep him talking until Matt got here.

"Where's my daughter?" I asked.

Piatkowski grinned. "Wouldn't you like to know?"

"Why are you doing this?" I asked.

He stared me directly in the eyes, and I felt my blood freeze.

"Because of what you did."

Chapter 86

THEN:

They took a twelve-page-long handwritten confession from Sánchez, each and every one of them bearing the distinctive "m" that looked like a "z," that had led them to him in the first place. He told them how he had seen Gary's wife, Iris, place the child in the carriage and how he had taken the child and left a ransom note.

Then they asked him to take them to the baby. Sánchez agreed to this and Gary was allowed to be in the front seat as they took off. It took all his strength not to point his gun at this man and kill him on the spot. But he kept himself calm, for Oliver's sake. Finally, the bastard was talking, and finally, he was taking them to the boy.

Sánchez wasn't very intelligent, Gary had realized, and he had to admit he didn't trust him much. Not until he actually held his boy in his arms again.

"Take this exit," Sánchez said.

They did as he told them to and they left the highway. On Sánchez's directions, they drove through town and entered a small neighborhood, very close to where Gary and Iris lived.

Has he been this close all this time? Gary thought, terrified, to himself. It was unbearable.

"Take a right here, and then stop by those bushes over there."

Gary looked out the window, his heart beginning to pound.

"But…but…?"

"Right here," Sánchez said. "Stop the car."

He pointed ahead.

"Right over there in those heavy bushes. That's where I placed the child. When I went to the first drop off site—I had the baby in the car. But I was scared away by all the press and police in the area. I drove away, then abandoned the baby close to the house. I figured you'd find him at some point… but I guess…you didn't."

Gary stared at the man in the back seat. Before he got into the car, Peterson had made him hand over his weapon. For this, Gary was very grateful at this moment.

Petersen got out of the car and opened the door for Sánchez in the back seat. He approached the window, and Gary rolled it down.

"Stay here, Gary," Peterson said.

Gary watched Peterson walk to Gary's partner, Agent Wilson, and they talked for a few seconds. Sánchez pointed again, and next thing, they all hurried toward the bramble patch behind Gary's house. Seconds later, Agent Wilson pulled out a piece of clothing before falling to the ground and beginning to sob uncontrollably.

Gary got out of the car and stood like he was paralyzed as they all turned to look at him. It felt like everything inside of him broke.

Dear God, no!

It took him less than a second to make the decision. He ran to one of his uniformed colleagues and, before he could react, pulled his gun out of its holster. Then he turned around and fired a shot at Sánchez before turning it toward himself.

Chapter 87

"It wasn't my fault," I said and tried to sit up.

Piatkowski pressed the gun against the skin of my forehead. He was sweating with distress, his white shirt getting soaked.

"Of course, it was. It was all your fault…Agent Wilson. See, you were there all the time. You were the one responsible for keeping an eye out on the house and its surroundings. And you failed to see the baby. You failed to see a small four-week-old infant in the bushes, crying helplessly for his mother. That baby died because you didn't find him. That's the reality."

Being confronted with this made me want to throw up. Even the name, Chad's last name, Wilson, made me sick to my stomach. I had gotten rid of it when he told me he was moving out, and I had taken my maiden name Thomas instead. I had spent years trying to get over this event. The guilt had eaten me up and forced me to work even harder, neglecting my family in the process. I had wanted to make amends; I had tried to work my way out of it, thinking I owed it to Gary, my old partner. Over the years, I had taught myself to let go of the guilt, telling myself it wasn't my fault, that anyone could have missed the baby, but still it nagged inside of me. Of course, it did. It always would. My partner had killed himself afterward, leaving Anthony Piatkowski—his child from a previous marriage—fatherless.

"But that's not all," Piatkowski said. "There's more. Not only did you fail to find the baby, but it was also your fault it was taken in the first place. Iris, his wife, told me everything. She told me how you and Gary, a week or so earlier, had stormed a house and rescued a kidnapped man, a gang member who owed money. When doing so, you shot a man. This man was the brother of Diego Sánchez. That was why he stole the baby in the first place. It wasn't random. He didn't just walk by on coincidence and decide to grab the baby. It was planned. It was revenge for what *you* did. The FBI believed it was coincidental until Sánchez wrote his confession. That was when the real motive came out. He wanted to revenge the death of his brother, and that was why he stole Gary's newborn. To revenge a killing that you, Agent Wilson, had committed. I lost my little brother and my father because of you. That is why I want you to be in pain. I researched you over the years and read all of your books about the many profiles of serial killers. My dad had told me about all the cases you worked together. I was just a teenager back then, but I remember each and every one of them, especially the one about the exploding bodies."

"You laid it all out like breadcrumbs for me to follow," I said, hearing tires screech outside of the house. That had to be Matt and his colleagues. I just had to keep him going a little while longer. And then, somehow, lead them to our whereabouts behind the house. "And now you have led me to you. You have my daughter, and you have me. You've won, Anthony. What do you want? What will it take for this to end? Money?"

That made Piatkowski laugh. "Do I look like I need money? I live here. I'm engaged to a Hollywood star who has no idea where her money goes."

"How did you know she was my sister when I didn't even know?" I asked.

"I've been following you for a long time, Eva Rae. Ever

since my dad died and I started to ask questions, I realized it was your fault. I spent hours in Afghanistan preparing for this, letting the anger fuel my planning. I have followed your every move since. Six months ago, you went to a PI and started to ask questions about your sister. I broke into her office at night and went through her files. Back then, she didn't know that your sister lived right here, or that she had changed her name to Kelly Stone, but it didn't take me long to figure that one out. I went to New England while she was filming there and then made sure to be at a charity event she attended while there."

I heard yelling coming from inside of the house and knew it wouldn't be long before they came out here. Unfortunately, Piatkowski heard it too. He growled, then grabbed me by the arm and pulled me up.

"You're coming with me," he said, then pushed me ahead of him, holding a hand over my mouth, gun pressed against my back.

Chapter 88

He pulled me into the underground garage and toward a car. I tried to scream, but nothing but muffled sounds came out of me. Piatkowski opened the passenger door and told me to get in when a voice yelled from behind us.

"Let her go, Piatkowski."

Anthony smiled and turned around. "Ah, the knight in shining armor. Matt Miller, is it?"

"Let her go, Piatkowski," he said, pointing his gun at him.

Piatkowski grinned. "Well, you can hardly kill me now, can you? See, then you'll never know where her daughter is. Besides, if you try anything, I'll shoot her."

Piatkowski stared at Matt for a little while, waiting for his reaction, while I stood pressed up against the open door, holding onto the edges, pressing against it, trying to fight him.

Matt lowered the gun.

"I didn't think so," Piatkowski said.

He turned to face me, grabbed me around the throat, and pressed, grinning. I couldn't breathe and had to let go of the edges of the car. It happened so fast; I'm sure Piatkowski didn't even have time to react. I leaned on my hands on the seat and lifted both my legs into the air, shaping them into a V-shape, wrapping them around his neck. I then twisted them hard, and Piatkowski went down onto the cement floor with a loud thud.

"Eva Rae!" Matt yelled as he came running toward me. Piatkowski was on the ground as Matt called for backup over the radio. Soon, they stormed inside the garage, while I had my foot planted solidly on Piatkowski. I held his arm twisted behind his back.

"Where's my daughter, you pig? Tell me!"

But no matter how hard I twisted his arm or even when I pressed my gun on him, he didn't care. He just laughed at me, then said. "That's the beauty of it. I don't even know."

"What do you mean you don't know, you sick bastard? What did you do to her?"

He turned his head slightly, lifting it from the floor, and managed to look at me while he said the next thing. It was like he wanted to make sure he saw my reaction when the words fell.

"I sold her. You have no idea how much money some people are willing to pay for a beauty like her on the dark web."

"You did what?" I shrieked. The realization made me let go of his arm. I felt like my throat was closing up…like I couldn't breathe.

He sold her?

Two CBPD officers grabbed Piatkowski and pulled him away from me while I screamed in deep pain, Matt holding me back, grabbing my gun from my hand. As they dragged him away, I looked into his icy eyes and his grin sent chills down my spine, while desperation and hopelessness made me sink into the arms of the man I loved, crying.

"What did he do to her, Matt? Where is she?"

Matt held me tight while I sobbed, missing my baby girl, wanting to wake up from this nightmare.

"I don't know," he whispered. "But we will find her. Trust me."

I let him hold me tight for a very long time and cried till I had no more tears. Then, I finally agreed to go back to the car with him, so he could take me home. I cried all the way back and held my two youngest children tight in my arms all night while I tried to sleep.

Chapter 89

Three days later, I went to visit Molly at the hospital and had a long chat with Melissa. I told her everything that had happened, but most of all, I was happy to be able to tell her that we got the guy, that he was in our custody. I had kept my promise to her, and for that, I was proud.

Molly was doing a lot better and would soon be discharged. She was learning to cope with the fact that she was now blind, and they had ordered a service dog for her, while they were training her how to maneuver by using a support cane—or white cane—at the hospital. She had also begun speaking again, even though what came out of her was sparse. She would, however, soon be able to give her entire testimony and help put another nail in Piatkowski's coffin.

"I am so sorry about Olivia, though," Melissa said and held my hand in hers. "You must feel awful. Let me know if there is anything I can do. I'll do anything for you; you know that."

I told her to take care of her own daughter for now and hold her tight, enjoying that she was still here.

I then checked on Carina Martin, who was with her mother. Carina hugged me and cried when she heard we had caught Piatkowski. She told me she would be willing to testify as soon as we wanted her to, and she would even go back to the house and the bunker if we needed her to. I told her she was a very brave girl. I also told her mother to be proud of her before I left. Tears were springing to my eyes as I hurried down the hallway of Cape Canaveral Hospital, while I wondered if I was ever going to see my daughter again.

After crying in the car, and slamming my fist into the steering wheel, I drove back to the station to watch the interrogation of Piatkowski through the glass. They had been at it almost non-stop for three whole days, and he still refused to say where my daughter was, repeating the same thing over and over again.

"That is the beauty of it. I don't know. You can keep asking me till we both die from thirst or even old age, but I will never be able to tell you because I don't know. Girls are sold all the time around this world, and who knows where they end up?"

As he said the last part, he looked at the glass window, like he knew I was behind it, which he probably did.

"To whom?" Matt asked, tired and angry. "Who did you sell her to?"

"I don't know his name. He called himself *The Iron Fist.* He buys girls online—through the dark web—and probably resells them. Some he might keep to himself. What do I know? I took the girl to the airport, where we met some of his associates. They took her. Where, I have no idea. She could be anywhere in the world by now. But they paid me good money, and that was what I wanted…money."

Financial gain, I thought to myself. *The last motive.*

He had covered all four serial killer typologies from my book. Lust, anger, power, and financial gain.

I stared into the icy eyes of Piatkowski, and in that very instant, realized that there was no way we were ever going to get him to tell us anything. If I wanted my daughter back, I'd have to find her myself.

"I am sorry," Matt said as he came out of the room. He leaned forward and kissed me. He ran a hand gently through my hair. "I'll keep trying."

I nodded determinedly. "Do that, Matt. Listen, I'm gonna…I'm gonna go back."

He examined me. Our eyes locked for a few seconds, and that was when he knew. I had made up my mind, and he couldn't stop me. I started to back away from him, biting my lip, until I finally turned around and left him, my heart crying.

"Wait," he said. "I don't like that look in your eyes, Eva Rae. Eva Rae? Where are you going? Eva Rae? Don't do anything stupid; do you hear me?"

That was the one thing I couldn't promise him.

THE END

Want do know what happens next?
Get Book 3 in the Eva Rae Thomas Mystery Series, **NEVER EVER** here:
https://readerlinks.com/l/642585

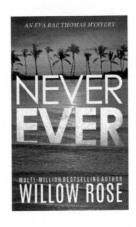

Afterword

Dear Reader,

Thank you for purchasing *What You Did (Eva Rae Thomas #2)*. I know I left you on a cliffhanger but rest assured, this story isn't over. We will know what happened to Olivia in book 3.

Now, the backstory for this book is based on a true event that took place back in 1956, when a young infant named Peter Weinberger was kidnapped from his baby carriage while he was sleeping outside. The kidnapper then asked for a ransom but was spooked by the press and police and left the child in a bush where he wasn't found until it was too late. It is such a devastating story, and, of course, I knew I needed to write about it. Here is a link in case you want to read more.

https://www.fbi.gov/history/famous-cases/weinberger-kidnapping

Thank you for all your support and don't forget to leave a review if possible.

Love,
Willow

About the Author

Willow Rose is a multi-million-copy best-selling Author and an Amazon ALL-star Author of more than 60 novels. Her books are sold all over the world.

She writes Mystery, Thriller, Paranormal, Romance, Suspense, Horror, Supernatural thrillers, and Fantasy.

Willow's books are fast-paced, nail-biting pageturners with twists you won't see coming. That's why her fans call her The Queen of Scream.

Several of her books have reached the Kindle top 10 of ALL books in the US, UK, and Canada. She has sold more than three million books all over the world.

Willow lives on Florida's Space Coast with her husband and two daughters. When she is not writing or reading, you will find her surfing and watch the dolphins play in the waves of the Atlantic Ocean.

To be the first to hear about new releases and bargains—from Willow Rose—sign up below to be on the VIP List. (I promise not to share your email with anyone else, and I won't clutter your inbox.)

- SIGN UP TO BE ON THE VIP LIST HERE :

http://readerlinks.com/l/415254

Tired of too many emails? Text the word: "willowrose" to 31996 to sign up to Willow's VIP text List to get a text alert with news about New Releases, Giveaways, Bargains and Free books from Willow.

FOLLOW WILLOW ROSE ON BOOKBUB:
https://www.bookbub.com/authors/willow-rose

Connect with Willow online:

https://www.amazon.com/Willow-Rose/e/B004X2WHBQ
https://www.facebook.com/willowredrose/
https://twitter.com/madamwillowrose
http://www.goodreads.com/author/show/4804769.Willow_Rose
Http://www.willow-rose.net
madamewillowrose@gmail.com

 facebook.com/willowredrose

 twitter.com/madamwillowrose

 instagram.com/madamewillowrose

Books by the Author

MYSTERY/THRILLER/HORROR NOVELS

- IN ONE FELL SWOOP
- UMBRELLA MAN
- BLACKBIRD FLY
- TO HELL IN A HANDBASKET
- EDWINA

MARY MILLS MYSTERY SERIES

- WHAT HURTS THE MOST
- YOU CAN RUN
- YOU CAN'T HIDE
- CAREFUL LITTLE EYES

EVA RAE THOMAS MYSTERY SERIES

- DON'T LIE TO ME
- WHAT YOU DID
- NEVER EVER

EMMA FROST SERIES

- ITSY BITSY SPIDER
- MISS DOLLY HAD A DOLLY
- RUN, RUN AS FAST AS YOU CAN
- CROSS YOUR HEART AND HOPE TO DIE
- PEEK-A-BOO I SEE YOU
- TWEEDLEDUM AND TWEEDLEDEE
- EASY AS ONE, TWO, THREE
- THERE'S NO PLACE LIKE HOME
- SLENDERMAN

- WHERE THE WILD ROSES GROW
- WALTZING MATHILDA
- DRIP DROP DEAD

JACK RYDER SERIES

- HIT THE ROAD JACK
- SLIP OUT THE BACK JACK
- THE HOUSE THAT JACK BUILT
- BLACK JACK
- GIRL NEXT DOOR
- HER FINAL WORD
- DON'T TELL

REBEKKA FRANCK SERIES

- ONE, TWO…HE IS COMING FOR YOU
- THREE, FOUR…BETTER LOCK YOUR DOOR
- FIVE, SIX…GRAB YOUR CRUCIFIX
- SEVEN, EIGHT…GONNA STAY UP LATE
- NINE, TEN…NEVER SLEEP AGAIN
- ELEVEN, TWELVE…DIG AND DELVE
- THIRTEEN, FOURTEEN…LITTLE BOY UNSEEN
- BETTER NOT CRY
- TEN LITTLE GIRLS
- IT ENDS HERE

HORROR SHORT-STORIES

- MOMMY DEAREST
- THE BIRD
- BETTER WATCH OUT
- EENIE, MEENIE
- ROCK-A-BYE BABY
- NIBBLE, NIBBLE, CRUNCH
- HUMPTY DUMPTY
- CHAIN LETTER

PARANORMAL SUSPENSE/ROMANCE NOVELS

- IN COLD BLOOD
- THE SURGE
- GIRL DIVIDED

THE VAMPIRES OF SHADOW HILLS SERIES

- FLESH AND BLOOD
- BLOOD AND FIRE
- FIRE AND BEAUTY
- BEAUTY AND BEASTS
- BEASTS AND MAGIC
- MAGIC AND WITCHCRAFT
- WITCHCRAFT AND WAR
- WAR AND ORDER
- ORDER AND CHAOS
- CHAOS AND COURAGE

THE AFTERLIFE SERIES

- BEYOND
- SERENITY
- ENDURANCE
- COURAGEOUS

THE WOLFBOY CHRONICLES

- A GYPSY SONG
- I AM WOLF

DAUGHTERS OF THE JAGUAR

- SAVAGE
- BROKEN

Hit The Road Jack (Jack Ryder Series Book 1)
EXCERPT

For a special sneak peak of Willow Rose's Bestselling Mystery Novel **Hit the road Jack** turn to the next page.

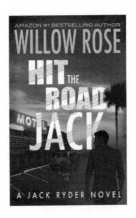

Prologue
DON'T COME BACK NO MORE

Prologue
MAY 2012

S he has no idea who she is or where she is and cares to know neither. For some time, for what seems like forever, she has been in this daze. This haze, in complete darkness with nothing but the sounds. Sounds coming from outside her body, from outside her head. Sometimes, the sounds fade and there is only the darkness.

As time passes, she becomes aware that there are two realities. The one in her mind, filled with darkness and pain and then the one outside of her, where something or someone else is living, acting, smelling and…singing.

Yes, that's it. Someone is singing. Does she know the song?
…*What you say?*

The darkness is soon replaced by light. Still, her eyes are too heavy to open. Her consciousness returns slowly. Enough to start asking questions. Where is she? How did she end up here? A series of pictures of her at home come to her mind. She is waiting. What is she waiting for?
…*I guess if you said so.*

Him. She is waiting for him. She is checking her hair in the mirror every five minutes or so. Then correcting the make-up, looking at the clock again. Where is he? She looks out through the window and at the street and the many staring neighboring windows. A feeling of guilt hits her.

Somehow, it seems wrong for this kind of thing to take place in broad daylight.

...*That's right!*

A car drives up. The anticipation. The butterflies in her stomach. The sound of the doorbell. She is straightening her dress and taking a last glance in the mirror. The next second, she is in his embrace. He is holding her so tight she closes her eyes and breathes him in until his lips cover hers and she swims away.

...*Whoa, Woman, oh woman, don't treat me so mean.*

His breath is pumping against her skin. She feels his hands on her breasts, under her skirt, coming closer, while he presses her up against the wall. She feels him in his hand. He is hard now, moaning in her ear.

"Where's your husband?" he whispers.

"Work," she moans back, feeling self-conscious. Why did he have to bring up her husband? The guilt is killing her. "The kids are in school."

"Good," he moans. "No one can ever know. Remember that. No one."

...*You're the meanest old woman that I've ever seen.*

He pushes himself inside of her and pumps. She lets herself get into the moment, but as soon as it is over, she finds herself regretting it...while he zips up the pants of his suit and kisses her gently on the lips, whispering, *same time next week*? She regrets having started it all. They are both married with children, and this is only an affair. Could never be anything else, even if she dreamt about it. The sex is great, but she wants more than just seeing him on her lunch break. But she can never tell him. She can never explain to him how much she hates this awkward moment that follows the sex.

"They're expecting me at the office...I have a meeting," he says, and puts his tie back on. "I'd better..."

...*Hit the road, Jack!*

She finally opens her eyes with a loud gasp. The bright light hurts her. Water is being splashed in her face. She can't breathe. The bathtub is slippery when she tries to get up. Her eyes lock with another set of eyes. The eyes of a man. He is staring at her with a twisted smile. She gasps again, suddenly remembering those dark chili eyes.

"*I guess if you said so…I'd have to pack my things and go,*" he sings.

"You," she gasps. Breathing is hard for her. She feels like she is still choking. She is hyperventilating. Panicking.

The man smiles. On his neck crawls a snake. How does that old saying go again? *Red, black, yellow kills a fellow?* This one is all of that, all those colors. It stares at her while moving its tongue back and forth. The man is holding a washcloth in his hand. She looks down at her naked body. The smell of chlorine is strong and makes her eyes water.

"You tried to kill me," she says, while panting with anxiety.

I have to get home. Help me. I have to get home to my children! Oh, God. I can hear their voices! Am I going mad? I think I can hear them!

"I guess I didn't do a very good job, then," he answers. His chillingly calm voice is piercing through every bone in her body.

"I'll try again. *That's right!*"

Prologue
MAY 2012

She had never been more beautiful than in this exact moment. No woman ever had. So fragile, her skin so pale it almost looked bluish. The man who called himself the Snakecharmer stared at her body. It was still in the bathtub. He was still panting from the exertion, his hands shaking and hurting from strangling the girl. He felt so aroused in this moment, staring at the dead body. It was the most fascinating thing in the world. How the body simply ceased to function. And almost as fascinating was what followed next. The human decaying process. It wasn't something new. Fascination with death had occurred all throughout human history, characterized by obsessions with death and all things related to death. The Egyptians mummified their dead. He had always wished he could do the same. Keep his dead forever and ever. He remembered as a child how he would sometimes lie down in front of the mirror and try to lie completely still and look at himself, imagining he was looking at a dead body. He would capture cats and kill them and keep them in his room, just to watch what would happen to them. He wanted so badly to stop the decaying process, he wanted them to remain the same always and never leave.

The Snakecharmer stared at the girl with fascination in his eyes. He caught his breath and calmed down again. He still felt the adrenalin rushing through his veins while he finished washing the girl. He washed away all the dirt, all the smells on her body. He reached down and cleaned her thoroughly between her legs. Scrubbed her to make sure he got all the dirt away, all the filth and impurities.

Then, he dried her with a towel before he pulled her onto the bathroom floor. His companions, his two pet Coral snakes, were sliding across her dead body. He grabbed one and let it slide across his arm while petting it. Then he knelt next to the girl and stroked her gently across her hair, making sure it wasn't in her face. Her blue eyes stared into the ceiling.

"Now, you'll never leave," he whispered.

With his cellphone, he took a picture of her naked body. That was his mummification. His way to always cherish the moment. To always remember. He never wanted to forget how beautiful she was.

He dried her with a towel. He brushed her brown hair with gentle strokes. He took yet another picture before he lifted her up and carried her into the bedroom, where he placed her in a chair, then sat in front of her and placed his head in her lap.

They would stay like this until she started to smell.

Part I

I GUESS IF YOU SAY SO

Chapter 1
JANUARY 2015

He took the dog out in the yard and shut the door carefully behind him, making sure he didn't make a sound to wake up his sleeping parents. It was Monday, but they had been very loud last night. The kitchen counter was still covered with empty bottles.

At first, Ben had waited patiently in the living room, watching a couple of shows on TV, waiting for his parents to wake up. When the clock passed nine, he knew he wouldn't make it to school that day either, and that was too bad because they had a fieldtrip to the zoo today and Ben had been looking forward to it. When they still hadn't shown up at ten o'clock, he decided the dog had to go out. The old Labrador kept sitting by the door and scraping on it. It had to go.

So, Ben took Bobby out in the backyard. He had to go with him. The yard ended at the canal, and Bobby had more than once jumped into the water. Ben had to keep an eye on him to make sure he didn't do it again. It had been such a mess last time, since the dog couldn't climb back up over the seawall on his own, so Ben's dad had to jump into the blurry water and carry the dog out.

The dog quickly gave in to nature and did his business.

Ben had a plastic bag that he picked it up with and threw it in the trash can behind the house.

It was a beautiful day out. One of those clear days with a blue sky and not a cloud anywhere on the horizon. The wind was blowing out of the north and had been for two days, making the air drier. For once, Ben's shirt didn't stick to his body.

He threw the ball a few times for the dog to get some exercise. Ben could smell the ocean, even though he lived on the back side of the barrier island. When it was quiet, he could even hear it too. The waves had to be good. If he wasn't too sick from drinking last night, his dad might take him surfing.

Ben really hoped he would.

It had been months since his dad last took him to the beach. He never seemed to have time anymore. Sometimes, Ben would take his bike and ride down there by himself, but it was never as much fun as when the entire family went. They never seemed to do much together anymore. Ben wondered if it had anything to do with what happened to his baby sister a year ago. He never understood exactly what had happened. He just knew she didn't wake up one morning when their mother went to pick her up from her crib. Then his parents cried and cried for days and they had held a big funeral. But the crying hadn't stopped for a long time. Not until it was replaced with a lot of sleeping and his parents staying up all night, and all the empty bottles that Ben often cleaned up from the kitchen and put in the recycling bin.

Bobby brought back the ball and placed it at Ben's feet. He picked it up and threw it again. It landed close to the seawall. Luckily, it didn't fall in. Bobby ran to get it, then placed it at Ben's feet again, looking at him expectantly.

"Really? One more time, then we're done," he said, thinking he'd better get back inside and start cleaning up. He picked up the ball and threw it. The dog stormed after it again and disappeared for a second down the hill leading to the canal. Ben couldn't see him.

"Bobby?" he yelled. "Come on, boy. We need to get back inside."

He stared in the direction of the canal. He couldn't see the bottom of the yard. He had no idea if Bobby had jumped in the water again. His heart started to pound. He would have to wake up his dad if he did. He was the only one who could get Bobby out of the water.

Ben stood frozen for a few seconds until he heard the sound of Bobby's collar, and a second later spotted his black dog running towards him with his tongue hanging out of his mouth.

"Bobby!" Ben said. He bent down and petted his dog and best friend. "You scared me, buddy. You forgot the ball. Well, we'll have to get that later. Now, let's go back inside and see if Mom and Dad are awake."

Ben grabbed the handle and opened the door. He let Bobby go in first.

"Mom?" he called.

But there was no answer. They were probably still asleep. Ben found some dog food in the cabinet and pulled the bag out. He spilled on the floor when he filled Bobby's tray. He had no idea how much the dog needed, so he made sure to give him enough, and poured till the bowl overflowed. Ben found a garbage bag under the sink and had removed some of the bottles, when Bobby suddenly started growling. The dog ran to the bottom of the stairs and barked. Ben found this to be strange. It was very unlike Bobby to act this way.

"What's the matter, boy? Are Mom and Dad awake?"

The dog kept barking and growling.

"Stop it!" Ben yelled, knowing how much his dad hated it when Bobby barked. "Bad dog."

But Bobby didn't stop. He moved closer and closer to the stairs and kept barking until the dog finally ran up the stairs.

"No! Bobby!" Ben yelled. "Come back down here!"

Ben stared up the stairs after the dog, wondering if he dared to go up there. His dad always got so mad if he went upstairs when they were sleeping. He wasn't allowed up there until they got out of bed. But, if he found Bobby up there, his dad would get really mad. Probably talk about getting rid of him again.

He's my best friend. Don't take my friend away.

"Bobby," he whispered. "Come back down here."

Ben's heart was racing in his chest. There wasn't a sound coming from upstairs. Ben held his breath, not knowing what to do. The last thing he wanted on a day like today was to make his dad angry. He expected his dad to start yelling any second now.

Oh no, what if he jumps into their bed? Dad is going to get so mad. He's gonna get real mad at Bobby.

"Bobby?" Ben whispered a little louder.

There was movement on the stairs, the black lab peeked his head out, then ran down the stairs.

"There you are," Ben said with relief. Bobby ran past him and sprang up on the couch.

"What do you have in your mouth? Not one of mom's shoes again."

It didn't look like it was big enough to be a shoe. Ben walked closer, thinking if it was a pair of Mommy's panties again, then the dog was dead. He reached down and grabbed the dog's mouth, then opened it and pulled out whatever it was. He looked down with a small shriek at what had come out of the dog's mouth. He felt nauseated, like the time when he had the stomach-bug and spent the entire night in the bathroom. Only this was worse.

It's a finger. A finger wearing Mommy's ring!

Chapter 2

JANUARY 2015

"Hit the road, Jack, and don't you come back no more no more no more."

The children's voices were screaming more than singing on the bus. I preferred *Wheels on the Bus*, but the kids thought it was oh so fun, since my name was Jack and I was actually driving the bus. I had volunteered to drive them to the Brevard Zoo for their field trip today. Two of the children, the pretty blonde twins in the back named Abigail and Austin, were mine. A boy and a girl. Just started Kindergarten six months ago. I could hardly believe how fast time passed. Everybody told me it would, but still. It was hard to believe.

I was thirty-five and a single dad of three children. My wife, Arianna, ran out on us four years ago…when the twins were almost two years old. It was too much, she told me. She couldn't cope with the children or me. She especially had a hard time taking care of Emily. Emily was my ex-partner's daughter. My ex-partner, Lisa, was shot on duty ten years ago during a chase in downtown Miami. The shooter was never captured, and it haunted me daily. I took Emily in after her mother died. What else could I have done? I felt guilty for what had happened to her mother. I was supposed to have protected my partner. Plus, the girl didn't know her father. Lisa never told anyone who he was; she didn't have any of her parents or siblings left, except for a homeless brother who was in no condition to take care of a child. So, I got custody and decided to give Emily the best life I could. She was six when I took her in, sixteen now, and at an age where it was hard for anyone to love you, besides your mom and dad. I tried hard to be both for her. Not always with much success. The fact was, I had no idea what it was like to be a black teenage girl.

Personally, I believed Arianna had depression after the birth of the twins, but she never let me close enough to talk about it. She cried for months after the twins were born, then one day out of the blue, she told me she had to go. That she couldn't stay or it would end up killing her. I cried and begged her to stay, but there was nothing I could do. She had made up her mind. She was going back upstate, and that was all I needed to know. I shouldn't look for her, she said.

"Are you coming back?" I asked, my voice breaking. I couldn't believe anyone would leave her own children.

"I don't know, Jack."

"But…The children? They need you? They need their mother?"

"I can't be the mother you want me to be, Jack. I'm just not cut out for it. I'm sorry."

Then she left. Just like that. I had no idea how to explain it to the kids, but somehow I did. As soon as they started asking questions, I told them their mother had left and that I believed she was coming back one day. Some, maybe a lot of people, including my mother, might have told me it was insane to tell them that she might be coming back, but that's what I did. I couldn't bear the thought of them growing up with the knowledge that their own mother didn't want them. I couldn't bear for Emily to know that she was part of the reason why Arianna had left us, left the twins motherless. I just couldn't. I had to leave them with some sort of hope. And maybe I needed to believe it too. I needed to believe that she hadn't just abandoned us…that she had some stuff she needed to work out and soon she would be back. At least for the twins. They needed their mother and asked for her often.

It was getting harder and harder for me to believe she was coming back for them. But I still said she would.

And there they were.

On the back seat of the bus, singing along with their classmates, happier than most of them. Mother or no mother, I had provided a good life for them in our little town of Cocoa Beach. As a detective working for the Brevard County Sheriff's Office, working their homicide unit, I had lots of spare time and they had their grandparents close by. They received all the love in the world from me and their grandparents, who loved them to death (and let them get away with just about anything).

Some might think they were spoiled brats, but to me they were the love of my life, the light, the...the...

What the heck were they doing in the back?

I hit the brakes a little too hard at the red light. All the kids on the bus fell forwards. The teacher, Mrs. Allen, whined and held on to her purse.

"Abigail and Austin!" I thundered through the bus. "Stop that right now!"

The twins grinned and looked at one another, then continued to smear chocolate on each other's faces. Chocolate from those small boxes with Nutella and sticks you dipped in it. Boxes their grandmother had given them for snack, even though I told her it had to be healthy.

"Now!" I yelled.

"Sorry, Dad," they yelled in unison.

"Well...wipe that off or..."

I never made it any further before the phone in my pocket vibrated. I pulled it out and started driving again as the light turned green.

"Ryder. We need you. I spoke with Ron and he told me you would be assisting us. We desperately need your help."

It was the head of the Cocoa Beach Police Department. Weasel, we called her. I didn't know why. Maybe it had to do with the fact that her name was Weslie Seal. Maybe it was just because she kind of looked like a weasel because her body was long and slender, but her legs very short. Ron Harper was the county sheriff and my boss.

"Yes? When?"

"Now."

"But...I'm..."

"This is big. We need you now."

"If you say so. I'll get there as fast as I can," I said, and turned off towards the entrance to the zoo. The kids all screamed with joy when they saw the sign. Mrs. Allen shushed them.

"What, are you running a day-care now? Not that I have the time to care. Everything is upside down around here. We have a dead body. I'll text you the address. Meet you there."

END OF EXCERPT.

Order your copy
today!

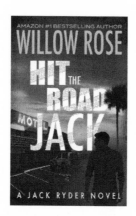

GO HERE TO ORDER:
https://readerlinks.com/l/190534

Contents

Copyright	iii
Prologue	1
Chapter 1	5
Chapter 2	8
Chapter 3	11
Chapter 4	14
Chapter 5	22
Chapter 6	25
Chapter 7	29
Chapter 8	33
Chapter 9	36
Chapter 10	39
Chapter 11	42
Chapter 12	45
Chapter 13	48
Chapter 14	51
Chapter 15	56
Chapter 16	58
Chapter 17	60
Chapter 18	63
Chapter 19	66
Chapter 20	68
Chapter 21	71
Chapter 22	74
Chapter 23	77
Chapter 24	80
Chapter 25	84
Chapter 26	88
Chapter 27	91
Chapter 28	94
Chapter 29	96
Chapter 30	100

Chapter 31	102
Chapter 32	105
Chapter 33	107
Chapter 34	113
Chapter 35	118
Chapter 36	121
Chapter 37	125
Chapter 38	127
Chapter 39	129
Chapter 40	132
Chapter 41	137
Chapter 42	139
Chapter 43	142
Chapter 44	145
Chapter 45	149
Chapter 46	151
Chapter 47	154
Chapter 48	157
Chapter 49	160
Chapter 50	164
Chapter 51	168
Chapter 52	171
Chapter 53	174
Chapter 54	177
Chapter 55	180
Chapter 56	182
Chapter 57	184
Chapter 58	187
Chapter 59	190
Chapter 60	192
Chapter 61	196
Chapter 62	199
Chapter 63	201
Chapter 64	205
Chapter 65	207
Chapter 66	210
Chapter 67	212
Chapter 68	215

Chapter 69	218
Chapter 70	220
Chapter 71	222
Chapter 72	225
Chapter 73	228
Chapter 74	231
Chapter 75	233
Chapter 76	235
Chapter 77	241
Chapter 78	244
Chapter 79	246
Chapter 80	248
Chapter 81	251
Chapter 82	254
Chapter 83	259
Chapter 84	261
Chapter 85	263
Chapter 86	266
Chapter 87	268
Chapter 88	271
Chapter 89	274
Afterword	277
About the Author	279
Books by the Author	281
Hit The Road Jack (Jack Ryder Series Book 1)	284

Prologue

| Prologue | 287 |
| Prologue | 290 |

Part I

| Chapter 1 | 295 |
| Chapter 2 | 299 |

| ORDER YOUR COPY TODAY! | 303 |